Just love
HER

A Journey into Love's Divine Essence

Copyright © 2024 Raz Mihal

Published by Mystic Publishing

Paperback ISBN: 978-1-0686300-0-2
Hardback ISBN: 978-1-0686300-2-6
eBook ISBN: 978-1-0686300-1-9
Audiobook ISBN: 978-1-0686300-3-3

All rights reserved

No part of this book may be reproduced in any form or by any electronic or mechanical means, including in information storage and retrieval systems, without permission in writing from the author, with the exception of short excerpts used in a review.

Raz Mihal has asserted his right under the Copyright, Designs and Patents Act 1988 to be identified as the author of this work.

Disclaimer:

Although the publisher and the author have made every effort to ensure that the information in this book was correct at press time, and while this publication is designed to provide accurate information regarding the subject matter covered, the publisher and the author assume no responsibility for errors, inaccuracies, omissions, or any other inconsistencies herein and hereby disclaim any liability to any party for any loss, damage, or disruption caused by errors or omissions, whether such errors or omissions result from negligence, accident, or any other cause.

This publication is meant as a source of valuable information for the reader; however, it is not a substitute for direct expert assistance. If such a level of assistance is required, the services of a competent professional should be sought.

For references and glossary, visit www.razmihal.com

Just love HER

A Journey into Love's Divine Essence

Raz Mihal

Contents

Daily Meditation:
Her 7

Daily And Walking Meditation:
Seoul – South Korea 117

Deep Meditation And Visions:
Thoughts Of Enlightenment 169

Memories Of My 'Self' 237

DAILY MEDITATION:
HER

MISSING HER

7 Aug 2019

Countless days passed, waiting for these feelings towards Her to settle down.

My life lately became Her, and the rest of my existence is like a picture where I am waiting to paint over the pen sketches with colours.

I try to remember at what point my heart became irreversibly touched by her soul image. I can't point out the exact time, though, just the feeling that my soul only felt Her instantly, as an echo of the timeless love.

Sometimes, I feel I must share my deepest feelings with Her in real life, like a pinch on my skin to feel it's not just a dream. Although it is like a dream ... A dream of Her whom the vision of divine love revealed to my wounded heart.

IN HER EYES

10 Aug 2019

I am lost myself whenever I look into her eyes.

That moment when the glimpse of her beautiful soul reflected in rays of the eye's light felt like an eternity.

How can you feel the eternity of love just by looking into the eyes?

It's the eternity of the soul that reflects eternal love. An infinite and absolute love beyond what words can describe.

This moment is the only way our souls meet and share their existence, just by looking into her eyes – the mirror of our souls. I can't even imagine the real feelings that would happen in reality and not only in thoughts.

That moment of reality feels like an eternity when our souls will meet the goddess behind the mirror.

In these moments, I feel whispers and shadows of past lives and present futures passing through the mind's screen. The emptiness of my mind reflects the vibration from my heart: love without the presence of Me – just Her and the Infinite Love.

STEP UP INTO THE LIGHT

11 Aug 2019

There have been so many years since I gave up making a place for my feelings into words.

Back then, I still agreed that words merely reflect real feelings. Words can't imprison Love. Just think about it. 'LOVE' and even 'L O V E' instantly make you aware of feelings from your heart.

Feelings can reveal lost relationships in ages or present futures and happiness just by living it. Go deeper after your feelings created by your awareness and delve into your heart beyond this simple word.

Warmth, happiness and the echo of eternity make a point in a vacuum. Your soul is bathing in those feelings encapsulated in a simple word like 'Love'.

This practice of divine love has been my daily meditation for dozens of years.

Few images in the past sat there close to my soul. Some have already left, and some still live there. It's like a wall of great paintings. Every painting has its value and meaning. Some pictures were alive at some point and now are just paintings.

Looking at Her, I feel her soul image is not a painting.

Her reflects that pure 'love' into my vacuum heart, filled with her existence.

When my mind escapes from this vortex of feelings, I look for a future related to this.

But my heart answers to all these meaningless thoughts:

The future is 'now'.

HEART VERSUS BRAIN: WHY MY HEART IS ACTING BEFORE THE BRAIN

13 Aug 2019

Long time, no see, my sweet 'heart' – almost forgotten times from the past when my heart aches, touching the love goddess.

My mind tried to conquer these feelings like 'God is Love'.

My heart intuitively created a space in my mind for the inception of the idea that 'Love is God'.

In a world dominated by men, I always thought about goddess love from our hearts. You can't think of love as a god but as a goddess.

The conception of our ancestral mind ruled by years of written code in our DNA is that God is of masculine origins.

Some scriptures tried to explain divinity as a duality or without a gender. Something that the mind can't comprehend.

There were some ancient times before this concept, now forgotten, when people believed God was a goddess who created the world as we know it, or at least that power was feminine, not masculine, as we perceive it nowadays.

When I look at Her, I feel her with my heart as part of it. With every breath in and out, my brain is aware of her inner touch. Our souls are connected in one because only her soul image is inside.

My soul is breathing love through her existence. That's the only feeling my brain perceives from her reality inside my heart: divine love – or at least the closest word that can describe this feeling.

The Goddess from my heart is Her, so I can't do anything about it. Just let this feeling live its origins. Since her soul image made my heart a place to live, I melted slowly and wholly into her existence. It's not a fight. It is surrender and acknowledgement of the Goddess from my heart. And that Love is God: my God, my religion.

JUST LOVE HER

14 Aug 2019

Thoughts come after other feelings and more views about destiny.

Since the first moment, I felt the connection; one thing led to another, and here I am, looking deep into her eyes for the first time and feeling infinite love for another soul after so many years.

And a voice long forgotten whispered inside:

'Just love Her!'

Why did I tell Her about feelings, love, goddess, and whatnot in the name of God?

Did Her even receive my soul messages, let alone know them?

And other dozens of thoughts passed through my mind, too gibberish to be out in words.

And again, the voice inside:

'Just love Her!'

Day by day, I feel Her through my heart in the wind, clouds, trees and rain. Her soul image and presence are everywhere, whether I close my eyes or open them wide.

Then, in the silence of my meditation, I understand the meaning of my voice inside:

'Why bother Her?'

What will change the echoes from my heart encapsulated into words for ears?

Maybe the hope or belief that will be heard and felt by heart and soul from past lives, or will it become the dream of an actual one?

And my heart, as always, whispers in the silence and echo of my soul:

'Just love Her!'

DIFFERENT CULTURES: HOW CULTURE AND TRADITION ACT THROUGH INFINITE LOVE

15 Aug 2019

Different cultures. Differences. Everything is different.

You wake up in one moment with your heart on fire, feeling the infinite and absolute love between two souls as fireworks celebrations.

In the first moments, nothing else matters; I mean nothing, just that pure love. You feel love because this is what rules your heart and nothing else. Then, as love settles its roots deep inside your heart, your mind wanders through every thought you didn't even know was possible. Nothing beats your mind to it.

Culture, tradition, and language are totally different. Life experiences are, of course, evaluated differently. And so, on and on, thoughts go on, questioning feelings.

Only one unseen can be on the same wave, and this is our soul.

Meditation without support is a blessing. You are just looking into your heart, feeling love close to the 'soul image' that your soul has chosen to be. And no thoughts, just pure love and adoration where you can feel the existence of the other one to the bone.

At the atomic level, everything considered different becomes 'clothes to the soul'.

The soul speaks only through love on different levels of vibration. Love is its root of existence, the living energy that is felt but not seen.

ACTORS OF OUR DESTINY – MOVIES OF OUR LIVES

16 Aug 2019

We all are actors of our own destiny, some good and evil, some beautiful and others just ugly.

In love, duality will melt its borders and become just existence. You will become the soul behind the actor awakened from the sleep of your life. Close your eyes and become conscious about your destiny, about your life.

The past is one part of the movie, and the future reveals how the film will continue. In the present, it seems that you are the director of your future life movie because you couldn't change anything in the past.

But can you change the future by acting in the present?

I remember some statements from *The Matrix*:

'Do you think that's air you are breathing now?'

'Do not try to bend the spoon. That's impossible. Instead, only try to realise the truth ... There is no spoon ... then you'll see that it is not the spoon that bends; it is only yourself.'

In so many years of love worship, I understood one thing: you can't change fate. Life and surroundings you can't change. You just have the impression that you can do something about it. Everything is as it is supposed to be.

Only inside can you do something about it, but outside, it's impossible.

Don't bend the life as you please; instead, try to turn your heart to love, and the experience will follow.

WORDS FOR MY SOUL – SOUNDS OF MY HEART

17 Aug 2019

Words are thoughts encapsulated in sound vibrations.

It's not the vibration or frequency that gives a word complete power but the meaning perceived by another person for that word.

Emotions also give life to a word. Saying 'love you' without that feeling is like eating nothing, just imagining the process of eating.

Words are also spoken in silence. The echo of feelings mixed with the vibration and frequency of thoughts in your mind are perceived telepathically by others, no matter the distance.

What gives absolute power to any word in existence is not the word itself but the soul that releases it with the meaning behind the name fuelled by feelings.

The accurate word for my soul is love, which means to exist as a deity in an absolute and infinite state. Love is the Goddess from my heart beyond any religion, although all faiths praise its presence.

When divine love inside takes form through a 'soul image', it's not something I thought. It's a gift for my soul. The highest reflection of its divinity is in love between a man and a woman. And the enlightenment starts when both acknowledge the source.

All these words and 'soul image' for my soul are encapsulated in one existence – HER.

TOGETHERNESS IN LOVE – MISSING HER MORE THAN LIFE ITSELF

19 Aug 2019

I lost my sense in this world due to my inner self, who hid my soul addicted to love.

I've considered and still believe life without love is empty and meaningless. And probably, I will die being entirely and irrevocably devoted to sharing the message that love is absolute and infinite in a divine state.

Forget about gods, deities and anything else mystical or fantastic. Love is the source of everything and is the 'blood' of our souls and existence itself.

That's why when universal love hits you, experiencing human love, although simple at origin, changes you completely into another person and life; it seems to be from another realm.

Love in the divine state as an absolute and infinite existence can be experienced straightforwardly and quickly. You don't need fancy practices or extreme rules to accomplish.

The only thing needed is to be in love with someone else.

Because you can search for love and still can't find it, it knocks you unexpectedly and without warning. So, when you experience love for another person, it's time to acknowledge its divine state through awareness and consciousness. Someone who has experienced love can understand what I will discuss further; otherwise, it won't make sense.

You feel love for someone, but the other person doesn't feel it, or not yet. Therefore, you start wondering what makes you be that way. Beauty maybe, but everyone is unique, kindness perhaps not, and so on. You start unwrapping every layer of another character or existence. Searching deeper and deeper, you will notice that, in the end, it's the feeling from your heart that makes you feel what is called love. It's not the person but the feeling from your heart for that person that makes you feel love.

The first time you see that love lives in your heart, it's like a mystery even if everything and anything is against your feelings. This feeling from your heart makes you feel unique and out of this world. You feel so close to the other, even at the world's end.

The mistake 'soul images' make when feeling love at some point in their life is that if they do not receive the affection back, love will be blamed and thrown away. They should be able to give up on the person, not on feeling, but connect that feeling to the 'soul image' of the loved one. They think that the other one has fired the sparkle of love inside. But it's the other way around.

Love from your heart has awakened your soul and made you feel that way. You feel love on different levels since birth but are unaware of it. Love exists in your heart for the family, country, people, loved one and anything else that gives the feeling inside.

You give different names to this feeling, but the source is the same. As it grows on higher levels, it is closer to the source. You will feel love inside your heart at the highest level, not because of a reason. You feel the love, and that's it.

The love between a man and a woman is the highest reflection of divine love because this is how the world was created from opposite sides. Yes, love is possible in unthinkable ways, but the highest form of it is how creation was possible.

Besides the nature of masculine and feminine, the connection is more in-depth. Both tend to become one being; sometimes, they do it for real. They melt into each other's existence in the most intimate and blissful experience of their love.

If you have already found a 'soul image' to share the love from your heart and both feel the same, then you are so close to feeling divine love. Just look into each other eyes without thinking of love and touch your heart.

You will feel that you have become one with your loved one. Nothing else besides your existence will matter. That moment will feel like an eternity.

When you experience divine love with your loved one's 'soul image', you will feel that love is beyond words and existence itself.

Love will become your God or Goddess, and that feeling of divine love will become your religion.

THE BEAUTY OF 'WHY?' – THE WONDER BEHIND IT

22 Aug 2019

Curiosity and search for knowledge from the ancient times started from this simple question:
Why?
Some answers proved to be accurate.
Some are just theoretical knowledge.
Others are just inception ideas.

The concept of 'love' is a part of all three categories from above.

1. *Love exists in every heart at the existential level, no matter the question.*
2. *How love breathes and manifests into reality is theoretical.*
3. *Love as an infinite and absolute state – the so-called God state or divinity state – is just an inception idea.*

The divine state can't be proven; it is known only by those willing to taste the existence of love inside their hearts and see it in their souls.

Questions of 'WHY' can be applied to both categories of love – existential and theoretical, and it manifests and receives an answer through experience.

The divine state of love stops at 'WHY' because it's without an answer. It's just the mystery and miracle of its existence. You feel love at that level just because of love itself.

There's no other motive or reason behind it. You feel the 'WHY' in this state and don't need the answer. The answer is in what you encounter and nothing else.

The difference between human and divine love is in awareness and consciousness of love's existence as a divinity state. Although the source is the same, the feeling is different.

Human love needs answers and proof, while divine love needs nothing more than the feeling and the awareness of its existence.

THE ECHO IN MY HEART

24 Aug 2019

I long thought about expressing through words what my heart feels with her 'soul image' in the background. Or maybe it's better to leave the feelings without words echoing to her heart. What is written in my destiny, it will happen anyway.

But if words were not spoken from ancient times through the echo of their messengers' hearts, the world wouldn't know anything about them. And who knows how many words are left unspoken from the echo of so many hearts. It's the fear or shyness to open and let the vibration of the sound of love into the world.

The sound of feelings is everywhere around us in the real world. But so many hearts close their 'ears' to listen to the beats of other souls.

Close your eyes and, for a moment, forget about your Self and start listening to the voice of existence. Feel the astounding rhythm of the music pumped out from nature and life itself.

MISSING HER ... MORE ... MORE AND MORE EVERY DAY
28 Aug 2019

I wrote about this feeling some time ago, but it keeps returning like a mantra.

So, my daily meditation starts due to missing Her. Feelings revealed in thoughts and writing help my mind and heart with the echo of 'Just Love Her'. My heart and mind often fly to Korea in my free time or just a moment of awareness. The sound of her reality speaks to my soul through her 'soul image'.

I feel her presence around me like a scent of her existence ... of her soul. I close my eyes, and the goddess from my heart is revealed and empties my inner self. In those moments, nothing about me is inside; only divine love fogging around her 'soul image' exists. It's like a dream of love that I don't want to wake up from.

Every glimpse of her life in my visions makes me believe Her is a reality, not just an illusion of my mind. In those moments, I feel everything, even the insignificant signs of her existence, and it translates into feelings handled by my heart.

Love is magical. Simple becomes unreal, and small things and tiny moments transcend life.

When the light in her eyes shines through her 'soul image' occasionally, revealed by sight, my soul feels eternal love closer than ever. Our souls are connected beyond time and space. These moments keep reminding me that feelings awakened by her existence are beyond my control. So, I just let it all out in the open through thoughts that bow to love melted into her existence inside my heart.

A dream is born whenever I send thoughts and feelings from my mind and heart to Her. And whenever Her touches that dream, it becomes a surreal reality.

Missing Her ... I want to beam my feeling of missing Her straight to her heart, searching for the reality of her soul image existence. In this way, Her would know that words are not enough to describe feelings.

'나는 그녀가 그리워 ... *(Naneun Geunyeoga Geuriwo ...)*
– I miss Her ...'
It feels even closer to her language in my heart.

NOTHING ELSE ... JUST LOVE ... FEELING HER

29 Aug 2019

Have you ever felt the love burning inside like a volcano ready to erupt?
Or have you felt your heart happy and sad at the same time?
Or do you find yourself lost in love that you see reflected everywhere around you due to fire inside your heart?

All these add to the awareness of the belief that love is your God (Goddess), and you feel humbled that it is housed inside your heart.

How can a mere human be so blessed with the immortality of divine love?

Love with the image of another soul that resembles, due to this fact, a deity through your feelings?

I am *literally* burning inside my heart. Oh no, it's not new to me. It was just dormant inside my heart, waiting to be awakened like an inactive volcano. And this lava of love inside my heart is dripping. Drops of her existence and her eyes follow me inside like a divine look.

I am grateful for her existence in these moments of pure

eternity, melted in eternal love. Without Her, I wouldn't experience love in its raw state ... I would still be moonstruck, dreaming of forbidden realms untouchable.

My love, which can be offered and received even unknowingly, is a blessing. If I confessed in writing, what I feel is due to my ego mindset, written in millions of years of DNA's so-called evolution. It is stagnation. It proves that I am a mere human with dreams of holy love.

The most significant gift to offer due to divine love in your heart should be to fire the spark of eternal love in the heart of the loved one. If the love in your heart is as strong and pure as divine love, it is enough for your soul to spread it to another soul. Words and actions mean nothing because no expectation is needed. Also, no recompensating is necessary for your feelings other than what you feel.

Love burning inside your heart and soul as pure awareness and consciousness of its divinity is more than enough. It is the greatest gift, and even gods dream of it.

In these moments, floating in love, I feel a pure connection with her soul, and I understand the echoing voice from my heart: '*Just Love Her*'.

LOVE FEELS LIKE DYING – DYING OF LOVE OR LOVESICKNESS ...
30 Aug 2019

There are many more moments lately when I feel my heart burning and fluttering as the echo of love feeling Her became so blatant. It is the sign that my life will have to endure crazy and blissful moments.

As good as it seems, these moments are not so easy to live with. Without proper control of respiration and mind, it's like being consistently high. Being high on feelings of love is not quite the best thing without control. It changes you completely, living in a world where only you dream. That dream you hope one day becomes a reality ... it mostly doesn't because it takes two to tango.

'Yesterday, I was dreaming of Her with eyes wide open. Next to the sea, sitting close to each other on the fine sand ... her head resting on my shoulder. I felt her short hair touching my face, cuddled by the wind. For one moment, our eyes crossed and looked deep into her eyes ... So beautiful that moment. Nothing else besides our souls touching together through our eyes existed. Oh, sweet life, it was like I was painted inside with her image ... My Self was dissipating into Her existence. It was unreal that it felt so real ...'

In that moment of infinite love, death was just another thing that it is a part of life ... If I had died at that moment, it would have been of pure happiness.

My heart is beating so hard even now. It's like a hum drum sound, and I still feel Her in my heart. Her soul image is freshly painting all my existence through my mental vision.

'너무 보고 싶어 그녀. *(Neomu bogo sipeo Geunyeo.)* – I miss Her so much.'

SEEING HER EVERYWHERE

31 Aug 2019

Usually, you must close your eyes to see the image of the loved one or at least to picture it in your mind. But the 'fire' in my heart is burning so intense. And the soul image painted with Infinite Love over my heart and soul is just in front of my third eye.

I see Her reflected anywhere around me in the shadows of existence. Her being is a part of me, either with eyes closed or open. Her eyes painted over my life are like a mirror to divine Love. And questions without answers are all over my mind ...

Does Her know and feel something inside through my messages sent by divine love reflection?

Am I crazy and imagining things?

'Just Love Her'? And the final 'Why'?

In the past, an answer was continuously released from above.

It happened in destiny, not in words but in life actions beyond my control, which amazed me and made me believe in the Goddess of Love – divine love.

Now, it is beyond any imagination and reality facts.

But who am I?

A mere existence knelt in front of Her ...

Nothing else has the same meaning as the feeling of Her in these moments. I see the beauty in other souls but don't feel that Love – divine love. Infinite Love is just for Her.

You know who Her is ... You feel it deep inside you, whether you admit it or not. You feel the hope of your dreams that you are Her.

Ultimately, it's just the destiny of souls to become one because 'Me' was lost a long time ago in Her existence ...

FLUTTERS OF LOVE –
SURRENDER TO LOVE FEELING

1 Sep 2019

Surrender. This feeling is the only option when the heart flutters. No matter how much you fight it, the heart ultimately wins.

The mind will try through every option available to turn around the heart. The only way the mind can listen to your heart is to be empty of thoughts, writing its feelings sincerely without words or ideas.

You are following the path of divine love reflected in your soul.

When your heart is vibrating at a higher frequency, you feel your heart all the time. You are aware that something is happening. The mind barely keeps up with the information, trying to translate feelings into thoughts to decide or act.

While your heart flutters with love and is enough to feel love, your mind will always try to do something about that. When you know the source of love – absolute and infinite love (divine love), goddess – feeling love is enough; otherwise, the mind may have a say about your feelings. The mind's intention is right and directed to bring the other soul closer to reality through every method or meaning available. But your heart full of love is following unseen destiny and past lives.

You think these flutters of love happen just because. But two souls are connected through many unseen things and beyond time and space.

My heart flutters with love for Her.

Why does it matter?

It matters because I have felt divine love inside my heart for dozens of years. When my heart flutters with love at high frequency, the painting in my mind is from the feeling of divine love through my heart and soul.

It means just feelings, no thoughts, and surrender to love for Her.

MOMENTS OF ETERNITY … ALONG THE WHEEL OF TIME

3 Sep 2019

Every moment you live is a moment of eternity, printed in the wheel of time forever. So be aware of every second in your life to leave for your soul-touching existence.

If you are in love with another soul, it's a must. These moments will be there to remember in other lives. If you weren't aware, it would be hard to recognise the soul who fired the spark of love inside you.

Living every moment with consciousness is essential because souls can connect hearts and minds over time and space. It is not magic; it's just the science of divine love reflected in souls' existence. That's why it's hard to fall in love again if you had deception in a past relationship. You don't see the divine love reflected in that pure human love. You can't see due to your closed third eye. The existence of divine love is reflected in everything around you.

Some perceived it as God reflected in all existence. Only a

few foresaw the actual source that connects and keeps everything together. Well, many called, few chosen.

It appears that you can truly love one person in your whole life, and that is your other half.

Maybe it's right for human love due to ego.

Human love wants to possess the other soul, being dependent, whereas divine love gives total freedom. It's a love without borders because feelings write rules and boundaries.

In divine love, the feeling of Her inside is always there. The 'soul image' painted over your soul becomes your other one. If the soul image wants to be free and doesn't feel the same, you can't do anything about it. You can't possess the other souls. It's a gift of love, not a purchase and indeed not a thing.

So, if you had deception in love, don't give up on the love you felt. Soul image is passing, but love is immortal. That's why if you love through divine love, you can't ever hate Her.

You will be hurt or suffer but never have hate, and no matter what, you will want the other soul's happiness. Love through divine love is a total surrender to another soul to become one due to your heart's feelings.

You don't exist inside. Only Her is your existence.

NO DAY GOES BY WITHOUT THE MANTRA OF LOVE

5 Sep 2019

My heart is in sync with me every day, so it repeats the same mantra dedicated to divine love.

Three things are required to keep feelings in their place and not disturb the other soul's image: respiration, the mantra of love, and the image of the loved one in the third eye.

Due to mind relativity, the soul wants to express love in seen reality, not just unseen. The mind can't see black and white as one. Only the soul can connect opposites.

It's easy when it happens for both souls the same way, but it usually doesn't. Furthermore, we are not discussing awareness of divine love reflected in human love. This awareness is what awakens and feeds your soul with love. The love mantra keeps the soul connected with both worlds – seen and unseen.

This love must be shared and directed to all beings from existence and expanding to manifested and unmanifested reality, to seen and unseen alike.

Divine love isn't just for the loved one but for all creation because divine love created everything from love to love. When you are aware and always living through divine love, it will happen at some point in your life to see love connecting everything around you – existing all around you in and out of everything.

That's why you become one with the other soul. When both will be free from the mind, each one will have the soul image of the other one inside, reflecting the love from their heart.

Enough for today. Let the heart do the talking through feelings – enough with the words.

OUT OF THIS WORLD ... OUT OF MIND

8 Sep 2019

Talking about divine love is like talking about the mystery of life.

Although it was considered the essential element in all religions and practices to enlightenment since ancient times, human life didn't acknowledge love as being divine. And still, it isn't. Maybe because everyone experiences it, or it has become a typical food for most of us. Also, nobody seems to see the source of its existence and the importance of the souls connected through it, and love is mundane.

It is no wonder that the world is close to collapse due to the heart being pushed away and love treated with ignorance.

Many people are interested in mystic and soul evolution-related things. But without practice, it's just talking and nothing else.

Although technology could help tremendously, it's not directed to help the body reach the connection with the soul but instead with pleasures and consumerism.

And what else could help if blind people direct other blind people?

Few try, but it's not enough.

All societies should have the same goal. Not power, nor greed, but love.

Love is the bridge between everything – science, religion, nature and people. You name it.

It will start to change our society when meditation and teachings related to the soul become an education in schools and universities. Until then, let's hope that divine love will not fade in the hearts of *soul images*.

I'M GOING TO DREAM OF HER IN THE MIDDLE OF THE DAY

9 Sep 2019

And I will dream of her in the middle of the day for the rest of my life …

Have you ever thought that your body isn't suited enough for your soul?

And does your mind need to prepare more for your intuition?

Did you feel that the ideas and information that come through your mind and brain are too much to handle?

Well, I felt it so many times, and I still believe that the body given to my soul to live in is too weak. The level of my brain's intelligence and memory can't handle the amount of information received and is struggling to decode my heart's intuition.

Many dreams are lost in the shadow of sleep. Many past lives are relieved in dreams forgotten as soon as eyes open. And dreams of love happened in reality as in mystical and magical stories many years ago. Now, just dust in the wheel of time. And yet, one true reflection of divine love cuddled my soul since it was awakened from the deep sleep of karma (law of cause and effect).

Now, I am living another dream of loving Her in the middle of the day.

Who knows where the path of love will bend time and space so that our souls can dance in the rays of the eye's light?

For the moment, any second away from Her is like a punishment for my soul.

The art of drinking tea from an empty cup is beautiful, but drinking natural tea from a full cup is way better. And I'm going to dream of her in the middle of the day until the end of time, and her soul embraces my soul in the dream of love – love beyond time and space …

WHEN DIVINE LOVE BECOMES ONE WITH SOULS

11 Sep 2019

When divine love becomes one with both souls sharing its reflection inside the hearts of soul images …

Everyone who experiences being in love for the first time knows it is unique and never forgotten. How about the second, third or several times?

One of the other essential things that makes a difference is knowing the source of human love – divine love. First love is not the most important or the next one …

It is important to keep love alive in your heart no matter what and to always be aware of its source – the infinite and absolute divine love.

Every time you share this love with another soul, you are thankful for it as a gift and happy just for living it and nothing else. Love in your heart becomes one with the loved one through divine love as a bond beyond any limits. You won't ever count or measure your feelings for a soul you love because every moment is unique. Every soul is individual. Your only hope is that love won't separate your soul images ever ... And even if it happens, you will never forget nor hate that soul image.

Because it happens ... Usually, neither soul image is aware of the reflection of divine love in their feelings. This is why human love, although highly praised, is not seen as its real value and enlightenment potential for the soul.

Conversely, when you become aware of its source, human love becomes one with divine love and steps up beyond boundaries and limits that the mind is constricted to.

My mind is blown every time the divine love chooses the soul image for feelings from my heart. Only divine love can foresee the potential of two souls to become one living it. When both soul images are aware of that and fight for it, magical and mystical things happen inside and outside. Time and space become obsolete.

The hardest part is being away from Her. I would be happy just by seeing Her every day, not only in my mind's eye. My heart aches to miss Her.

Will fate allow our soul images to connect and become one in this life or others?

AN IMPOSSIBLE YET POSSIBLE LOVE – HOPE DIES LAST

13 Sep 2019

Since the first time I experienced the divine love reflection in human love, every soul image chosen for the heart to represent divine love existence was a provocation for the soul. It seemed impossible to share divine love with the soul selected due to many factors and different views of life.

But in the end, the impossible can become possible.

Everything will be magical if both souls follow the feeling inside and know divine love. Both souls will feel its magic touching them. From a simple touch of hands to an in-depth look into the eyes, it will go beyond any movie or book description.

Everything will be broken if the material side corrupts the brain over love feelings. And even if you don't have a tough life, the mind will want more and more … and more.

In love felt with the awareness of divine love reflection in it, you must have patience … much patience because love isn't against living a good life and doesn't require you to live poorly to prove your devotion. Because of your feelings for the loved one, everything you own and represent as a material and spiritual being is given to the soul you love.

So even if you don't have wealth, your heart is given to the loved one, and your ideal will be to bring happiness to the life of the soul you love no matter what.

In love, following the rules of divine love, 'You' don't exist.

Your ego is melted and disappears, feeling the love for another soul.

This is the meaning of becoming One. Both souls melting and living one for the other gives birth to a new entity.

This is how I feel looking into her eyes. My soul is melting, and only Her exists inside. If I search for myself inside my heart, I only find Her and nothing else. Just feelings and her soul image.

MUSIC OF THE SOUL

15 Sep 2019

Feelings … like never before … or maybe it's due to divine love whenever sharing feelings with a soul image is new … feelings deep from the soul's music.

You will never get bored if human love is aware of divine love reflection in it. Everything will seem new and exciting every day due to your feelings.

Being high on love, even a simple meal eaten every day will become a ritual.

The mantra of divine love, although repeating the exact words and feelings all the time, will be like a drop of water that, ultimately, will make a hole in the stone.

It was like being struck by the lightning of love, seeing Her inside my heart ... My heart was pounding like crazy in my chest, and I had to cool down through some deep breathing. In the end, it left me wondering why I had these feelings.

Sometimes, I question whether everything is correct or if I'm going insane. How can you love someone without base, support, connection ... or nothing?

I know 'Just Love Her' is a good start ... but why?

I have crazy feelings ... so deep inside my heart. I desire to be with her soul, craving just a moment of reality with Her, even if it seems so natural, just inside my soul, like being connected with Her.

How can these feelings be shared with her soul?

Wondering if it's one-sided and dreaming of love of only one soul ...

Yes, the song seems connected with her soul image, and that's why my heart is fluttering with love just by listening ... And only her soul image is covering the sky of my mind. I can't even describe this feeling ... of Her inside ... being one with Her.

With eyes closed or opened, her soul image is full of life in front of my mind's eye. I feel her soul touch all over my being.

How many aeons passed since the last time our souls found each other?

INSPIRING MUSIC: Hey Laura – Gregory Porter

MOMENTS OF LOVE ...
BEYOND 'SIMPLE' LOVE ...
MOMENTS OF HER ...

17 Sep 2019

Burning heart, painful memories from the past, dreaming of past lives while sleeping.

Some people are born just to be loved, others to live in pain and others only to share their love.

Sometimes, I want to let go of myself to feel the love inside and not share any thoughts about feelings. But how else can the soul image, whom I see as the divine love reflection, ever be aware of its existence in this reality?

When I became aware of divine love reflected in human love for the first time, it was like discovering that I didn't know anything about the food I eat daily. There is so much more in the background, feeling the love. Understanding a simple thing happening every day has so much more meaning.

I often just wanted to immerse myself in the feeling of loving Her and shouting inside my heart that I love Her and nothing else. But the echo inside my heart didn't go silent until the words were released for Her to know.

What good is in Her knowing about my feelings?

It's enough that my heart is tormented loving Her. Why bother Her with mere thoughts about feelings?

I am searching for my Self but not being here. My Self has become one with Her near the Han River.

In some moments, I feel Her so close that my existence vanishes like a ghost of past lives coming to haunt me. Hearing about love around me instantly brings up her soul image from the depths of my heart in front of my eyes, like a shadow of her existence.

Is this love so real that I can't deny it even if my mind talks so much about illusions and lost sense of reality?

Only Her knows. I'm following my heart and only the path ahead of my soul.

Divine love is my life, so I will probably die loving Her, with or without me in her reality.

I cry with joy when I feel Her in my heart or with sorrow at the sad reality that I see numerous possible paths of destiny. I wonder if there's any possibility that our paths in the future will converge at some point or will be a story in the forgotten life path.

One thing is sure. I can't give up on reminding Her about

forgotten feelings from past lives, especially since the awareness of divine love was awakened deep inside my heart again for her soul image.

This connection isn't happening too often in one's life ... or at all.

ALWAYS THINKING OF HER ... BEYOND MY MIND ...

18 Sep 2019

I was reading past writings about my thoughts and feelings about her over time. Time passed, and I didn't feel it. Time and space disappeared from my mind since my heart became a shrine to Her.

Now and then, I must wash my mind of thoughts about the reality of my visions.

I understand why. My mind is anchored in the reality of now related to the past, while my heart is living now for the future and never in the past.

The other day, I prayed for her and her potential family. I would love to see her happy in the future and wish her life were as good as it was in her dreams.

From my soul's side, the only thing that will mark her existence in the future is my awareness of divine love reflected in human love through my writings.

When going to sleep, always my heart is cuddling Her close to it ... I feel her hair warming my face and her scent touching my soul. It is so unreal, yet I think I am next to her.

How is that even possible?

Can my mind still comprehend the numerous sensations my heart has spread its wings for?

One thing is sure: I am not here anymore. I live in a realm my mind can't touch; I dream of it. Instead, my heart is feeding and living within.

Love for Her is untouchable in my mind. And this means it's here to stay.

MAGICAL AND MYSTICAL LOVE – IT'S LIKE A DREAM, EXCEPT IT ISN'T

20 Sep 2019

When you feel divine love connected with human love, you lose the sense of time and space between you and your loved one. You wake up one day; looking back is like watching a movie or reading a fairy tale.

But you'll want those magical feelings back because reality is always sad. You are not yet with the loved one. It's like a beautiful dream from which you don't want to wake up until it becomes a reality.

Magical. Just closing my eyes and seeing Her inside me felt like being a part of my soul. I struggle to find myself because I want to feel her soul. The next moment, my heart opened, and I felt our hands touching and holding her hands into mine. And honest to God, I felt every part of her skin. It was like her soul was kept in her palms. It was so sweet that my heart was melting and my brain vibrating at such high frequency.

Oh ... And then I hugged her, tucking her chest close to mine and her lovely face resting on my shoulder. I couldn't resist touching her face softly.

And again, honest to God, I smelt her perfume, her hair touching my nose. And all my being just dreaming of her sweet lips touching mine like a wind blow. Then, both laughing, falling on the grass. Alone in a park where the sky was kissing the earth where we were falling. Her body is on top of me, losing myself in her eyes like in the eternity of our souls. Love beyond imagination, feelings not from this earth ... Not in this little life.

Mystical ... Silence ... of the thoughts against love. No cloud of negative thoughts. Just pure worship in the heart's beating – a warm feeling cuddling the heart and every atom of my body vibrating with love for her existence. It's like dying, but not that kind of death. My mind is dying, surrendering to the higher path of the soul.

Feeling ... the other soul's existence. Although so far, yet so close.

Intuition ... doing something simultaneously as Her, catching the moment of her existence. Happening once could be a coincidence, but occurring more times means a connection beyond time and space.

Bliss ... Nothing on earth gives more happiness than feeling Her. Nothing but love that reflects divine love. In these moments, my mind has no doubts about divine love as a divinity when proof of divine love reflection is everywhere around the existence while loving Her.

Oh ... and Her is everywhere I look and touch. It means that Her became one with love inside.

TELEPATHY – THE OUTCOME OF LOVE AND DEVOTION

21 Sep 2019

What does it mean to become one with the soul we are in love with?

One outcome could be telepathy. We are sharing and feeling thoughts and existence altogether.

Imagine having instant access to the other soul. Individuality will become duality, not because of differences but because of the same path of enlightenment. We can't imagine it because it's out of this world now, but who knows in the future?

Technology started to do something about it outside of our bodies, but we are born with this ability. This ability can happen in your daily routine. Just focus on the feeling of love from your heart and spread it through your mind around you everywhere you go. And use the mantra of love and breathing in and out, filling your lungs with air slowly and relaxing.

In time, you'll notice that people will start giving back your feelings of love. Those who are 'bad' will feel fear or at least will try to avoid you.

Love is a powerful 'weapon' if used constantly until it becomes your heart's breath. The scriptures call love 'the blood of God'.

I went further in my meditations, calling it divine love and seeing human love as a reflection of it. The soul is revealed when you become aware of the connection between 'human love', 'the divine love' and 'the reflection of the divine love'. These instances of love are the Trinity of God as I see it through divine love vision. All representations have an existence by themselves and are interconnected as one.

Love is the language of the soul, so feelings don't need words or actions to communicate. When you see a person in love, you will recognise the signs.

Could this be a way to communicate and share feelings with Her?

Only Her knows and feels if it's true or not.

LOVING HER JUST BECAUSE ... AND NOT BECAUSE OF ANYTHING ELSE

22 Sep 2019

When you love someone just because, without any expectations or because of different things that your mind considers suitable to be liked, your life is not a normal one for sure; it looks from the outside as of everyone else, but inside, it is a different world.

Every moment exists for Her, and all thoughts are related to feelings for Her inside my heart. This kind of living happens because her soul image revealed became one with the divine love reflection from my soul. It's not like I am doing that as a practice; it just happens. The only time when it is quiet, or it seems so, is when sleeping.

Many times, I looked inside, being an observer of what was happening. And I had to fight with my mind over beliefs and logic of what's better for my soul. My soul feels that it can't live without Her. In contrast, my mind feels the burden of this choice for the future of my existence.

One of the perks of awareness of divine love reflection is that even if you have different views, tastes or cultures, in the end, you will start loving everything that your loved soul image likes. It will enhance the experiences and feelings of your soul, keeping you closer to each other.

Listening to Oohyo or Gregory Porter for the first time because of feelings for Her, it seems the connection between our souls happens in a parallel universe. My soul feels the same way, even the most insignificant thing that Her inside likes or wants. Of course, my mind will always find a way to annoy my heart, but it's like a stranger who bothers my soul.

In the end, the love mantra prevails over thoughts, and only feelings of love exist. The hardest part is getting used to my destiny, which unfolds in front of my mind. It unveils all the obstacles I must overcome to love Her.

In these moments, it seems like a pain for my soul, the body's existence, feeling the limits of this passing life. I am struggling to write words because I want to let myself experience feelings of love for Her just because and not write about it.

But how else would Her know sometime in the future that my soul exists only for Her?

Her choice is to accept it or run away in one of the realities. My mind would be so happy if both soul images ran away. This way, no more troubles and finally, the soul vision is defeated once and for all.

It is easy for the mind to think of forgetting the feelings. Luckily, my soul beat my mind dozens of years ago due to awareness of the divine love reflection.

How else could I dream of an impossible yet possible love?

THE RIGHT TIME ...
FOR THINGS TO HAPPEN

22 Sep 2019

Why now? *Why* not another time in the past? *Why*? The beauty of *why*.

Everything happens for a reason. And the right time is now.

My mind is empty some days, and feelings are going to the roof of my mind. Some moments are like that. I can't do anything other than stay still and look at the shadow of my existence.

I know what's next. I have seen it for months in my visions. Troubling thoughts pass through my mind all the time. I understand the reason for logic, but my heart follows a different set of rules. These rules are not from this Earth and the past. They are from our destiny's future and our souls' hidden path.

The mind is always trying to understand the existence of the soul.

But how can something so limited and passing decode the mystery of eternity?

In the future, science will prove that we are way more things and forces than our bodies and that life will exist for love and enlightenment. Steps for this future have already started with quantum realm discoveries.

The right time is like in Schrodinger's cat paradox, where a cat is dead and alive until someone opens the box to find out. Until it happens, nothing is for sure.

It could occur if both souls are in 'the box'. If one soul is outside the box, it can free up another.

Love is the key to breaking out of the box. Divine love reflection awareness is knowledge about the clue. Divine love is the creator and energy contained in the whole process.

1001 THOUGHTS AGAINST FEELINGS OF LOVE

22 Sep 2019

The biggest enemy against love and our feelings isn't destiny or anything other than our mind. It's like a quiet monster waiting in the shadow to attack at the proper moment. One second of distraction and our mind will take the lead, and thoughts we didn't know before will bother our hearts and feelings.

Patience is not a mind virtue but a heart quality. The heart can wait as long as needed; in the end, the fact that love exists within it is all it requires. Also, the time and space in the heart disappear. Only the mind is obsessed with things that happen as soon as possible due to fear of death.

The heart follows the unknown and values immortality, unchanging energy and silence. The mind is always bored and unstable. Silence is like a killing virus for the brain. That's why meditation is a cure for the mind.

From ancient times, the heart mantra has been used to overcome the mind's control over the heart. One doesn't have time for other thoughts by keeping the mind focused on praying. Combined with controlled breathing and deep feelings of divine love, the mantra becomes a powerful practice for enlightenment.

At some point in time, people lost the knowledge and awareness of reflection of the divine love in human love. In this way, human love became ordinary yet the most desired accomplishment. Our souls have written in their existence the code of divine love. That's why searching for a soulmate was ideal for all of us.

A long time ago, I realised that some of us don't have only one soulmate for all our existence. There is a limit to finding one of our soulmates due to life expectancy and the place we live in, and if we believe in reincarnation, then obviously, we can't be only one in aeons of the soul's existence. And indeed, it doesn't depend on our soul other than the divine love that matches our souls.

In the same way, it just happened to fall in love with Her. It was like being struck by the light of divine love when I saw her eyes inside my heart. The thunder of love echoing in my heart at that moment came into my mind later.

Soulmate or long-time soul sharing love in the past lives?

Who knows how many unseen things lurk in the shadow of our destiny?

All I know is that my mind laughs at every downfall from receiving a sign from Her ... Any sign. But what my mind doesn't understand is that my heart is happy just living love for Her and nothing else. Any expectations are failures of the mind to see the beauty of pure love in our souls.

OUR BODY IS NOT OUR SOUL – IT IS ONLY A VESSEL

24 Sep 2019

In my adolescence, when, for the first time, the 'inception' idea that divine love is God and the scale of its representation into existence came to my mind, my brain was on fire. There was so much information and contradiction due to my past beliefs borrowed from the scriptures and books, that my mind often couldn't follow up the visions of what divine love signifies in the world.

When all information came at once, the brain couldn't handle it. Many times, when I wanted to unveil an idea or a vision that came to my mind, I had problems communicating in words due to too many simultaneous connections related to the concept.

Ultimately, the practice prevailed, and I was 'lucky' enough to experience and have proof of the statement. So, I had to throw out everything I'd learned from the books and test what's true by myself.

In those times, I realised that my body and brain were too weak to represent my soul. Instead, I've tried to do my best. But after so many years, I am still unhappy with my accomplishments.

How can you handle it when you know your body and mind are not good enough to represent your soul?

The only thing that kept me through my 'weakness' was the feeling of divine love inside my heart, even without a soul image to represent it. That's why nothing else matters when my heart chooses a soul image. It's not my mind's option; it's the divine love reflection into my heart's choice.

Sometimes, it looked like I was very bright, but I knew the difference instead. Intuition was the force behind my philosophy. It's more like a revelation than my reflection. If I had been more intelligent and had a good memory in this vessel, maybe I would have explained and talked more concisely or poetically about divine love representation and existence due to so many books, readings and information acknowledged in the past.

Because of my experience and practice over time, I understood the limits of my body and accepted its weakness. I also saw the difference when words or views about divine love came out of my mind and mouth that information received was beyond my human limits.

Many times, after some exciting concepts and explanations in my past writings or thoughts, I couldn't say that it was a creation of my mind.

Oh, and I am not a good writer at all. Too blunt, no beauty in expressing into words the divine love, no shining in describing my love.

Even so, to test my ideas' endurance and let others know about the divine love vision, I had to write when my heart was in awe of a soul image revealed. Maybe the connection between our souls was from past lives, or the soul's beauty or souls so evolved that soon we will be free from the shackles of destiny.

I always wonder how my heart chose a soul image to represent the divine love inside. Or better yet, how the divine love reflection reveals inside my heart that soul.

How could we know that a soul chosen is a choice of divine love?

It's pretty easy. It happens. We look around and see beautiful faces, people and souls. But none of them makes us feel like the soul revealed into our hearts.

Nothing and nobody makes us feel the connection with divine love and a higher state of consciousness as the loved soul image does.

THE SOUL REFLECTION INTO HER EYES

24 Sep 2019

Her eyes follow me everywhere and all the time.

Since I met her soul through her eyes, my soul has resurfaced before my mind, taking the lead. My heart has been beating at an unprecedented rate since then, and I sometimes wonder if I have some health issues rather than love inside. I mean, all the time?

I still remember the first time her eyes glittered in the depths of my heart.

My mind was like, 'Huh?'

And my heart was like, 'Finally, my prayers answered!'

My soul was next to Her.

In time, the feelings for Her evolved to the point of no return.

I said before that the right time was now. With technology nowadays, Her could navigate the wheel of time. One of my beliefs is that technology exists to elevate and ease the connection between soul and body through our mind. Of course, there are elevated and evolved souls out there with some 'powers' that are native without needing technology.

The technology brings these powers to the whole world, not just a chosen few. However, it is a 'weapon' with two blades; not everyone will use it for good.

Most of the time, my soul is not here but out there with Her. If destiny allowed it, I would probably disappear to be her guardian angel. And permanently, her eyes and her being are engraved on its aura when it returns.

Mystical? Magical?

Maybe not. It's just the way my soul feels close to Her.

There are moments when I barely feel my existence. Looking inside, only Her exists. It's like a dream, except it's not. It's the reality in which my soul lives. The shallow attempts of my mind to take control proved to be like a feather touch for my unbreakable soul.

For sure, logic and reason are not in the existence of my soul. My soul only breathes love for Her. It's not human love, as my mind is getting used to, hence the struggle to understand the path.

All this process exists as a contemplation due to divine love reflected in all my existence. Without it, blindness would be all over my vision. So, there is nothing to talk about and no knowledge.

MY PLACE IS WHERE HER LIVES

26 Sep 2019

The world should be without borders for the hearts of love ... and my place to exist is where Her lives.

If it were a country or place where 'love' lives, that would be the most sought after location. There are some places where love can flourish and be maintained more easily. Any place would be acceptable if the practice of divine love happens inside our hearts.

The place where I want to live is where Her exists.

Why? Even if there are no feelings back from Her?

The divine love reflection in human love is the same as adoring an entity in the divinity realm. Being a gift for our soul, we would also want our beloved soul to taste the nectar of the gods. This means that no matter what happens in the material world, we will keep the beloved soul image in our hearts as we cherish the divine love.

Suppose we talk about anything other than 'love just because' is pointless. The mind and the material world do not matter in this equation. The gift of divine love is enough for our souls. If both souls decide to be together or connect in the material world, it will happen with or without taking action through our minds.

Without the practice of divine love, the mind can't handle this kind of devotion. The mind can't think of a connection without results or materialisation in the real world.

The soul gives total freedom of choice for beloved soul image, even if it means suffering for the whole life of body and mind. Being driven by a devotion to divine love, love for another soul is not a possession. It's treated as a gift; the only outcome is the practice of praying to divine love. This way, we can protect the beloved soul image against the destiny chains.

That's why time and space don't matter for the soul.

Who knows in what multiverse or point of the axis of time both souls will be together?

Also, in this reality?

Walking on the same paths as Her, kissing the shadow of Her steps in the same places, tasting the same existence as Her in the real world – could we be a step closer to the heaven of love?

There is only one way to find out: to live in the same place as Her.

SILENCE SPEAKING ... THROUGH FEELINGS

26 Sep 2019

Thoughts gone ... Mind empty ... Words without sound ... Nothing is moving inside ... Staying still as a stone ... Just feelings ... Untranslated to the mind.

My heart aches when I miss Her. Something is always missing, and I'm just wondering how it happened.

How could I fall in love again after so long?

I lost my trust in human love a long time ago.

My heart is full of joy: What is so unique about seeing news about her on the screening of My Soul?

Or when taking a glimpse into a moment of Her existence, my eyes have a moist look.

Every day, I pray for Her happiness, with or without me in the picture. Her image became inside my heart, a precious icon shrouded by divine love.

All that is left are just feelings … So deep feelings are bouncing on the walls of my heart.

…

I have been trying for so many hours to translate feelings into thoughts, to put words in writing but to no avail. Words are embedded in the silence of thoughts, and my heart doesn't want more words, or thoughts for that matter. Feelings for Her are just what the echo from my heart told me from the beginning: 'Just Love Her'.

Maybe no more thoughts are wanted because, too many times, rational and logical thinking tried to overcome the heart's hopes for the reality of its dreams.

Like Her … Missing Her … Loving Her … Ultimately, all mixed in and kicking hard to the bottom of my heart.

Her Korean name in Hanja (自然) means Nature …

Since divine love was revealed to my soul, heart and mind years ago, I've seen it as the heart of existence in nature. That adds up to why 'Just Love Her'.

Because my heart chose Her to be the image of love inside, not my mind though, real love can't be measured, and not thinking of it while living it.

Is there a destiny for both of us? Or are only dreams left in this reality?

Love works in mysterious ways, and time will do the bidding.

LOVE TOO INTENSE – SPREAD IT TO THE WORLD

27 Sep 2019

Sometimes, love is so fierce in my heart that I need to close my eyes and spread it to the world, like praying for the good of all existence to feel divine love and be blessed. It's like being wealthy, but instead of money, you spread love. And let's be fair, I haven't yet seen a rich person acting as being driven by love.

A wealthy person should create all the things and services for the benefit of society for free. This means schools, libraries, education, hospitals, transport, food, etc.

The same goes for big companies. Everything should be free for their employees, and all the help needed should be provided as in a family. Instead, all companies and rich people act as if they own everything, not as if it were a gift received.

A soul who received the gift of divine love is so overwhelmed by feelings and happiness that the only way to be thankful is to spread the gift of love around like a fountain with overflowing water. And as well as sharing love, the same goes for receiving like a boomerang.

An unseen force changes the surroundings and the souls praying with love for the good of all humanity. The same power is leading monks, prayers, hermits and worshippers around the world to pray not only for themselves but also for humankind.

Without love, nothing will happen, as an empty vessel. It needs to be filled, not to be emptied.

When the heart is full of divine love and feelings are at higher levels, pray for the beloved soul image, for family, friends, country, world, nature … everything.

If the heart is still burning with love, pray for the whole Universe, all things seen and unseen, all the existence.

That's how I'm praying for Her …

SOUL'S HAPPINESS

28 Sep 2019

My soul happiness was the heart mantra praying for dozens of years and still is.

I am praying just because and nothing else. Nothing is expected in return. Happiness for the soul is when I see people loving each other, the world is in peace, and nature is preserved. Happiness in my heart is when I see and feel real love happening around me. When people choose love above anything else.

The mind always induces expectations for its happiness. Happiness is to be healthy, have food on the table, own things I supposedly want, and so on. The mind has the most difficulty satisfying its happiness. This happens because its needs must occur in reality and as soon as possible.

The soul's happiness is easy to maintain. It's enough to pray with the love mantra, be aware of divine love's reflection, and always have the precious soul image of Her in my heart and mind.

Deep breathing awareness keeps everything connected. It also cools down the heart's passion and the fire of love burning at high levels.

The soul doesn't need reality to make it happen. It follows unseen rules and experiences, gifted by the divine love vision. I don't know how it's happening … it just is, and I feel the results.

I often had to take steps back in my mind's desire to prove the reality of Her. My heart and soul feel 'Just Love Her', and the connection with her soul feels so real, but my mind keeps bugging me, telling me that it's only an illusion of my troubled soul and signs of Her nowhere to be seen.

As an observer, it's hard to think about free will between mind and soul while watching *Game of Thrones*.

My heart is the moderator, and its high vibrations keep telling me that the feeling of love for Her is natural.

진짜로*! (Jinjja-ro!) – Really!*

LOVING HER BEYOND MY MIND – TALES FROM THE ALTERNATE REALITIES

29 Sep 2019

Whenever the soul falls in love with another soul due to divine love reflection in its existence, although love is unique in feelings, the pattern of events is the same.

This is the third time my soul succeeded in bending the mind for another soul. Of course, I liked other beautiful souls but I didn't fall in love. The connection could have been stronger. Also, my mind never kneeled. For my mind to listen, it should be out of ordinary feelings.

And it's not about body, beautiful face, or anything else that men's minds are addicted to. It's like loving a flower. Many beautiful flowers are out there, yet only one moves your soul to the roots. And only that one makes your heart sing of love vibration. You don't know why, and if you start thinking and analysing, the magical connection could be lost. The flower won't be unique anymore. Because what makes the flower special are your feelings, not the flower itself.

When you fall in love, don't think about it. Just follow the river flowing of love and forget about the mind.

This happens when my soul feels a special connection. Initially, my mind was forbidden to make assumptions or think about what happened with my heart. The only thing allowed is to use the mantra of love – nothing else.

After the feelings settle in, the mind is accepted to do its work. It's a free world.

And how else can you keep in touch with reality if not through your mind?

Troubles begin from now on. Due to deep-rooted feelings, my mind can't overturn and contest the love felt, but it will analyse, check and question everything my soul dreams of. The mind wants to accomplish the soul's vision. The sooner, the better.

Action is my mind's motto. I called my mind 'the beast'. If it listens to my soul's needs, it's a necessary annoyance in the real world.

The next stage is the accomplishment of so-called 'fake it until you make it'. Some of the soul's visions will happen. The mind will transition from a noisy and annoying troublemaker to the constructor and builder of dreams. What started as a possibility will become almost a reality.

That's the beauty of 'nothing is certain'.

Is the free choice an option or a dream of mind?

Or is free choice another thing in predestination?

Is it just another settled choice that we know will happen, and afterwards, we must understand why it occurred?

The fact that I love Her with my mind and soul will make things happen in one of the realities. Otherwise, it would have been just an echo of my dreams.

THE WARMTH OF MY HEART – MANA OF MY SOUL

30 Sep 2019

If something I love is related to my physical Self, it is my heart. Everything else seems to be unrelated to my soul. My heart has never deceived me since it became the sanctuary for divine love's reflection.

At the beginning of my practice dozens of years ago, I had to endure a lot of pain, trials and deceptions, but in the end, the love persisted and settled in forever. It pleased my soul being the 'instrument' that tests and measures the rates of love breathing inside. It was the unseen Master who guided me through the uncanny path of living with love as the purpose of my life.

Many years ago, my heart proved my belief that divine love lives inside and won't ever leave. Everything else could fail, but not the tremble of my heart.

After the deception of failing to be with my beloved soul due to its decision to have a better material life related to a job, my heart broke up into pieces. Instead of giving up on love tremors, it made me become a beacon for other souls in search of that feeling that love is way more than it seems.

Why the need for another soul, though, if the love lives inside no matter what?

Only another soul gives me a reason to exist in this material world with all its shallow existence. It also proves that the connection between souls through divine love is not my imagination, and following the unwritten rules of it, the other soul becomes one with the feelings from my heart. The other soul can choose the same path or a different one. Divine love proves its existence, but the decision is ours to follow the path or give up on the belief that love is much more than another simple thing from our material existence. That's the issue when you are not possessive and give total freedom to the choices of another soul due to this principle. Ultimately, it can hurt you more than anything else in the material world.

Because the connection can't be broken after, you only learn to live with the pain.

Is it worth following the warmth of the heart, even knowing it could repeatedly cause pain?

In the past, I thought our souls would be together in the material world forever when life is dedicated to accomplishing the desires and ideals of the beloved soul image chosen through my heart's feelings. That time, living together for years meant an infinity for my soul. I could have been living my whole existence like that. So, I don't feel sorry for that time. It's not a time lost for me if the beloved soul image is happy with the choices and becomes aware of the divine love reflection. I can't do anything about it though, for the happiness of my beloved soul image falling in love with another soul. Their destinies will write the story of their life.

Now, what after feeling the warmth of my heart for Her?

It's just wild to think about it. Although nothing points out a connection in this existence, my heart feels the relationship between our souls as it happens. Maybe it's only for my heart, but this feeling is a fact ... and only Her knows about it.

BLESSINGS – PRELUDE TO 'JUST LOVE HER' BOOK

1 Oct 2019

Living life through the rules of divine love is a blessing and a curse at the same time.

These rules are simple, and the fundamental principle is to surrender to feelings of love no matter what, even if it means you will disappear.

'If one is lucky, a solitary fantasy can totally transform one million realities.'
– Maya Angelou

The biggest problem is that most of the time, your visions and feelings are not of other souls. Also, your feelings are exacerbated by your heart and soul beliefs and experiences.

At the beginning of my practice, many years ago, without experience and proof of my beliefs, I was like a blind man speaking through the experiences of other well-known writers, thinkers, saints, gurus or whatever. My thinking was influenced by information borrowed from reading a lot in my adolescence, mostly religious scriptures but also spiritual writings, hypnotism, practices of yoga and teachings from India, China, Tibet, you name it.

I was blessed enough to have access to information that nowadays you can find easily online, but back then, there was no option other than old books in libraries or the market.

I have read everything representing religions and practices on this Earth in those times.

I always felt an emptiness in my heart, a void that no information succeeded in filling. Praying was dull; reading was a better option. But also, nothing happened, just life in search of the unknown.

In my childhood, I finished all the fiction sections from my town library, all books written by Jules Verne, for example, and started to read anything else. The end led me to read about hypnotism in one of Camille Flammarion's books written in French. This was the first contact with the unseen realm and psychic powers hidden deep inside of our soul. Because of successfully testing hypnosis with my younger brothers, the search for knowledge moved to spiritual and religious beliefs.

From then on, my life has completely changed. Through experience, yoga exercises, visions and constant prayers, my heart and soul opened the forbidden door, seeing the light from the other side.

Rereading the scriptures and religious practices gave me new meanings and a more profound understanding. It was shortly after my 18th birthday.

Long story short, in the end, the concept and vision of divine love reflected in human love and a simple way, accessible to everybody, to prove and understand this belief were born. Because of everything I wrote in one of my visions during practice, I later realised that it was a book.

That's how my book *Hearts of Love* has seen the light in reality.

In December 2019, almost twenty years since its publication ... after that, not too much writing. This happened due to failures in my personal experience with human love. And because this was and is the most essential thing in my life, my heart closed the doors, waiting for another fire to burn them.

> *'Have enough courage to trust love one more time and always one more time.'*
> **– Maya Angelou**

And here I am again with 'no doors left' burned by Her.

My mind bought 'popcorn and juice' to watch the sad comedy of my life because my mind experience is from the outside while my heart and soul knowledge is from inside.

Since I met Her through the divine reflection in our souls, my heart started breathing again the love scent, cuddling my soul in the arms of holy love.

Once again, I've been blessed to surrender to human love because of Her.

THE GODDESS WITHIN

2 Oct 2019

The Goddess Within revealed Her ... The Goddess Within is ...
> *'That feeling of something inside us giving hope when there isn't any, caressing our soul through awkward moments or painful memories, tutoring our mind through unbearable sins inherited from years of programmable religious and traditional teachings.'*
>
> *'The other self-inside is talking with us, giving clues, blaming it for our mistakes or wondering why we didn't listen to that advice.'*
>
> *'The soul image that we are falling in love without understanding or knowing how it happened.'*

The Goddess Within, for me, is the divine love.

We have a special relationship. I try not to exist, which gives me meaning to at least the final departure. In the past, divine love chose a few soul images inside my heart.

Why only some souls? Why not all souls?

It is so hard when a soul image from the inside can't relate with the soul image outside and must let go of feelings, not because of feelings or choices of the other soul image but due to fate. Nothing else is to blame; otherwise, it would be unbearable for the mind. I would go crazy after so many beautiful moments under the shelter of love.

Many souls are going crazy without awareness of the divine love reflected in their souls. If they knew about it, they would return to worship the Goddess Within instead of doing stupid things or making final decisions for their life.

People have done this to get over the pain after the soul image vanished outside. Being chosen by the Goddess Within wasn't easy. It's like giving up one of your body parts. Even if you let go, you still feel it inside all the time.

I blamed destiny on every occasion and myself for not being

good enough to keep it together with the connection. But you can't do anything if you want the other soul's image to be happy.

Fate always wins. Once the soul image chooses the path of fate, this is it. You help accomplish it and hope you will be a part of it forever or as long as possible; you are just a dream.

I say 'soul image' because that's how I perceive other human beings as an image of their soul. There are so many beautiful soul images. It's not that all soul images aren't gorgeous, but rather how much they are aware of the existence of their soul or the divinity hidden inside.

And now the Goddess Within has chosen Her inside … And I pray for the future that my soul won't be only a dream in her existence. At least a part of her life, I would like to help accomplish her dreams in destiny, even if it wouldn't be forever.

I must finish writing a fiction book about this Goddess Within in the middle of one of the years somehow …

CONNECTING THE DOTS … OF COINCIDENCES

3 Oct 2019

Looking back in time, I still wonder how it's possible.

Three months have passed from nothing that would have made me believe in human love again. One tiny dot of coincidence at the beginning created the connection with Her. Back then, if anybody had told me the future of now, I would have said it's ridiculous – no way to fall in love again, at least not this way.

In these moments of introspection, I realised that it had been exactly nine years since 'The Fall of My Heart'. In the meantime, I lost hope that divine love would allow another soul to take shelter in my heart again.

Now that it happened, my mind bothers me from time to time, lately often, about the reality of my feelings. It's an impossible dream because, after the mind's logic, there is no chance our souls will find a way to be together. And how are my soul and heart so sure when no sign of Her exists?

It's weird when you hear your mind laughing out loud at signs that soul and heart are feeling it, and it was like heaven opened its doors. It's even weirder to be an observer, an outsider, wondering what the hell is happening inside.

As an observer, I follow the soul and heart from the beginning. But the mind can't be neglected. Its logic is foolproof.

If love were logic, it wouldn't be called love. It would be called marriage. Joking, but love can't be logical; it's out of this world, so rules of reality don't apply to it. Also, 'Just Love Her' echoes the connection between souls, the essential connection dot. That's how it all started, after all.

EVERY TIME ... HER EYES ...
THE LIGHT IN HER EYES ...

3 Oct 2019

Long time no see ... Beautiful eyes ... Beautiful soul ... Divine light into her eyes.

I had to write about it.

Every time I see and meet her soul through her eyes, I'm thankful for the divine love reflected in our souls. Without it, we could not have recognised each other. That spark of light behind her beautiful eyes communicates with my heart and soul on different frequencies. It's the language spoken only by our souls. Feelings result from this communication, but many more unexplained things are behind it. Direct communication between our souls can't be translated into words. Feelings could be formulated in words, but not that deep connection of unspoken communication between souls.

A glimpse of her soul tells me more than a real talk can do. Only seeing her eyes would mean the whole world to my soul. Would our destinies allow an incredible divine moment like this in the future?

When I see that light of the soul in her eyes, it is like a moment of eternity captured for my heart to decode. Everything stops inside me, like a bridge of our souls beyond space and time. I would like to know what our souls communicate in their unknown language yet feel through the feelings in my heart. I wonder how many other souls are unaware of this communication between them through divine love reflection.

One moment like this keeps my heart on high vibrations for days and nights. It's like another world opens instantly inside. The mind can't even think about a world where only our souls are allowed. It's like a forbidden realm to the mind.

Only the heart can feel it because it's the sanctuary for the soul. In these moments, I think that dying is just another life. No matter what, when the souls meet in their world, everything else kneels in front of their shared divine love.

How many aeons will be needed to release our souls from the slavery of body and fate?

The divine radiation of love is felt all around our existence in these instants of connection, and you can quickly notice how other souls around you can perceive the scent of their life as well. But their existence is yet to uncover the miracle of divine love reflection into their souls. They are so used to their 'glasses' that they forget that they are gods among gods, not through their bodies but their origins.

How can all these beautiful souls be freed sooner from the dream of their existence?

That's the message of divine love when her eyes allow my soul to glimpse her soul. A way and path for every soul on this Earth to be freed in this life, not after aeons of suffering.

TRUE TRUTH LOVE ... BEYOND YOUR MIND

6 Oct 2019

When everything is against your feelings, there is not even the slightest sign of accomplishment from destiny and nothing else left inside other than the divine love reflection and your loved soul image, then you can say it is true 'truth' love.

If you fail to pass the trials of divine love, you are not worthy of receiving the nectar of gods.

Loving the soul image through divine love resembles loving the sacred goddess of love.

To reach the enlightenment of your soul, the narrow line separating the terms and meanings of both representations inside should be 'void'. It sounds unbelievable, but it's not if you trust and leave your ego in the hands of divine love. Give up entirely on your Self to become one with divine love. Then nothing and nobody can touch your soul and make you suffer.

The circle of rebirths will be broken, and your mind will vanish. Reaching point zero of rebirth requires tremendous sacrifice for the body and mind. If you can imagine and think about this process, your fate allows it. However, it doesn't mean it can be reached when you want or in this life. It indicates that you are on the right path.

Your mind will be the greatest obstacle to overcome. The mind can't comprehend the information and knowledge of the rebirth because it also means understanding its death and temporary existence.

THE AGONY OF LOVE – A CURSE TO THE MIND

6 Oct 2019

Today struck me with the nonsense of my mind's logic.

Finally, my mind is happy, thinking that that's it; one problem is gone after beating my soul to the ground in the unbeatable proof of my undoubtful destiny.

I stayed in the shadows as an observer. I noticed the peace of my mind while my soul went into agony. A sorrow as never before clouded my heart, although there was no real reason. It happened after a message sent in the abysses of existence was ignored.

The reason for my heart and soul suffering is not because of communication, but due to agony behind my mind having doubts about divine love reflection revealing her soul image.

Thinking it is the worst outcome for my feelings. Just feel the love and don't analyse it. It is unnecessary to think about helping the beloved 'soul image' in the future or whether there is a fate for soulmate souls. 'Just Love Her'.

Then I found these notes below, trying to digitise some of my written notes. In the past, many ideas or things passing through my mind have been lost. Due to the fall of my heart, I gave up writing them to share with other souls. But lately, thanks to Her, I have left notes whenever my phone wasn't at hand.

<u>Sonmi (Cloud Atlas – movie):</u>
'Our lives are not our own.
From womb to tomb, we are bound to others …
Past and present …
And by each crime … and every kindness … We birth our future.'

<u>The Matrix – movie:</u>
'There is a difference between knowing the path and walking the path.'
'There is no spoon …
Don't try to bend the spoon.
That is impossible.
Try instead to realise the truth:
There is no spoon.'

<u>Shakespeare:</u>
'Love is barely a madness.'

<u>Love Alarm – TV Series on Netflix:</u>
X: 'I don't have the time or intention to date anymore, so forget about me and …'

Y: 'You don't have to like me back … Just because I like you.'
X: 'How's that fair for you?
Just receiving your love …'
Y: 'I just … wanted you to know how I feel.
All that matters to me … is that you act on how you truly feel.
If you ignore my text messages, I'll let myself be ignored.
If you stand me up, I'll let myself stand up.
And if you dump me, I'll let myself be dumped.
All of that is romance to me because we'd be doing things together
… that I can't do it on my own.'

Well, the last part sums up everything. There are so many things I can't do on my own related to human love.

Without sharing thoughts and feelings out in the open, nothing will matter. Even if the echo from inside is revealed through the soul image in the outside world, it is never to be found.

Just continue the path to becoming one celestial body and soul, no matter the agony of the mind. This agony is tolerable and passes fast, while the suffering of love is like a storm wiping out everything on its way.

The agony of separating from the matrix of love between two souls is a curse for the mind, which is aware of divine love reflection in their existence.

I FEEL HER – I SEE HER – BEYOND OUR PHYSICAL BODIES

6 Oct 2019

It amazes me how, after so long, it still comes to my mind, with so many words and feelings to think and talk about, inspired by the deep depths of love from my heart.

Her soul image is reflected all over my mind screen like a virtual reality of our souls.

How can I see, hear, smell and touch the existence of the loved one – her presence through my mind's eye?

I don't know how it happens or if it's possible to feel Her. I haven't met or seen her soul image in reality, only through my soul, but this kind of connection has never happened before.

Could it be the wish of my soul to work my mind in the minor details and then transpose those thoughts into reality?

Yesterday, I dreamed with my eyes wide open again, her beautiful eyes melting my soul. Without knowing, I had entered a dream while sleeping. When I woke up, tears and heartaches poured from my eyes because the feeling of her was heavenly.

I still feel her hand holding my hand, her short dark hair touching my face, and her head resting on my shoulder. It's a dream of another dream born into another vision of our souls wanting to be together beyond time and space in the reality of an unknown universe somewhere in an undiscovered galaxy.

I have said it before and will say it repeatedly: it's unreal that it feels so real – more real than anything in my life. Love is so real and intense that it makes feeling Her so real.

Anywhere I turn my head, her eyes follow me like a shadow of Her. I feel it in the bottom of my heart. Like an abyss, I'm falling into her being. I'm cuddling next to her soul, whispering to my soul, 'I Love Her'.

It's not from this world. It's way beyond our temporary bodies. It's feeling like touching the immortality of souls. And I'm just a humble nobody.

Prayers to divine love rise from the human mind, bringing feelings of hope for a future that is now. If not in this reality, these dreams are happening in one of the multiverses (a hypothetical group of multiple universes). Of course, I want this reality to happen here in this universe.

But is it possible for a mere human dreaming of infinite love, which seems impossible, to think of it and to live it here in this world?

I could whisper to her soul love mantras that only our souls could hear. I am thankful to Her for the bliss that covers the cloud of happiness from my heart. I wish to have the power to share with her existence the same feeling that passes through my heart like a flood of love. It kept me in the heaven of her existence for hours, so close that I could feel the touch of her skin. Feeling Her beyond our bodies seems like a connection between our souls and hearts from both sides of existence.

We could have become one in these moments.

BEHIND HER EYES …

7 Oct 2019

The eyes are the mirror of the soul.

That's true. You can see that in pictures and by looking into the eyes of a soul image. Of course, it depends on the quality of the image and other factors. The identity of the soul is revealed no matter the eyesight.

That's how I met Her: through her eyes revealed in visions. I looked into her eyes deeply and felt her soul – a connection beyond my mind's comprehension. Although many soul images exist, no one else made me feel like that.

Since that first connection awakened my soul because love reflected my heart's feelings, I notice the beauty and magic behind them whenever I look into her eyes.

Many times, I took a glimpse of her soul image in the mirror of my soul. Sometimes melancholic sight, other times with the joy of living. Watching into her eyes, respectively, to her soul, feels like looking behind the curtain of her life backstage. The more recent the soul image in vision, the more information is received from her present life. The soul image captures the moment it was taken with its corresponding data. Decoding what's hidden in that look reflects the soul's stance; it's a feature that only my soul can read and understand. It is translated into feelings for my heart. My mind is quiet or absent during this communication.

I remember being amazed when I read the look from her soul image for the first time. I can't even think or dream about it. How would it be to look into her eyes in reality?

It is too heavenly for my soul to expect a moment of divinity from my destiny. I hope, though, that it will come to that moment of eternity one day.

I once told her (in my heart) that I missed seeing her beautiful eyes. It was a subliminal message to open her heart through her eyes. Instead, Her revealed an image of her soul without eyes, making my soul pick crumbled pieces of hidden thoughts. This way, my mind attacked my soul with fury. And I couldn't do anything about it as the observer that I am.

Assisting in this battle became even more challenging: the desire to abort my mind and to transcend it entirely. Maybe opening once and for all the third eye?

The reasoning behind my mind's actions is worldly and understandable. But the soul's actions and divine love reflect feelings not from this world into my heart. I feel it more and more as time passes, loving Her. That's what I would call the unearthly game of destiny.

Luckily, my soul and heart have the experience and strength from the past to cease hopes for a future. That's why I should never worry about mind games. Thoughts are mind games, and feelings are soul tools to fight against them.

Never surrender. This is the motto of my heart and soul. Never give up in front of unruly destiny, especially now that I found Her.

As long as we are alive in this world, the divine love reflected in our souls through our soul images will be a realm where fate can't do anything to change our lives to forget about love.

WHEN TWO SOULS BECOME ONE

8 Oct 2019

When mind troubles are gone, the soul can finally feel divine love. The soul feels the beloved soul without restriction or annoying mind interference.

Dancing in the inner world on the rhythms of divine love

reflection, both souls become one move, interconnecting through the energy of divine love beyond time and space. When the souls become one being, a new entity comes into the realm of the unseen universe in the shadow of our natural world. It feels like, at the same time, both souls have access to the inner essence of their existence. They sense each other as one, being aware of their individuality at the very moment.

The 'soul images' combine into one appearance with both identities as one with two faces. One that is aware of its existence and the other as of the loved 'soul image'.

The consciousness also feels like one but is aware of its duality.

It's not the most accurate description of words about this connection as there are not yet any words created for it. A glossary of word descriptions for this new entity should be completed. Time, evolution and awareness of our souls' existence will make the new science of the future for this entity.

Every moment of her life makes my heart tremble like a flower in the wind. My soul is bathing in her being's scent, melting into her soul existence surrounded by a love shrine while we became one.

DREAMING BIG YET FEEL SO SMALL

9 Oct 2019

Sometimes, I feel the pressures of big dreams' inception from my mind.

Either imposed by feelings from my heart or my mind target. Usually, those from my heart seem impossible to accomplish at first sight, but after seeing the energy and motivation behind my feelings, I realise they are not entirely.

Looking back in time, fair enough, my dreams nowadays are reasonable. But to compare the accomplishments from the past with real ones, well ... I'm feeling so small.

I had published a book twenty years ago, experienced enlightenment and lived in extreme conditions imposed on my body. The divine love reflection was revealed for the first time, with the beloved soul image in real life due to holy love.

OK ... To sweeten the old me now, back then, I always dreamt of retiring from this world to be a hermit, staying in monasteries, and ultimately thinking of a religious life before accomplishing a divine love experience that changed my life completely.

The fact that I gave up a religious life dedicated to my childhood was a good thing. Being conservative is not the way of evolution for the soul. You take it from one kind of prison and put it in a dignified one, which is even harder to escape. Of course, not being at all conservative leads to the other extreme with the same result.

Being moderate is the key, as Buddha said.

Returning to the present, due to Her, my soul assigns new impossible dreams through my heart's feelings, so twenty years later is like starting again.

Once again, coming back from the mind clouds, nowadays I consider myself a modern hermit. Living in the world, a healthy life, yet not entirely in this world. Past experiences and practice built the fundament for the rest of my life forever. Divine love is the key to the unknown.

Following my heart's instructions, the path ahead looks like an impossible dream.

But how will it be to accomplish easy dreams ... Boring?

I'M BREATHING HER AETHER ... JUST LOVE HER

10 Oct 2019

These days, I have a troubled mind, and I feel my soul for the first time uneasy due to my existence. It craves to fly, be free next to Her, and follow and watch over her being.

Sadly, I'm still limited to my body, although sometimes I can fly with my mind and heart wherever I feel her.

I love it when I see happiness and joy all around other souls, especially Her, when art and creation of any form use the soul's hidden source reflected in unusual compositions.

People tend to forget that we are born to live free and respecting divinity and nature; instead, they are enslaved by the material side and destiny. Art and nature are representatives of human essence, bonding soul with mind and body. That's why, reflected in many creations, there are sparks of the unseen world of souls behind our sightless eyes.

When the third eye is opened, life will be different, seeing behind the curtain of existence.

I will make up for my soul in the middle of the winter, breathing the same air, walking in the same places and enjoying the same life as her being. How will it be to exist for once at the same time and place as Her?

Will the connection feel at higher levels, or won't it matter?

What I discovered lately is that I never felt before what I feel now.

The divine love reflection never ceases to amaze me with its tricks related to soul existence and connection with the beloved soul image of Her. I felt a strong connection with Her, embalmed in her aether beyond our passing existence.

In these moments of unnatural reality, time is flying, and I would relive endlessly, on and on, her heavenly aether touch with my soul. Nothing else exists other than our souls' aether, the divine love surrounding us, and the mantra of love chanting …

Aum mani padme hum …

ODE TO HER …

10 Oct 2019

I confess: 'I love Her … with all my heart and soul.'

No day goes by without Her in my mind and heart. It's like a ritual of love.

Although human, for me, Her looks like a goddess who

represents the most beautiful qualities of feminine divinity. Glancing around me, I see that no one makes me feel like Her does. That's the divinity of her nature. Only if her soul is unique can it give my heart so many heavenly feelings. For so long, I forgot who I am or how everything started.

I want only her 'Being' inside; my Self is forbidden.

Listening to her voice inside brings tranquillity and whispers of feelings for my heart and soul. Memories unknown before are born in the corners of my mind. All I am hearing are the beatings of my heart, touching her eyes.

What's more beautiful is that I don't even know if my messages touched her heart. Does Her know there is a soul that loves her more than life itself?

My mind pushed me over and over to confess. But I understand. Who would believe there is possible a love without borders?

A love without facts and reasons ... A love between souls.

Would destiny allow a friendship of our soul images in the foreseeable future in this reality? Wouldn't giving a feather touch to an unknown soul image be uncommon?

Because love is not supposed to be on both sides if destiny won't allow it, if her heart is untouched, that's what was written a long time before our existence.

I wish I had been born close to Her in these moments. I would have accepted anything close to Her, and I am jealous of nature and life because they wrap up her existence.

I pray to divine love for all her friends and family to make Her happy if 'Me' is not in the picture. I will pray until the breath leaves my body, and my soul will remember Her for countless lives.

That's why I make this confession. At least Her will remember that once was a soul image that saw the goddess in her heart.

그냥 헤르 사랑해 ... *(Geunyang Hereu Saranghae)* ...

Just Love Her ...

THE CHOSEN PATH TO ENLIGHTENMENT THROUGH DIVINE LOVE

12 Oct 2019

What if my visions are only my visions?

Maybe that's why my message must spread to the world.

Without understanding, the divine love reflected in human love messages are misinterpreted by many soul images without spiritual practice, which leads to more suffering.

It doesn't have to be both ways, the reflection of divine love into the hearts of loved ones. It can be only one side, even if you are a seer and your visions look real. Maybe you can feel and see past lives or a future connection, but this is not a reality for both souls.

What you can do instead if your soul draws you on this path of spiritual love reflection practice and to help with your understanding and bring happiness to your beloved soul image is to pray for its health, fate and enlightenment. Of course, you can be a good friend or more if destiny will allow it, but other than that, nothing more.

Your loved one will be the soul image chosen by the divine love reflection inside your heart, and that's it. Your sacrifice and practice will be geared to the divine love inside, no matter what, and with no conditions regarding the beloved soul image. This way, you won't produce suffering to the chosen soul image.

I said it before, and I will repeat it. The path of divine love reflection is challenging. It could mean much misery until you reach enlightenment. After that, the connection and awareness of divine love will give you comfort and a vision of your soul.

Usually, two soul images already in love or in search of enlightenment can smoothly test and follow the divine love reflection practice. They have settled in the environment prepared by their destiny for their chosen path. Of course, this doesn't necessarily mean that it will be a fact in the future.

The life and personality of every individual soul, heart and mind will also influence their destinies. You might fail in your relationship, but do not fail to keep the divine love inside your heart no matter what.

If you had proof of God from a chosen religion, you would surely follow that religion no matter the suffering. Moreover, having evidence of love in your life makes it even more important to follow the divine love in your heart, and never give up on feeling it.

Please don't believe anything of what I said until you prove it to yourself. Just follow my advice and your heart's feelings to reach the enlightenment of your soul in this life. If not in this life, at least you chose your path for your immortal soul, being aware and awakened in this life.

Also, don't try to be a saint; you better be a sinner full of love. Ultimately, divine love will correct your path to avoid so-called sins due to your heart's feelings and free up your soul.

LOVING HER, AND NOTHING MORE

12 Oct 2019

Why not give up if there have been no signs of destiny to find and meet Her for a long time?

It's the journey and the feelings that flow from the divine love reflection practice, and keeping it real is of tremendous help. I know Her is out there somewhere, but not for me or my destiny. My prayers and path of divine love can help us both even in this destiny, no matter the chosen soul image for Her to live with.

You think you are exceptional, but you are not. Unique is what you feel inside, the gift of divine love reflecting into your heart. So, you are the same as everybody else, if not more responsible and awakened, due to your awareness of divine love reflection. You should not bring suffering but also help for the good of humanity and the enlightenment of souls.

If you do nothing, your heart will be broken to pieces due to love inside.

Yes, prayers can be beneficial for the enlightenment of the soul. Ultimately, it will lead to actions, if not through your heart and mind, then through others. Sometimes, it is even better to pray than to get the wrong results due to your ego.

The correct action is to do without doing. It means don't do it for yourself or think it is the right path to enlightenment. Just do it, and don't expect the results or reward for yourself. Be thankful if other souls, hearts and minds let you help them, not vice versa.

The same mindset should be for sharing divine love reflection with the chosen soul image from your heart. Be thankful and happy that the sacred love decided to feel and be the vessel for the sacrifice of living divine love. Don't expect, ask or hope for results, accomplishments or a return of feelings from the chosen soul image.

If it happens, you must be even more grateful and dedicated; if not, you must pray harder to the divine love inside. It could mean many things, the awareness of divine love reflected inside, but you don't want to make it suffer the other soul believing that you are the chosen one, giving your mind ground for incorrect decisions.

It doesn't mean your beloved soul image won't feel your love; maybe at the same time, the loved one shares your feelings and is aware of it. It implies that every soul can choose the path with or without you due to destiny.

Remember that the divine reflection into your heart is a gift, not a given, and realise a connection with the beloved soul image. You love what you feel inside and work towards your enlightenment and nothing more. If it is more in your destiny, so be it; if not, you have already received the greatest gift for your soul.

That's why I'm just loving Her and nothing more …

WHEN LOVE IS NOT STRONG ENOUGH
13 Oct 2019

You love the chosen soul image with all your being, though nothing related to happiness and feelings of love happen in the real world other than inside you.

Love means sacrifice from your side most of the time, sometimes the whole life. The ideal of divine love reflection is not the accomplishment of your desires in real life but the practice and concentration of your mind through the love mantra to keep divine love alive in your heart.

Sometimes, I wonder if my practice wasn't strong enough in time, giving up some energy to learn and gain the material things while losing a fight with fate for the beloved soul image in the long run.

Yes, you can blame both sides for many things that didn't work out in the end, but after such numerous beautiful moments, you came to wonder why or how it was possible to break off.

Maktub ... It is written!

In the end, what matters is the journey and experience, no matter the result.

Of course, it would be nice to be with the beloved soul image, at least in this life, if not forever. Destiny will allow it for a short or extended time; this way, you will have memories, experiences and feelings left from that encounter.

Always be prepared for the unknown. Once settled on a path, don't think that this is it. Give all your best as long as it happens, and bring happiness and enlightenment to the destiny of your beloved soul image. After that, if everything fails, carry on your journey, and continue praying for your favourite soul images.

Isn't there any way to settle forever with a soul image in this life?

It is when both soul images follow the same path of enlightenment and believe in the power of divine love reflection in their hearts. Throughout your journey on this Earth, don't forget the existence of divine love as a deity if you are blessed with its acknowledgement.

And a Sufi joke:
'Oh, Imam! Which of my actions is of my free will, and which is predestined?'
'Lift your right leg.'
'OK.'
'That's free will. Now lift your left leg.'
'I can't ...'
'That's predestination.'

WHEN THE DIVINE LOVE REFLECTION IS BEATING THROUGH YOUR HEART
14 Oct 2019

The heart is the best instrument for testing the feeling of divine love reflection.

The main difference besides human love is the awareness and consciousness of living it; the source is the same. Knowing and feeling that love from your heart is of divine roots, your heart will become a shrine dedicated to love. A new world will open in front of your inner eyes, a world as magical as you have never seen before.

Sometimes, I feel my heart cool and refreshed as I rest after numerous intense feelings. Other times, it's burning like a fire, melting any thoughts and impurities inside. It burns to feel Her inside, like a connection beyond my physical self.

I let myself loose on this feeling, staying in this kind of meditation of senses that is unstoppable inside. I can't think of anything else in the meantime. The image of her soul image rises like a flag fluttering in the rhythms of the wind of love.

It happens while I write about it, and I must stop due to intensity and continue writing after when it will allow my mind to think.

A few hours later ...

Again, I felt Her beside the Han River, close to a bridge. I was hugging her close to my chest, feeling her heart beating in sync with mine and touching her hair – so close to me. I thought I had lost connection with Her since this kind of vision was paused for a while. It resembles a work of art by David Hockney on an absolute scale, happening in a dream of visions. I don't know if it's from past lives, future destiny, or alternate reality ...

I love it when my mind is troubled by love feelings inside. It can't concede the connection of our souls beyond time and space, and it can't believe that Her at least knows about me, my soul vision, and so on.

How can my soul trust these beliefs when there is no real reason?

If I hadn't opened my heart to words my mind could understand and others could read, no future is possible for the divine love reflection message in this reality, not now or never. Also, it wouldn't have been a burden for my mind if I only practised meditation with no thoughts allowed at all.

The message is my destiny on this Earth since I was born with or without my choice. So, my soul doesn't need any proof or actions because the belief is inside my heart, not outside of it. Sometimes, I wish to have been silent because if words were spoken, fates could be influenced.

Her is the soul image chosen by divine love reflection inside my heart, and I can't do anything about it. It wasn't an option. Maybe it was a blessing for my soul, not my mind. Not for any reason that will try to understand it in the future of now.

THE FALL OF MY HEART – ACCEPTING FATE

15 Oct 2019

Nine years ago, my heart had a more significant fall than at any other time before. It happened because what was supposed to be forever ended unexpectedly.

I never felt the aversion of fate like those times ever. And I was so stubborn that I didn't give up even after nothing left to be achieved fighting with destiny. I believed it was enough for one soul to love, and things followed. Later, I understood that destiny can't be changed if not written to reverse. You can try, but isn't this another way of predestination?

The problem was that I felt the changes a long time before destiny's grim path. But one thing is to see or sense it and another to walk on the trail. I couldn't give up without giving all the chances that my soul can do, mainly a time for reflection. But time changes, as well as our minds and concepts, in the end, going to the point of no return.

So, after many years of sorrow, I had to give up on trying. At that moment, after years of trials and fighting, when I gave up declaring unwanted destiny a winner, my fate has wholly changed, and here I am … It changed the country, transformed me, changed everything.

The lesson learned is that if it's going to happen, you can't do anything about it other than accept it and move on.

WHY HER? ONLY MY HEART KNOWS …

17 Oct 2019

I'm doomed … I thought whenever silence settled in my heart, my feelings would return to normal and wouldn't go overboard anymore. Feeling the love inside at high levels for my body and mind takes much energy. It's a good thing that keeps me fit, in any case.

But it was enough of an instant moment with Her for my heart to flutter. So here I go again to the long road of feelings over the limit.

It's not something I haven't experienced before, but every time is different. And although knowing the symptoms and problems that come with it, it's still hard to keep pace with my soul. It pushes me to the limit as never seen before. And visions and the feeling that this time will be a more compelling message and the story of my present future higher than before; I wonder how it happened.

Her is the inspiration and fire of creation, seeing new things in the light of shining love inside, motivated to realise and spread the message of divine love reflection to the world.

I didn't imagine before feeling her that I would have the energy and determination to do things that seemed impossible at first sight. I connect with Her beyond my mind's imagination and facts. What's weird is that I don't care if destiny will favour finding Her in this life.

I've often asked myself: 'Why Her?'

Only my soul knows why. An unseen bonding connects us beyond space, time, destiny, reality, etc.

Loving Her also connects me with her surrounding existence, including her parents, siblings and friends. All that Her feels close to becomes familiar to my soul.

I've tried everything to take it out of my head, but nothing works. My heart journeys through the sanctuary of feelings on levels never seen before.

Somehow, I see where my heart and soul are heading, but would it be at the end of the journey or in between?

THE WIND OF LOVE ... MISSING HER

17 Oct 2019

Today, I was missing Her so much. Nowhere around me in my reality was a touch of her being. That's what I thought, and I felt deep inside me missing Her.

But as I left home and walked down the road, the wind started blowing to my ears, whispers of her scent and being, reminding me that Her was everywhere around me. I was looking up at the sky. Her sweet face was smiling at me in the shadow of a cloud. And seagulls flew all around me, passing her feelings to my heart.

The wind of divine love keeps fighting close to my soul, giving me strength and assuring me that I'm not alone. If I miss Her, the whole existence is missing Her. Also, my entire existence will take her soul close to mine through all of nature around me.

The sun threw a shadow of a smile behind the clouds that gathered to chill my heart, aching after the image of her beloved soul. Soon after, the sky started to shed tears for the missing soul, accompanying my heart through the sorrow.

All I know in these moments is that I would give anything to be with or at least next to Her. My life feels meaningless without Her. Her soul image feels like a blessing for my heart, covering the mind screen with blissful moments touching the eternity of our souls.

Flashes of her soul image make their way inside my mind's eye with instances of her daily life. A smile, touchable eyesight, a wave of her hair in the wind, it's healing for my soul and heart.

And from the void of my existence, a revolt of thoughts rose against the implacable destiny. A fate that didn't follow the feelings from my heart and the divine love reflection from my soul.

One step back, another few steps ahead. A fight against time and space that separate our soul images, but our souls not keeping away from the union in the realm of divine love.

A whisper covers all my being with its echo:

'If not in this life to be with Her, then in the next one …

And if not even in the next one, not even eternity will stop from missing Her.'

'너무 보고 싶어 *(Neomu bogo sipeo). I miss you (Her) so much.'*

These words keep coming through my mind, and I feel Her in my heart. It feels like a wheel of touching sounds for my unfortunate reality.

INSPIRING MUSIC: Dirty Dancing – She's Like the Wind …

THE POWER OF YOUR MIND

20 Oct 2019

Mysterious and otherworldly … How else would you call an event that happens at once in your mind?

You are working on something that takes all your attention as part of the job or action you are involved in. But instantly, the soul image of the beloved one pops out on your mind screen, simultaneously with a flash of hyper feelings inside your heart.

I understand why the heart feelings event is happening, as it's created by divine love reflection from our soul existence, sometimes being aware, other times not, but always present. My mind can't constantly pay attention to the soul image reflection from the heart feeling, especially when busy with everyday life. And still, in some moments, out of nowhere, the soul image fills up the mind screen unexpectedly. What strange and unseen forces make it happen?

The divine love effect creates events and actions without our interference. When you are aware and conscious of your actions, you know that they are with your participation or that you have a say in some moments due to your efforts. But when it just happens, these are pure moments of divine love reflected in the beloved soul image.

Occasionally, I wonder … Could it result from our souls' communication, unseen and beyond time and space? Or, because of the soul image, does the mind act as a result of divine love reflection?

Our mind is a powerful tool. We have yet to be fully aware of how powerful our minds are. That's why, in the scriptures, it is said that even with our minds, we can be sinners. Our mind starts the action, so our mind is the source of all good and evil acts. Our mind creates good and evil gods and forces.

Miracles happen due to sharp minds and not because of the existence of all deities. Or bluntly speaking, without a powerful mind praying, miracles can't occur. The unseen realm can't change our reality without a powerful mind or a soul behind it. So, remember how strong your mind is when you are full of hate and rage because this is destroying your inner self and health. Instead, try to cultivate the divine love awareness in your mind and practise the love mantra of divine love reflection of the soul image in your heart and soul.

This mindset will generate happiness and joy in your life and your beloved soul image. Also, it is the path to enlightenment through the divine love reflection, starting with the pure feeling of human love.

HER SOUL IMAGE

24 Oct 2019

The soul of Her is hiding behind her soul image, which transformed my life and destiny lately. Whenever I look into her eyes, I can feel her soul through my heart feelings.

Living and following the unwritten rules and perception of divine love allows me to see the reflection of divine love onto her precious soul through her soul image. That's how we could recognise each other's souls.

When our souls connect strongly, her soul image appears clear as the light of the day on my mind screen. My dormant heart evolves due to the butterfly effect.

Is her soul image aware of these moments as well due to her soul? Or are they forgotten in the pool of divine love eternity?

I'm waiting for my destiny to make the big turn in changing my life. Finding Her was only the beginning of the journey through the shadows of my visions.

That's the beauty of the unknown path. You feel it, but it's different walking on it. Sometimes, it gives you moments of life bliss; other times, it is just dreams – unaccomplished visions.

Soulmates are destined to be together in this life, in multiverses, alternate realities or eternity. A soulmate can't be found searching or wanting. It happens unexpectedly and only through your heart's feelings. With a soulmate, you are happy just living divine love with them, and that's it; nothing else is needed. You are pleased with its happiness and given total freedom with no restriction, even if it means living without you in this life and destiny. Your life is not yours but dedicated to the other soul's happiness and enlightenment.

There are times when my heart goes silent waiting ... I don't know what for or why. It just goes silent ... so quiet. It doesn't speak to my mind at all, just feelings left without an echo.

Then, Her appears in the waves of existence on the present timeline, and my heart suddenly awakens. Life starts breathing through my heart because of a moment with and from Her.

All this time, I have had to wait even days to translate those feelings into words, and her soul image is the catalyst for my soul and heart. It also means that Her is well. Always without a sign from Her, I worry if Her is feeling well and happy.

What can I do to make fate follow her heart?

And the echo from the bottom of my heart: *'Just Love Her!'*

LIVING THE DREAM

25 Oct 2019

Recently, I've been told that I live the dream ... Maybe it seems so from the outside.

It also seems so inside due to my higher feelings for Her. It's more than a dream.

I lived the dream in the days, being with the beloved soul image many years ago. But fate and a material side took it away from me.

To live the dream again, I should be with Her in this reality and destiny.

It is still okay because, in my heart, the divine love reflection is always burning, but it would be heavenly to be with her soul image, not just in my visions and not only in my dreams.

Looking inside, I can see the difference only when I see Her as a reality. Every atom of her being touches my soul when her eyes melt my heart to tears. Nothing else in my reality can surpass that.

Without divine love, reflection, awareness and practice, it wouldn't be a dream or reality vision. It would be just another story of human love, passing and life-limited, not with a touch of eternity nor a drop of divine love over the shadow of our existence.

This is the message of divine love through time. By being aware and living through the divinity of love reflection practice, the dream of love will become a living and touching reality of divine love. Love will become our God/Goddess.

Many soul images think that the dream of this life is to be accomplished materially and professionally as soon as possible. And the higher, the better. But other soul images prove it wrong. They were achieved in both aspects, yet they gave up on this life due to the emptiness inside. A void that life's dreams can't fill. Human love could fill it temporarily, but it is not enough sometimes if you don't see the source hiding behind it.

Only divine love awareness could give us a real meaning of life. And it wouldn't be just a dream if you were feeling and living it. Then, the soul image revealed through the feelings from your heart due to divine love reflection awareness will not be only another human love. That soul image revealed in your heart will become the image of the divine love and the meaning of your life. The boring and usual tags of human love will lose their sense in the realm of divine love.

The divine love reflection practice with the soul image of your beloved soul will open the forbidden door to heaven in this reality, not in the afterlife as all religions and spiritual practices promise.

LOVE WILL SET YOU FREE

26 Oct 2019

Looking around daily, I see so many soul images caught in the net of destiny. They are blinded and unaware of their freedom. Freedom is fancy and not quite the right word, but there is a place where the soul can be freed from the bonds of our minds and bodies.

People have always fought for freedom from different cultures, traditions or mental limitations. The battle for liberty reflects our souls' struggle to escape this world and destiny.

There is a place where the soul can be free and follow the path of its enlightenment. This place is inside our bodies, not outside of us. Our heart is the only place where the soul can live as its sanctuary.

For the first step to enlightenment, you must follow your heart, let feelings free and start the fight with your mind to overcome the ego. You must understand that you are not your mind. The flood of thoughts that clouds your heart and feelings every day keeps your soul in shackles. And even after awareness of your soul's existence, your mind will block your feelings. In front of your feelings of love and trying to stop your thoughts from disturbing your heart, kneeling can bend your mind and ego to follow enlightenment.

The second step will be the acknowledgement of divine love's existence. There is proof of its presence through your feelings of love. Of course, if you've been lucky enough to feel love for someone. If not, you can follow the feelings of love for your family, country or whatever gives you a feeling in your heart. That feeling is living proof of divine love's existence. Every day, following and paying attention to that feeling and giving priority in your mind to make that feeling stronger will allow you to see and sense the divine love's reflection in your heart to some point. This feeds your soul's existence and provides consciousness and awareness of your Self.

The practice to make your feeling stronger is different from how it looks. That feeling from the source of divine love existence is the same all the time, like a river of life. The awareness and consciousness becoming clear and settled in your mind through time make you feel it strongest this way.

A mirror represents the best analogy for divine love existence. You have the mirror, the soul reflected by the mirror, and awareness of this process. The mirror itself is divine love. Awareness of the process of reflection between soul and divine love existence is the divine love reflection. Finally, the soul is why all these are connected and appear to exist.

Tested discoveries and theories of quantum entanglement and quantum superposition principles from quantum mechanics represent the unseen world of our souls at an atomic scale.

> *'Quantum mechanics (QM; also known as quantum physics, quantum theory, the mechanical wave model, or matrix mechanics), including quantum field theory, is a fundamental theory in physics which describes nature at the smallest scales of atoms and subatomic particles.'*
>
> – **Quote About quantum mechanics**

These principles state that a particle can exist simultaneously in two locations or states and will change its properties only when observed.

That's why being aware and conscious of the existence of the soul and divine love is so crucial for the path to enlightenment. The only acknowledgement of this fact is enough for your soul to bend the mind and free up from its chains.

Love between a man and a woman is the fastest way to enlightenment through spiritual love practice. It's also the highest representation of divine love reflection. Nothing else can give us more happiness and blissful moments than the connection between our souls through soul images. Love has no restrictions for the path chosen, but in my vision, this representation is the purest and at the highest level for enlightenment.

In a world dominated by patriarchy, divine love finds it difficult to spread its wings and be acknowledged for its actual value. The future looks bright, though, because only women can change our world. It's their nature to give birth and influence other souls to embrace divine love. A random factor can permanently block and divert even this path. But I can trust that femininity will prevail in the end, and the world will be enlightened through divine love, awareness and consciousness.

> *'The biggest happiness is to feel that someone loves you, not to know, but to feel.'*
>
> – **Nichita Stanescu** *(one of the greatest Romanian poets)*

MISSING HER – SHIVERS IN MY HEART
27 Oct 2019

Some days are quiet and shadowed in my daily life. These times make me think my visions are just a drop of forgotten memories from my past lives.

Then came that moment when shivers struck my heart. I suddenly missed Her. I miss Her so much that it burns my heart and moistens my eyes with tears of sorrow for my unhappy soul.

In these moments, I let myself loose on the feeling inside, closing my eyes and emptying my mind of any thought. It is a moment of eternity accumulated with pain from all past lives and present futures, and the universe is crying out for painful memories. I feel the sadness and agony of all beings on this Earth along the timeline of existence – a never-ending bounce of suffering on the rope of destiny.

The ache of missing Her is happening, expecting her soul image in my reality and destiny. The connection inside our souls feels the broken link with the present destiny and reality of our soul images.

Time and space act like a barrier separating eternity from the timeline of existence.

Inside, it feels the eternity of our androgynous being as portrayed by Leonardo da Vinci's visions – our souls' images becoming one through divine love reflected in our souls. Hence, the pain felt when, in reality, not yet an incarnation of this vision from inside.

Nobody can understand androgynous visions until two soul images look into each other's eyes, being aware of divine love's existence. At that moment, both souls become one and soul images feel the same way inside the heart and mind.

That's how I feel Her inside my heart and mind – a part of my being inside my heart. And with wishful thinking to be outside of her soul image as well. Looking around outside, there was no sign of Her, yet closing my eyes, I found Her inside my heart; instead, there was no sign of Me.

WHEN DIVINE LOVE FLOWS THROUGH UNSPOKEN WORDS

31 Oct 2019

It's hard sometimes to write about my feelings inside. Although divine love awareness is always present inside my heart and mind through practice and consciousness, emotions cannot always be encapsulated into words.

I prefer feeling divine love than describing it. But how else can the message be spread to other souls searching for divine love to fill that void inside that nothing else could?

After the fall of my heart, I gave up on writing in time, choosing to live with my practice inside. Without feeling it through the revelation within my heart, no relationship is possible for my soul with another 'soul image'. Only a soulmate through the 'soul image' revealed in my heart can fire up the burning love.

That's what happened when I found Her. Glimpses of her existence had occurred before without seeing Her. When I looked into her eyes instantly, my heart started burning with love for Her. That moment opened the door to the past and present futures that nothing else could.

It's enough one instant with her eyes to see and feel her soul. Every new instance with a look from Her gives me a spark of the eternity of divine love reflection into our hearts and souls.

Unspoken words … Real feelings don't need words to listen to. An open heart is required, and unspoken words will follow. It's a different and unique language that only the heart will understand through feelings. It's the realm of divine love. These unspoken words shared by divine love reflected into existence will touch some souls' images; others will run away, but they will change some destinies.

That's how I speak to her soul through heart feelings with unspoken words. These messages will last beyond our minds and bodies are gone. We don't need words or facts to share our feelings, only an open heart. And her heart is opened for sure.

How else is her soul image revealed to my heart visions as the Goddess of my heart and soul?

THIRSTY FOR LOVE

1 Nov 2019

Are you feeling bored reading and constantly hearing the word 'love'?

Well, my sad soul image, who is feeling like that ... No wonder divine love isn't happening in your life. It's not because divine love evades you but because you are running away.

Feeling the divinity of love in your life should be like air, water and food. You'll die if these necessities are not provided.

Advancing daily in awareness and consciousness of divine love existence will feel more like an air necessity. Sometimes, your soul will feel suffocated if you do not allow your heart to worship the divine love. All your existence will be dedicated to the divine love existence practice as soon as you reach enlightenment.

If the soul image is revealed in your heart, feeling the divine love and feelings out of this world happen, don't give up no matter what. Your life won't be yours anymore. Devoting yourself to love for the soul image chosen in your heart by divine love gives you a reason to live happily in this world on the brink of extinction.

We are like a virus on this planet. We are not respecting life and nature around us. We have eradicated and annihilated most of the species and environment around the world.

I hope for the younger generations to come and for the technology that could help humanity on the long road of enlightenment for all beings, not only a few chosen ones.

All ancient religions, beliefs and concepts used divine love to enlighten humans. Raising awareness of divine love's existence as a deity could help the present future of soul images in search of the unknown to accept the concept of love being our God/Goddess. Moreover, human love is an experience that most of us have already tested and experienced. Also, it is the most pursued ideal in our passing lives.

Why not acknowledge the divinity of divine love reflected in human love and free our souls from the limitations of the human body?

WHAT'S GOING ON? TIMES WHEN …

1 Nov 2019

There are … times when I feel love burning my heart to tears, missing Her … times when I feel the craving to listen to 4 Non Blondes – 'What's Up?' … times when I ask myself from the bottom of my heart, 'What's going on?'

Indeed, I have peculiar feelings: happiness, divine love and sadness, and I miss Her with all my being.

And I pray for my heart's revolution against destiny, time and space, keeping my human body restrained in the chains of this limited life.

There are times when patience is unbearable, knowing that no 'cards' hold in the pockets of my soul for the present and future in this life with Her. Other than inside feeling Her with all my entities, there is no reason behind my unusual feelings.

I still wonder when the echo of my feelings will occur in her heart, and will destiny be affected by the connection between our souls.

There are times when the thought of following the voice inside telling me 'Just Love Her' gives me belief in our soul images' fate, which will conquer the seemingly unthinkable togetherness in this life and for eternity.

My heart and mind abyss are painted with her soul image, keeping my soul from vanishing into the depths of the divine love realm.

These are times when, because of feelings for Her, this reality still makes sense to spread the message of divine love reflected in our souls' existence. And our soul images can reach enlightenment through human love, knowing its origins.

There are times when ... I beg the divine love for a sign from Her to ease my heart from the torment of unnatural feelings of missing Her.

Since the flame of love burns again, my heart's destination is always to feel the soul image of Her and offer the rest of my life for her blissful future.

SIGNS OF DIVINE LOVE REALITY

3 Nov 2019

> *'If you would have known ... the divinity of love ... you will feel remorse ... to be worried!'*
> *'I'm looking at you, and I see only the love inside ... I'm looking inside, and again, I see you ... but you grabbed the face of love.'*
> *– RAZ MIHAL*

I'm only human, after all.

Looking back in time, I've found some relics' words from the past that prove unchanging divine love inside. It's a blessing and a curse at the same time. The curse has a good connotation.

Although I trust the divine love inside, I still have doubts about my ability as a human being to cope with the divinity of the love message revealed too many years ago.

Because of all the time, I'm asking myself: 'Why Me?'

Many other beautiful souls have better skills and opportunities to deliver the message. However, this is my destiny.

I've asked for a sign from Her. And now I feel shame because it shows how weak my human being is. Feeling the divine love inside shouldn't ask for anything. The gift inside needs no confirmation or proof of its existence. Yet my heart feels so heavenly that Her sees signs of divine love everywhere – even in clouds shaped like love.

Time has been flying like a magic carpet since Her became the soul image chosen by divine love inside my heart. Last night, a vision of Her growing old together in love happened, having two daughters, and seeing the grandchildren, spreading divine love all around us. Too much happiness allowed to dream of …

> <u>Nichita Stanescu:</u>
> 'And I have been loving you so much that I forgot you,
> believing that you are a part of me.'
> 'If someone can love, it is an emperor.
> If someone is being loved, then it is infinite.'
> 'What is a woman?
> It is the only gift that chooses you.'
>
> <u>Pablo Neruda:</u>
> 'I want to do with you what spring does with cherry trees.'
>
> <u>Osho:</u>
> 'No man understands the woman,
> no woman understands the man,
> and that is the beauty of their being together.'

FEELING HER SO DEEP … DEEP … DEEP … TOO DEEP

4 Nov 2019

More than a dozen beliefs are being drafted. But the soul image of Her keeps covering the walls of my heart and the screen of my head.

Deep feelings and a touch of her closeness made me believe that if I turned my head, I could see Her next to me. Wishes that are buried in the long-forgotten destiny of our souls.

I wish I could tell Her with my eyes and lips through unspoken words and feelings, whispering how much I want the present future of this reality to be with Her.

I was often close to leaving messages to Her in the 'past of present', confessing only for her soul image the human love of my soul image with roots in the divinity of love. Unspoken words only for our human beings are like whispers of mirroring souls.

I don't know how many times tears covered my sight, feeling Her so deep ... deep ... deep ... too deep. Tears of joy, sorrow and missing her soul image ... all of them at once?

All I know is that these feelings come from the depths of my heart. Hence, my soul is missing her soul on the long road to the present future of this reality.

너무 너무 너무 보고 싶어 *(Neomu neomu neomu bogo sipeo)* ... – *I miss Her so so so much* ...

Words born from the depths of my heart flow through my mind like a river of sorrow for my soul image, missing her soul image.

DREAMING OF PAST LIVES AND VISIONS OF PRESENT FUTURES

5 Nov 2019

There is a difference between dreams and visions.

Dreams are a window to the unseen universe around us. Some relate to feelings, mental troubles and so on. Some give a glimpse of our soul connection with the divinity realm.

In the past, I dreamt of heavenly places with many beautiful and vibrant colours in nature, birds, and all surroundings like a fantasy – or spiritual dreams with hidden messages connecting with evolved spiritual beings from the past. And some darker dreams where I fought with evil forces. I happened to dream déjà vu events happening later that day a few times. Over time, it also happened to heal my pains through my mind and the inner energy of divine love.

Visions happen when you feel what's next to come in your destiny or others. It doesn't have to be as in a dream seeing images. It's more like a feeling of the future. It always happened before bad or happy times came to my life and destiny. As I've welcomed the good ones, I had to do the same for the worst ones.

Before the fall of my heart, I felt the hard times come a few years before. Even so, when junctures in time happened and warnings of the future changed, I still supported the dreams of the beloved soul image.

The hardest part of the destiny of our souls on the path of divine love is when you must break the connection with the beloved soul through soul image. Although you can be in friendship as suggested often, in the future, the connection with the soul image running away from love should be suspended totally like it never happened. However, it takes years to heal the wound of separation completely. Because of divine love, it's like ripping off a part of your soul and throwing it away. You can't forget the connection and feelings inside, but the memories ... Yes, you can.

I never felt sorry for the happy times together; I was just sad for the destiny that separated us. And I must admit that there should have been so much love between our souls to accept my modern hermit life in devotion to divine love practice. Our soul connection was at the right time and moment to help our souls and destinies and ease our future. We also shared and proved the reality of divine love's existence; still, the sorrowful destiny happened ...

Once it's a coincidence, twice maybe again a coincidence, but the third time it's destiny.

Nine years alone with divine love inside, without any other soul image reflected in my heart ... And now, for months already, Her made it through.

This time, the most challenging destiny awaits me because I won't be able to break the connection even if fate makes fun of my soul image again.

REMINISCENCE OF PAST LIVES AND MIND TROUBLES

5 Nov 2019

Always for me was more attractive in the future than in the past of myself.

While most soul images yearned after the past when they were younger, I always wanted the time to pass faster and sooner to reach the end of my destiny. I didn't think that I would live to see the older Self.

The greatest mystery in our life seems to be the so-called 'death'. When your soul is revealed inside your heart, and you cuddle your life at the breast of divine love existence, 'death' becomes just a door to the present future and not a reason for sadness but a celebration when your destiny reaches the end.

I keep forgetting the past and mind troubles completely, keeping my dreams clean of residues and allowing me to see the past lives and present futures instead. This way, the divine love existence is always alive in my heart and soul without mind interference.

For years, I dreamt of seeing so many past lives – from woman to child and so many faces – it is no wonder my actual Self understands so many character portrayals inside my mind.

Also, it is unsurprising that one of my hobbies is other languages. If my mind and memory helped me, I would learn all the languages in the world. But no worries, there will soon be an app for that, better than any human being.

Suppose I would consider the vision from twenty years ago from the mountain, and an essential part of the revelation happened soon after that night; at the end of my life, I will be released entirely from the cycles of life and become one with divine love. So-called the final nirvana.

Yes, my past was way more exciting and thrilling than the present.

I hope the present future will be even more impressive since Her awoke my soul and raised the awareness and consciousness of divine love's existence as a deity once again in my life, which happened through her soul image revealed.

IN THE SHADOW OF MY SOUL

6 Nov 2019

My mind's voice is the greatest critic of them all.

If I am worried that my ego will go haywire, feeling that it is above anything else in this world due to the sanctuary of love in my heart, my mind's voice is always present to remind me that I don't have an ego anymore.

I called my mind voice 'The Thinker'.

No subject won't be debated in any way possible. The same goes for my heart's feelings and visions with Her. That's why I often had to shut down the door opened to my mind to snoop around my heart's feelings to translate them into words. Sometimes, it becomes a nuisance to the mind's voice.

The difference between my mind and heart is how I see the action in reality.

My heart feels like 'Just Love Her', to leave fate to write the path. If meant to be with Her, it's for the best; if not, so be it ... 'Just Love Her'.

My mind voice feels there's no point in bothering about destiny as there's no chance to be with Her, an impossible task and vision. My mind sees my visions more like pleasant dreams to sleep about.

My mind is overwhelmed when the feelings and thoughts touch the unseen realm of soul and divine love, so I can't function anymore. The same goes for my heart when feelings go over the standard limit.

The most exciting personality inside, born out of the divine love existence revelation, is the heart voice, called 'The Observer'. It's like a judge who does not take sides, either mind or heart.

'The Observer' is the only entity inside that can lead them through the labyrinth of the divine love realm. This entity also translates feelings from my heart into words that my mind can comprehend. Also, it oversees the practice of divine love reflection inside my mind mantra and all the things inside my mind can't handle.

'The Self' represents my soul's hidden shadow inside. This entity oversees the divine love practice, meditation, heart mantra, and everything that keeps a connection inside the unseen realm of divine love. Things are done without doing anything or taking any action or words needed – only complete silence and feelings inside the heart. Becoming one with the feeling of love inside means becoming one with divine love. It is the only entity inside my heart who can recognise and approve the chosen soul image. It can see the difference between passion and love as one reflection of another. It can distinguish the soulmate among souls in the present reality and can see the visions as they are without any interference.

The last decision inside is always 'The Self', taking it because its ruling is based on the feeling of divine love in my heart. That's why when the final decision that Her is the chosen soulmate, all the mind's blubbering voice went silent.

From time to time, I can hear the babbling of my mind's voice complaining that destiny and her soul image never will accept the divine love existence as a deity and also that my soul image is doomed to be alone forever because nothing sustains my heart's feelings from her soul image.

Nonetheless, I somehow feel Her – closer than ever before.

As time passed, what started as an echo of the feelings from the heart, the present future became a deep pulse of heart feelings for her soul image covering all my being.

MUSIC OF MY HEART AND SOUL

6 Nov 2019

I was always blessed to have more access to music and movies than I needed. And this life is not enough to enjoy all the films and the music passing through my hands.

Back in time, I had a collection of thousands of movies and all the music that would cross anyone's mind or taste. Long story short, I watched and listened to maybe a quarter of it. All that collection was gone so many years ago due to unforeseen circumstances of destiny's path.

In the past, I had to watch movies and listen to music that wasn't to my taste. But this opened my mind, and I saw beyond the preconceptions related to time, message and influences of the artists.

As I said, I will keep repeating that my mind isn't suited and prepared for the tremendous perception of my soul's existence. Because of this, too much information is lost or forgotten.

When my soul and heart vibrate at high levels, feeling divine love, there is always a sound inside, like a continuous humming. And it doesn't have to be complete silence around. Sometimes, I listen to this sound, going deep into the abyss of it.

When the divine love reflection makes the connection between souls, the taste in music, culture, art, passions and ideals, one's preferences become a common ground for another. When you love through divine love, there is no such thing that you don't like the same things. You start to like even the most annoying thing or hobby your beloved soul image pursues in its destiny.

What I like the most about the present future with Her is music as part of her destiny, among other heavenly talents. I am blessed this way to listen and catch glimpses of her soul echo in pure existence. Acting can hide the real soul behind walls of emotions and character portrayals, but in music, the door to the soul must be opened wide to let the feelings out to express oneself.

Often, I caught my heart listening in my mind, her voice singing to my soul. A glance at her laughing is pure bliss for my soul. A touch of her voice makes my heart shiver.

THE MASTERS OF MY LIFE

7 Nov 2019

The masters of my life to reach the knowledge of my soul and enlightenment were the soul images revealed in my heart by divine love reflection.

Through every step and experience, a master instructed my mind and heart on the path to enlightenment and understanding the divine love, existence and reflection into our souls. In the end, all the suffering and agony that besieged my heart for years in the past led me to an accurate understanding of the fundamental practice between two soul images, from human love to transcending it to divine love.

The divine love process isn't new and not at all unusual. The difference is in the idolised soul and the energy behind this process. The adored soul is the soulmate chosen by heart feelings and represented by the soul image revealed by divine love reflection.

Most of us, if not all, experienced precious human love, but nobody believed in its divinity, nor was it revealed as the God/Goddess reflection from our hearts and souls.

Some beliefs and practices use the concept of love adoration, yet there needs to be a clear message that divine love is above all there is.

Divine love has been used for aeons in religions, doctrines and all existence without knowing its presence as energy, as a deity – God/Goddess – the purest state of life and the source of all existence. Without divine love, there would be no enlightenment, no knowledge of souls' existence, or any other powers or deities anywhere in reality.

Divine love is more even than the idea or belief in God. It is above all religions, concepts and practices in the world. And it is so simple ... that's why it's so hard to be seen as it is. Who would believe that what's hidden behind human love is the most potent force called divine love?

Her has been my most crucial master since I was born as a soul image in this reality. After years of practice, her soul image was revealed to my heart, and then I thought, that's it in this life. There is nothing more left to new experiences until the final departure to the unknown.

Ultimately, Her cuddled my soul again in the abyss of divine love existence as the final practice.

THE SADNESS OF MY HEART ... MISSING HER

8 Nov 2019

Occasionally, not even heaven can help you feel better inside.

There are moments when I feel the physical space between our soul images harshly, and the sadness inside is felt as *Gom Jabbar* device testing from *Dune*.

Although everything is happening inside my mind and heart, there is no injury to feel the pain. The sadness feels so real, slashing through my heart. There is nothing else to do – just let it go. Feeling divine love can pass over any pain.

Why and how it happens?

There is no point in answering because I feel it. Missing Her will feel stronger and stronger as time passes because of the connection between our souls. It's the agony of destiny.

Maybe these moments are the result of heart prayers for the destiny of the beloved soul image to ease her life and clear the path to enlightenment. Negative energy and blasts of *karma* have been washed away through the divine reflection in our souls.

It can also reflect the feelings of the beloved soul image, passing through some difficult moments in destiny. Due to the strong connection between souls, the ripple effect of destiny echoes on each side of the images of souls.

The humming drum of the divine love mantra rises from the depths of my heart. Although I became one with the praying mantra from my heart and mind long ago, my consciousness and awareness are stronger than ever in these instances. Like wearing glasses and getting used to them or forgetting about them, wearing them helps you have clear sight no matter what.

I prefer suffering all my life if that will ease life and erase the negative effect on the destiny of her precious soul image.

THE FACE OF DIVINE LOVE

9 Nov 2019

The door opened in my heart to divine love's existence in the most significant experience of my life. It changed my destiny and life for aeons to come.

With eyes wide open, I can see Her. Her face covers my mind, heart and soul like a hollow of divine love. This happens whenever our souls make a connection beyond time and space.

One moment of her existence reality is translated inside my heart with feelings so deep as being together. It doesn't even happen to look for or to meditate about this process. It's only happening. The environment and place won't matter. For example, my surrounding space is noisy, full of people, voices, faces, machines and much work. Yet, all I could feel and see was her sweet 'soul image' face and the echoes of her voice singing to my soul.

These events reflect the present future with Her in my destiny. It's not an option or feeling you can run from it.

Who would want to run away from the feelings of divine love inside?

Who would give up on happiness and blissful moments like these?

Of course, it doesn't compare, and it's not even close to a moment in reality with her soul image. But if this happens, missing Her, I can't even imagine how it would be a moment in the present reality with Her.

I feel divine love reflected inside my heart. I contemplate her face and existence in this present reality, which is worth more than all the possible futures combined without Her. If there is a reality of Heaven in the Multiverse where feeling Her in these moments is the existence, then it would be my home for aeons to come. A version of my Self is probably out there feeling Her. And a reflection of that dimension is thought in this present reality with Her.

Time is disappearing in the infinite void of divine love feelings.

One moment of pure bliss, feeling Her, and eternity become that moment. I wish I could share some of these moments of pure bliss with her soul image in the present. Or maybe they are already felt by Her.

As I let myself bathe in moments of sadness from my heart, the same happens in moments of pure bliss. These moments comfort my soul image, missing her soul image. Otherwise, life without Her in the present reality would be unbearable.

The connection between our souls feels so strong when the face of her soul image covers my entire being with her existence.

The divine love sanctuary from my heart is filled with her presence. My mind is 'lost in the translation' of these feelings. And the present future vision with Her seems more relevant, seeing and feeling the connection out of this world inside.

I sometimes wonder if her soul image feels any moments of divine love. Is it only one way around this present reality, or is it the past of the present?

What sign from the divine love reflected in our soul images' existence won't be seen as a coincidence but an actual sign from Her?

THE HIDDEN SECRETS OF OUR SOULS
11 Nov 2019

How many times in one day are you aware of what's happening around you, especially inside you?

We live our lives as biological robots, throwing ourselves into the hands of destiny. The most significant change starts when you become aware of every moment. I'm not talking about your desires, material accomplishments in the profession, or whatever else your mind dreams of … I'm speaking about your soul.

Outside, everything is overruled by your destiny … Even if some sceptics say that is their will. It is, but with the help of destiny, which surrounds you with the proper moments and relations, good health and so on. Don't get me wrong, it doesn't mean that if you become aware of your soul's existence, your life won't be governed by destiny.

I can confirm only one thing from my experience. You will be freed from the shackles of destiny in your heart and mind. When you become aware of your soul and its divine reflection, hence the divine love existence, you will walk on the path of enlightenment and become free from the cycles of life, past and present.

You will live in the world following your destiny, but only your human body will be affected. Your soul will be free and conscious about its existence and divinity.

> *Buddha:*
> '*Believe nothing, no matter where you read it or who has said it, not even if I said it ... unless it agrees with your reason and your common sense.*'

> *Rumi:*
> '*I belong to no religion.*
> *My religion is love.*
> *Every heart is my temple.*'

> *Albert Einstein:*
> '*Science without religion is imperfect. Religion without science is blind.*'

WHERE IS HER? WHERE IS HER SOUL IMAGE IN PRESENT REALITY?

11 Nov 2019

I asked 'Destiny' so many times:

'*Where is Her?*'

I'm looking at my destiny of present reality, and her soul image is nowhere to be seen ...

Or is it only in my imagination?

Or is Her only in my heart but not my destiny?
Or is it not in my destiny yet?
Or will it ever be in this life around me at some point in time?
Or will it be a chance to meet Her in this present reality?

Too much 'or' and possible 'maybe' – too many probabilities. No wonder my Self and 'Destiny' are not such good buddies in the present.

I breathe Her ... That's how I feel lately. I feel her presence inside my heart from morning to morning, whether sleeping or awake. It's unusual to feel Her inside my heart. And still, her soul image is so far away in my present reality, literally speaking.

Soon, I will be closer to her soul image in the present reality. Will this be an opportunity for a present future to find Her in reality, or will the destiny of our soul images remain the same?

I love it when my heart is burning with her presence inside. This feeling eases the suffering sparked by the distance in our destinies between our soul images. Why a destiny where Her is only inside but too far outside, physically speaking?

I know that the next step of enlightenment is due to Her, but it's unbearable without her soul image closer.

Sometimes, I ask myself why I bother writing about my inner feelings. How would this help other soul images search for enlightenment in the future? Or is feeling Her the only reason that I'm writing?

I close my eyes and let my Self disappear in the presence of Her inside ... And a wish rises inside my heart: that my destiny would have been to be born inside her soul image, living together close to her soul for aeons to come.

HER IS SO BEAUTIFUL ... TO ME

12 Nov 2019

While looking in awe at her soul image inside my heart and mind screen, the song lyrics of Joe Cocker's 'You're so Beautiful ... To Me' came to my mind, expressing my feelings for Her.

I still wonder what moves our hearts to tears for the loved one chosen from billions of souls out there. What mystery is hidden behind our connections, preferring a soul image and sharing our love inside, most of the time with no love back?

On the contrary, the beloved soul image usually loves another who doesn't care about heart matters and then suffers. This is supposed to help the soul image on the path of enlightenment. Or maybe it must clean the karma of its existence.

It does not matter if you are devout to divine love inside. Sometimes, following only human love is even more harmful.

The game of suffering will have the same rules applied. But the pain felt will go way over the board than human love because all your existence is dedicated to divine love, and nothing else makes sense in your life. And then you wonder why you still follow divine love in the name of love.

The divine love in my heart gave me so many moments of pure bliss that nothing from the outside could ruin the purity of love. It also gave me many experiences and proof that when we share back our beloved soul image, even gods envy our feelings. Living most of my life cuddling at the existence of divine love in my heart became the second nature of my being.

To feel and awaken the consciousness of connection for her soul image, Her should be a true soulmate after so many years, including the fall of my heart.

Months passed, and my mind – 'The Thinker' – tried every possible reason to let go of Her.

'Yes, just love Her, but don't dream of destiny with Her ...' I have been told so many times.

I must break it to you, my dear Thinker, but Her is already my fate.

The fact that Her is always in my mind and heart without any hope of a present future makes it look already like a fairy tale. Well, sometimes life beats up the movie, especially when it is a life dedicated to divine love.

THE MODERN HERMIT

12 Nov 2019

Be in the world without being in the world ...

Following the practice of divine love reflection into our souls doesn't require us to retire from the world in a monastery or live secluded, but it does require us not to reject the world as a system. It embraces everything from existence and adapts to the destinies of our soul images.

The rules are that there are no rules other than what you feel in your heart. This means that if you feel love, then feel it ... never give up on that feeling. These so-called rules are not imposed and consist of being constantly aware of divine love reflected in our souls.

The instrument that makes you follow and respect the practice is the heart's feelings. That's why when you fall in love with a soul image through divine love reflection, it is induced by heart feelings and nothing else. It looks like a gift because it's not something you analyse before, nor is it decided by the actions of other involved relations (parents, tradition, culture and so on).

In the end, you become aware of the divine love existence as a deity, although it's not the best representation, more like a state of absolute and infinite existence embracing forms and energies, seen and unseen, manifested or not.

The modern hermit in the present reality will always be alone in the outside world but not inside.

Even if other soul images embrace the vision of divine love, our bodies and minds are not prepared yet to live connected inside. In the future, when so many soul images are enlightened, the inner world will overcome the outside world, and the connection between souls will be awakened as a part of our human bodies.

Religions will be a thing of the past. Who needs religion when divine love is revealed inside our hearts?

Also, racism, discrimination of any form, prejudice and hate will be seen as a documentary of the primitive human beings from history. Who will want to suffer when all enlightened soul images are connected inside through divine love?

Word of advice: *'Be a sinner ... But full of divine love.'*

MOMENTS OF HER

15 Nov 2019

My mind is so empty ... and there is only the presence of Her in a vacuum space where I am the Void surrounding her soul image.

No thoughts ... Only feelings and breathing through her existence inside.

As time passes, Her becomes more than I imagined inside my heart. No corner and shadow of my soul remained that was not shrouded in her existence.

I always wonder if her soul image is doing well and implore my soul to watch over Her. That is the game of destiny, setting us apart in our bodies but keeping Her closer through our souls.

Soon, I will sit next to my beloved friend Han River and listen to stories and memories of Her.

And I will see my soul image echoed next to her soul image in the mirror of its reflection ... from past lives.

And I will engrave in its waves my heart whispers for her soul image when it passes by the river ... to let Her know that my soul image is yearning to hug her and look into her soul image's eyes.

And I will be one with the Earth, kissing her feet with my existence while walking around under the sky of Hanguk ...

And I will wish to be with Her forever in the first snow.

And I will greet her soul with hums in the wind of winter:

'괜찮아, 내 사랑? *(Gwaenchana nae Sarang?) – You alright, my Love?'*

THE ART OF PRAYING ...
TO DIVINE LOVE

15 Nov 2019

It is a common belief that praying is only seen in religions, doctrines or any other form of faith.

After years of praying, I saw that even animals are praying – all nature is a devotion. The only difference is that nature praises divine love through raw love.

Look around you and start seeing things hidden behind the curtain of your human eyes. Start viewing with your heart, and the secrets of your soul will be revealed.

Human beings pray in the wrong way. When we pray, we ask God for many things: health, money, power ... and the best for our Ego. Sometimes, we pray for others or, in the family business, for each other.

I don't say it's not good to pray – quite the opposite. But we must learn to pray.

Do you think the mighty God (divine love) doesn't know what you need?

Have you wondered why you are hungry and homeless?

Or why you have all that you need and more?

There are laws above everything, and destiny is written from the moment we are born. So, to pray for you makes no sense, but for others, yes. Praising God and His creation (nature, the universe, the multiverse, galaxies, the divine realm and so on) makes even more sense. The more you expand your mind, vision and heart, the more you will get in return. So don't ever have a small mind. You must pray, think and know the actual scale of existence.

When you feel divine love in your heart, the feelings become prayer. What else do you need when feeling the love inside gives you more happiness than you can handle?

The only reasonable devotion is to thank divine love for its existence and never leave your heart in emptiness again. So, praying will become one with the feeling from your heart through the existence of divine love.

The praying inside will go unattended once you experience enlightenment. You must be aware of it initially, but prayer becomes one with your existence in time, like the divine love reflection inside.

Sometimes, you suddenly feel the praying inside stronger than usual because you become conscious and aware of the praying inside your heart and mind. Usually, it happens due to future events in your destiny or the beloved soul's image.

Praying is like a shield against the blows of destiny. That's why you must become one with devotion. You are praying not only in need because of suffering and hard times but also in moments of happiness and bliss.

One or a few words are needed to pray, but it's more than enough. More important is the feeling of divine love from your heart. You must feel how the divine love from your heart spreads throughout your existence, and your mind will repeatedly focus on words representing your heart's feelings. Ultimately, your prayers will cover your destiny, like a drop of water making a hole in the stone.

There are other forms of praying, some that you might think are not a prayer. A moment of listening to music that you like and moving your heart to tears, a moment in the middle of nature admiring the greatness of its existence in clouds, trees, water and mountains – everything reflects the divinity of love. Divine love created all the existence, so that's why you feel love and connection through nature.

Other forms of praying are art, culture, tradition and human love. Anything that moves your heart to tears or focuses your mind (an idea, an accomplishment in life, a mindset) could be praying. It doesn't matter what you choose in your heart to pray as long it's filled with divine love.

It helps when you pray that the soul image represents the image of divinity from your heart, revealed through divine love's reflection in your heart. This makes sense since the flame of love in your heart started with your beloved soul image.

The soul image divine love chose through feelings from my heart while praying is Her.

Oh ... Why did I choose a human being to represent divine love?

I didn't choose. Divine love, reflected in feelings from my heart, does it because divine love is my God/Goddess.

TEARS OF DIVINE LOVE FOR HER
18 Nov 2019

If I could count the tears I have shed since divine love was awakened in my heart, I could take a good shower.

Sometimes, sorrow rained in my eyes; other times, bliss poured from my heart.

Missing Her always feels like an open wound dropping shades of agony that don't heal with visions, dreams and hopes. In these moments, being the Observer happens to cause me to feel the tears seldom outside and more often inside. The line between sorrow and bliss is so thin that it blends both feelings simultaneously.

And I wonder how destiny will make it happen for me to see or glimpse her soul-image eyes in the name of love!

When will the veil between coincidence and a real sign from Her fade away in divine love?

Does the Book of Life write about our soul images being together in a present future or one of the unseen worlds?

If the present reality offers me recent information that her soul image is doing well, my sorrow withers with each update. The more, the merrier.

If it takes more time between, my soul starts wandering in the unseen world of the aether and connects with Her. These moments bring up tears of bliss inside my heart. It feels as natural as being with her soul image in reality.

Her eyes follow my heart and mind like a candle, keeping the light burning so I can see and feel the path traced by divine love's reflection into my soul's existence. These moments bring up tears of love clouding my eyes, missing her soul image.

I feel empty and incomplete without Her in my shallow daily life. Moments with Her became the only way to feel that my efforts were not in vain and that magic was bound to happen in destiny just by loving Her.

THE SILENCE BETWEEN WORDS

18 Nov 2019

Once in a while, start listening to the silence between words spoken. In that silence, it is breathing out your heart and soul.

Silence empowers words and gives strength to their meaning. Imagine there is no gap between words. It will be chaos to express your feelings and thoughts. A reflective silence can give words meaning and feel heard by other hearts and souls searching for enlightenment.

Listen to the words of great masters and enlightened souls from the past. Their words contain significant meanings and force your mind to take a break and listen to the silence between words. This way, your heart's feelings can be translated by your soul.

Feelings awakened in your heart by the silence between words will have a say in your destiny towards enlightenment.

Divine … Love …

Listen to the silence between both words with your heart. Feeling the meaning of both words connects you with the unseen realm of the soul. No other part of your body can recognise the divine love realm; only your soul is bathed in the rays of sacred love reflection.

Love … Her …

It's the same thing I'm doing in my daily meditation. I listen to the silence between words chosen through my heart's feelings. And quietly, information starts pouring into my mind's screen, expressing the sense of Her inside.

Sometimes, all that's left is silence – no words, just a stroll under the rain of feelings inside my heart.

Seldom, it's going even more profound, and I listen to the silence between perceptions from my heart, where only the divine love in the raw state resides.

THE FIRE IN HER EYES

19 Nov 2019

Oh, my God! That's all my mind can think of, glimpsing the fire in her eyes.

Finally, after a long time, my heart is full of genuine bliss, without any shadow of sorrow – only real happiness and no mixed feelings.

Seeing her eyes, the flame of love struck my heart, instantly taking me into the divine love realm. What has Her done to me?

Do you know the excitement that something good might happen when you feel your heart fluttering with love?

My heart trembled all day while I felt Her and waited. I expected something to happen, but not at such scale.

Why does a pure moment of Her make an overwhelming statement profound inside my heart and soul?

I didn't feel my body for hours because I was living with her soul image through her eyes in my heart. It's too much love for a mere human, covered with blissful moments of divine love due to Her.

Floating in clouds of love reminded me why I would vanish happily anytime from this world blessed with divine love for Her.

My face is burning … It is the same as the first-time crush of a teenager that catches a look in the eyes of a loved one.

I must pinch my skin to remind myself I am still here and not in my dreams. All my being is in awe of her presence inside my heart.

It was only one moment, enough to squeeze all my existence into her eyes. I could live in this moment for eternity.

I don't want to think of words born from feeling Her anymore.

I wish to go deep into my heart, lie down next to her soul image and lose my Self looking at her eyes.

Her existence inside melts any trace of my being. All that is left from the shadow of my being is a humming sound of love:

'고마워, 내 사랑*! (Gomawo, nae Sarang!) – Thank you, my Love!'*

KNEELING TO FEELINGS FOR HER

19 Nov 2019

I feel such strong feelings inside my heart due to the presence of Her ... that I must kneel my soul, seeing her soul image on the screen of my mind.

I knocked out everything from the old 'Me' inside, and now there is only Her inside.

How can I cope with the new version of 'Me' when all I feel is Her?

I should rename 'Me' into her existence.

All I wish for in the future is to be with Her forever, not as long as destiny allows.

I have never dreamed in the past of being with a beloved soul like I do in the present reality. And the agony is more significant than ever.

All I asked my Self was, what if Her really loves me back when our soul images meet in the future, and fate allows us to be together?

My belief was Her to acknowledge the existence of divine love and to feel its presence in any reality. My life feels worthy due to feelings for her reality inside my heart. The problem is, what if Her is and will be just a dream and not a vision?

Is the reality of her existence only in my heart and never in my physical proximity whatsoever?

That's why ignorance is bliss, not knowing and not asking your mind to voice existential matters. And I return inside my heart to listen to the echo of my feelings for Her:

'사랑해, 내 사랑*! (Saranghae, nae Sarang!) – I love you, my Love!'*

HER SOUL IMAGE IS A BLESSING TO MY HEART

19 Nov 2019

Do you know that feeling when you look at a painting by a great artist, let's say David Hockney, and you are lost in that moment and forget about your existence?

Before divine love revealed Her to my heart, I tried to picture who would settle in my heart for aeons.

Amazingly, the main features I can see now in her soul image are exposed in my heart artwork. Seeing her soul image repeatedly, I lose myself in her eyes. I forget about everything and anything. I am lost in Her.

The greatest gift from Her was her soul image with her eyes uncovered. It's way easier to look at Her on the walls of my heart and see her soul image so clearly on my mind screen. It seems closer to the reality of Her.

That's how lovers can resist being apart for a long time – always keeping a picture of the loved one close to their hearts. Nothing beats reality, though.

The only dilemma is that my mind – 'The Thinker' – is boiling. It's like her soul image perceived so clearly opened a new chapter in its existence.

Is there too much information to process?

Or, because of the thin line between coincidence and certainty, it seems so confusing. Once, twice … and three times, coincidence is too much to account for. Fate moves with quick steps ahead of anything.

It's the feeling that starts from the beginning – the first time I look into her eyes, when I fall in love with Her, when I express my feelings for her in words. That's the power of divine love, and you can't ever get bored living human love this way. You are constantly feeling like new beginnings with your beloved soul. Every beginning seems to have stronger feelings as your human heart expands the limits imposed for its protection. The moment you choose divine love over everything else in your life, the magic world inside opens its gates to know your soul.

If both souls chosen by divine love revealed onto their hearts accept the gift of holy love, knowing the source of their feelings, a new type of human being would be born out of their infinite and absolute love.

CLEAR YOUR OLD MIND PROGRAMMING

20 Nov 2019

To access the higher state of mind, you must clear your mind programming and start from the beginning.

Our genetic code is written by fate, what you like, how your physical self will look and feel and so on. Our genetic code has a backdoor allowing us to access hidden features and modify anything the karma coding writes.

The human microcosm is a small reflection of the macrocosm. This also means that what is happening today in technology and programming already occurs on a much bigger scale in the universe.

Advanced practices from religions and yoga and other systems of deconditioning try to clarify what is written in the hidden program of our destiny. Through concentration, meditation and physical exercises, it overcomes the limits imposed by the unseen laws and rules in our genetic code. This way, a new set of rules and conceptions are added to the genetic code. So, in a way, we are biological robots or any other term that must be invented to describe what we are, but we are not born free.

Those who access the secret information about our soul's existence without the practice of understanding the bigger scale of our life's programming have primitive minds; they are bound to become despots, dictators and dark souls. A dark soul means that the mind lost the path to enlightenment, not that the soul is evil. The soul is not good or bad. It is melted and enslaved by your destiny and genetic code written in your existence. These dark souls are more prone to desires and rules they impose because they can't control them due to their lack of spiritual practice. That's why they cause suffering to other soul images: they repress their weakness.

For a long time, I wondered why many saints and visionary beings praise God's mighty power and divinity, but they limit the power and laws of divinity according to human existence. If God has unlimited power, it means it can do anything literally ... Like an oppressor or a liberator.

The concept of divinity will be overwritten in the future because what exists now is just a copy of our limited human mind's ideas. Some people had a vision and spread it worldwide according to the code written in their existence. But nowadays, the old coding is obsolete, and we must create a new one from the ground to evolve to the next step of enlightenment. The existence and concept of divine love are fundamental to the new code. They are included in the old code, but as we can see, it's not working anymore. It's outdated.

In a world where technology and advanced genetic coding give anybody powers like the gods praised in old scriptures, it's time to build a new code inside our human beings, which is the message of divine love. You take something from the old coding of love for God and adapt it and include the new features for the present future of our human beings and society.

The message of divine love is that love lives within our souls through our hearts as a temple. Instead of praying and devoting to outside temples, it's time to pray inside and dedicate our lives to the beloved souls revealed through our hearts by divine love reflected in our souls.

THE ONLY ONE ...
DO YOU THINK WE HAVE TIME?

21 Nov 2019

I pray with all my being to my lovely friends to pass my feelings to Her, to let her soul image know and feel the touch of my heart on her existence.

My lovely friends are the sky, water, earth and wind. When I feel lonely, I look up at the sky, and the clouds tell me stories of past times. When I want to see my heart, I look down at the water, and the waves tell me stories about the present reality. When I am upset, I look down on earth, and the sand tells me stories about the suffering of all existence. When I want to spread my love and feel the love back, I whisper to the wind feelings from my heart, and its whipping on my cheeks gives me shivers to my heart.

These moments make me want to shout from the top of the mountains in the echo of the abyss that I love Her. I just wanted to let it all out in the open, to chill the burning fire sparked by her presence inside my heart since I met Her.

Loving Her fades away anything else in my existence. No thrill can move my heart as her soul image does.

Feeling the need to listen to George Michael's 'Praying for Time' as the time required for our soul images to get together is shortening out in destiny with every day that passes.

Do you think we have time?

LOOKING AT HER

21 Nov 2019

Whenever I look at Her, I can't get enough. I want to see Her one more time ... and one more time. And no thoughts were going through my head, just pure silence, stunned by the shadow of her soul light reflected in her eyes.

I wonder what's changed inside her heart that looks brighter than before. It can't just be the quality of visions in my heart. Or maybe I'm changed since I am irrevocably bound to her existence.

I would cuddle to her heart to feel the warmth of her being. To ease the tears of my heart, yearning for a touch of her feelings. I would aspire to her scent clouding my senses, to forget that I am just a human dreaming of an unseen divine love realm. I would kiss her sweet eyes, glaring with peeks of enchantment, keeping my soul in a net of rays of love.

Looking at Her is perceiving like being under the spell of love. I can't belong to anyone else but Her. Even if her soul image doesn't want me, my heart is addicted to her presence inside.

I pray to divine love to be as close to Her as possible. It is better to be gone in the abyss of oblivion than not to be under her charm.

Yeah … I don't know why the longing to listen: '*Nina Simone – I put a spell on you …*'

NOT GOOD ENOUGH

21 Nov 2019

It hit me finally … What else other than love can I offer to Her?

Unconditional and absolute love … it's all I know to give. There is nothing else I've learned over the years of spiritual love practice.

But … It's not good enough …

Finding a soul to share the same values is more than a dream. It's a fairy-tale story that happens once in a century or a millennium. The scale of the sacrifice in the name of love determines the outcome.

I have experienced in the past the value of '*not good enough …*' – not even money and love offered are good enough. Life is boring without sins, the so-called desire for more and more, professionally or materially speaking. This is typical for any human being, myself included.

The new wave of human connections suggests that relationships as we know them will disappear in time or become something else. It reflects our sick society, which is blind to the destruction waiting to happen on a big scale. Humans can't learn from love and happiness, only from suffering. It's the only language they know on the path to enlightenment.

And yet suffering failed to raise the consciousness of human beings for a higher state.

Happiness and a life without worries connect many of us with the inner Self and occur in art, culture and technology.

It's still not good enough ...

The past of suffering is quietly hunting us all.

Pollution and lost connection on a deeper level between souls are, however, leading and affecting great minds who are blind or close their eyes to the brink of disaster we are living.

Around the world, there is worry about economic growth and more ways to make easy money from nothing.

There are more sustainable ways of thinking. This is while many species around us have disappeared, and the space allocated to wild nature is shrinking.

Indeed, we are like a virus as suggested in *The Matrix*, spreading and using all resources from one location and then moving to another. Soon, we must move to other worlds to destroy it because if nature doesn't do something against us, we will surely erase it.

Love is not good enough because of the limits imposed by our mindset and ignorance of its roots.

Why not want more and more love instead of any other shallow things in our lives?

We are fortunate enough to find and live with our beloved souls. And that's it. We think that's the limit of love's existence. We lose because of our limited vision and can't see the absolute and infinite state of love existence – divine love.

Why choose suffering over happiness?

Surrender completely to love, knowing its divinity, raise the bar to infinite in achieving a love connection with your beloved soul and voilà ... You must learn to accommodate too much happiness in your heart instead of suffering.

Not good enough, though ...

After reaching your happiness, what's good, a world where only you are happy?

You must spread your happiness to other souls in search of enlightenment. Otherwise, your joy won't be *global*, just *local*. In the past, I felt this local happiness where love was only upon yourself. It's like drinking tea from an empty cup.

Of course, other than opening the minds of others and spreading the message of divine love, there is only so much to do. All the other souls should accept divine love into their hearts, make it a shrine to happiness, and forget about suffering.

So, in the end, it's not good enough that happiness is only in my heart because of Her. I also wish her soul image to be happy because of Me.

And lastly, not because of Me ... entirely due to divine love.

DAILY AND WALKING MEDITATION:

SEOUL – SOUTH KOREA

THE LONG ROAD TO S(E)OUL – THE DESTINY AWAITS ...

24 Nov 2019

Flying to Paris ...
À Paris mon cher s'il te plait!

I finally started the long journey to 'Just Love Her'.

Destiny settled my path to Her months ago without even noticing. And now, just following the clues along the road.

Someone asked me why I was not thrilled about my trip and not shouting and dancing as Seoul's destiny awaited in front of 'Me'. I have been thrilled for months, loving Her. And I jumped, cried, laughed, sang and danced for a long time together with Her inside and out. I feel mixed emotions of happiness and sorrow inside my heart as reality and coincidences play with me.

How can I communicate with Her or touch her being in the noisy existence of our soul images?

I feel her soul, though ... But I forgot how to be 'Me' in the real world and connect with a beloved soul image. However, it will be enough to take one moment to look into her soul-image eyes, and the connection will feel like more than thousands of words.

Above the clouds ...
Seoul flight – Birmingham to Paris – Above the clouds ...

This is the first time I've thought of Her literally above the clouds.

Walking on the clouds to Her ... My heart is filled with divine love, cuddling her soul image. It feels closer than ever to her soul.

Tears of joy flow through my heart as I feel Her. I have so much love for Her in my heart ... that I must spread it all over the clouds to all soul images that run after divine love in their lives. I can barely keep the tears of happiness from dripping from my eyes. Too crowded around me to let my feelings for Her flow outside my heart.

> *How do you choose the fastest way to her heart?*
> *(그녀의 심장에 가장 빠른 방법을 선택하는 방법은 무엇입니까?!)*
> *(Geunyeo-ui simjange gajang ppareun bangbeobeul seontaekhaneun bangbeobeun mueosimnikka?!)*

Ah, divine love, I implore you; please give me a sign from Her that I am walking on the promising path to Her!

I could test whether the closer distance between our soul images gives us more strength and whether it is faster to communicate inside our hearts through divine love.

I will feel her footsteps in my heart around Seoul. Until then, I will run on the clouds to …

À Paris … Paris Airport …

Ah … Mon amour, la langue française …

I promise that at some point in time, I will see you 'mon cher Paris'. I haven't needed to speak in French for dozens of years, only a few times with a colleague from Ghana for fun.

The French language is one of my favourites.

Flying to Seoul … (서울로요) (Seoulroyo) …

I have an authentic feeling while flying from Paris to Seoul.

My heart is burning, feeling closer physically with every minute passed toward the destination. My lovely friend, Han River, flows through my mind, washing away doubts and sorrow, missing Her. Her soul image is clouding all my being, touching every corner left untouched in the past of the present.

My soul is already flying above all places around Seoul, with her soul sharing feelings from their existence. Although I feel their language, I can't translate any words through my mind. I sense just pure Love … divine love.

The angelic voice of Nina Simone is singing 'Feeling Good' to express my emotions above the limit that our souls' connection throws out in the depths of my heart.

'It's a new dawn, it's a new day, it's a new life for Me …

And I'm feeling good ...'

Because soon – so soon – I'll be closer to Her, not just through souls but also our human bodies. My heart is reminiscing every second passed being nigher and nigher to her heart, feeling the pulse of love passing through.

41 NIGHTS OF DIVINE LOVE IN SEOUL
26 Nov 2019

One year ago, I wouldn't have believed if someone told me my life would change this year because Her, the divine love, would send me to Seoul.

The best thing is that I feel Her closer, and it's way easier than being far away. I couldn't understand why Seoul was due to divine love until I came here, and the real impact of Her started to unravel. I feel Her in every space around my existence in Seoul.

Wandering around Seoul while walking, feeling divine love and meditating are bliss for my soul. My mind is empty, and I am just rambling, loving Her. Divine love takes my steps and surprises me at every moment. It carries me to places where I wish I were in that time and place, past or present, to see Her and feel its soul-image existence.

My mind is not happy, however ... All the time here will imply its non-existence. It is not needed other than the usual things the mind should do. But in matters of the heart, access is not granted. It means no actions, expectations or reality, just pure love and bliss due to Her.

Sometimes, I struggle to keep my tears of love flowing outside. But inside, rivers of divine love and tears pour all the time.

It feels like stepping on the clouds of love walking all day long. Love inside flushes away all tiredness, and my heart sings the melody of eternal souls.

I start to feel my soul's past lives touching the earth of Seoul. It feels like home.

Looking at people's faces, I feel the divine love covering the sky.

And I'm just wondering … Am I the only crazy one feeling it?

In those moments, I closed my eyes and started spreading the love that felt like an ocean to all existence. I dream of times when people will be happy living in eternal connection with the divine love.

How can I thank Her for opening my heart to divine love for this world again?

A long time ago, my heart was broken to pieces, and I lost my trust in existence. I thought I couldn't share divine love with a soul image.

That's the beauty of destiny. You don't have to be with the soul image chosen.

Sorrow and happiness mixed is the feeling of enlightenment – the happy, sorrowful feeling.

INSPIRING MUSIC. Sew Your Heart 김경희 *(Kim Kyung Hee)* | *It's Okay to Not Be Okay (사이코지만 괜찮아)* OST

SO MUCH LOVE AT NAMSAN TOWER

27 Nov 2019

So many padlocks of love are all around the Namsan Tower.

There is much love around Seoul, and Namsan Tower is undoubtedly the heart, like a lighthouse for soul images sharing the love.

Any place where soul images share hearts and minds becomes a shrine dedicated to those feelings.

My heart shivers, feeling divine love for all soul images in search of romance. It doesn't matter how long or if it will be shared back. The important thing is to search for and feel love. That's the first step to enlightenment through divine love between two soul images before knowing their souls.

My soul spread the wings of divine love onto existence from Namsan Tower.

I hope that someday, more souls will acknowledge its existence by visiting places in Seoul where my consciousness felt divine love.

Some tears of joy couldn't be stopped, feeling so much love. As usual, I close my eyes and spread divine love to all the souls around me, then around Seoul and Korea. Finally, to the whole world because it's too much love to keep only for my soul.

Looking from the top of Namsan Tower, there is no place in Seoul where I didn't take a glimpse of Her. And my heart can touch her soul image through feelings, wherever the place, and unfold the beacon of love to let Her know that I miss Her so much. Yet, somehow, I don't feel lonely.

Her is closer than ever to the top of Namsan Tower.

WALKING MEDITATION WHILE FEELING DIVINE LOVE FOR HER

28 Nov 2019

Long walks around Seoul while feeling the divine love for Her settled me in meditation for hours.

It became a daily habit to stroll around Seoul, aware of every step touching the earth while walking. Feeling space around me, people's emotions and lives, and running on the path of their destinies led me to experience the oneness of Korea.

In other travel locations I explored I didn't experience these sensations, although I felt a connection with the past. It's all because Her opened the doors to divine love for her soul image. It returns to the Joseon Kingdom and recognises my soul's past life.

Past existences of my soul came to chase me, contemplating the events from Namsan Tower and places re-enacting the history of once a vast empire. Although I did not understand words, I felt the tears, the shadows of the past lives' feelings slicing through my heart.

Seeing the monuments dedicated to the freedom movement

from the history of Korea opened the door of my heart, feeling tears of sorrow and suffering for past lives of my soul long forgotten.

If I was in doubt about dreaming about my past lives and why I was travelling to Seoul, not anymore.

Who knows what troubling existence shared with Her over time?

Under the spell of feelings, I had a short vision of Her sharing the past in a small village, washing clothes, her face full of joy and laughter. Her beauty overwhelmed my heart to tears.

Souls carry the love over aeons and never forget the beloved soul. If there is a time in the same destiny to come together with the precious soul, the soul image you are born with will not have peace until death.

WALKING MEDITATION FOLLOWING HER STEPS

29 Nov 2019

My spiritual journey to Seoul is to complete the visions of my soul, feeling Her closer and following the shadow of her steps. It's now a part of my destiny from the present reality and future, not just a dream anymore.

My meditation footsteps are guided daily by divine love inside feeling Her. A few places where I wanted to sense her presence in the past or present are revealed daily. Sometimes it happens in a place where feeling Her is so intense it hits me instantly in my head:

'Oh, this is one of the places where I wish I were in the past to see Her in reality, not just in my dreams!'

Walking close to my beloved friend Han River, I felt its calling, talking through the whispers of its waves. I promise you, my dear friend, that we will communicate together, whether in snow or rain. For the moment, we shared the first sunset, feeling Her. Anyway, I admire your beauty, and soon we will cuddle, feeling the touch of her soul image existence.

I had to write while walking because my weak mind memory was lost, and I needed to translate feelings from the depths of my heart. I wonder if Her feels these moments simultaneously, or is it only one way?

Although cold, the sun warms my heart and soul with its rays of divine love, and my precious friend Han River takes away my thoughts and worries above its tides.

These times with Her require listening to Adele ('One and only', 'Take it all', 'Set fire to the rain') ... My heart is crying inside and out, feeling Her too close.

From the deeps of my heart, my soul whispers are passing through the echo of its sorrow:

'And I miss Her so much ... more than ever!
그리고 그 어느 때보다도 그녀가 너무 보고 싶어*!*
(Geurigo geu eoneu ttaebodado geunyoga neomu bogo sipeo!)'

So close now through our soul images, yet Her is so far away in time. It is good that no one is close by to see a stupid, mature person shedding tears of nothingness while feeling Her.

Some visions have already happened in a few days since in Seoul.

So, what's come next to my sweet-sour destiny?

INSPIRING MUSIC: Adele – Songs Playlist 2020 ...

HER SOUL IMAGE PROFILE

29 Nov 2019

A strong character and lovely presence represent a beautiful soul.

Looking at a person in the beginning, after the glamour has passed, you will notice the differences between body and soul. The body presence is average but attractive compared with the standards of so-called beauty appreciated by *experts* in the field. For those connected with their soul, even if they are unaware, a cheerful and likeable personality reflects their soul.

What makes the difference is the awareness and consciousness level of enlightenment attained in past and present lives. Meeting a soul aware of divinity reflected in its existence will make you feel the difference. Unseen forces surrounding the soul image of this soul awakened will make other souls in search of enlightenment see the light within.

Some souls aren't aware of their enlightenment, like glasses on the eyes, forgetting about it. They might even reject any ideas or practices of enlightenment. Why must one search for and learn knowledge if one's soul is enlightened?

You will find a lot of enlightened souls through artists, musicians, actors, writers and any other creative soul images. Their work expresses the proof of the soul within. The only thing missing is the acknowledgement and authentic experience of the divine love inside. The energy accessed is in the raw form. It's enough to have one moment of divine love for them to reach the consciousness of enlightenment. Other soul images must search and practice their entire life or a few lives to attain enlightenment. Even if they experience enlightenment, they won't be able to recognise it.

I hadn't searched for enlightenment my whole life, but I ran from it initially when it happened. Because of the beliefs imposed by religion, I thought that only by being dedicated to a closed environment could you have a spiritual experience. Later, the divine love inside revealed the truth about religions.

There is no better religion than others, and there is no different truth in each. Human beings make religions look like systems, while enlightenment is individual. It is known only by personal experience of the soul.

There is no heaven and hell, nor good or bad soul image. Like in movies where actors play their roles, the same happens with souls in destiny. Souls are so clouded by their role that they become one with it. That's the problem because waking up from their dreams will be tough.

Her soul image reflects her soul way more than mine. Noblesse's strong personality spreading joy around is the mark of her existence. It also means that her soul image reflected her soul from the beginning of her life.

Some soul images are born with the reflection of their souls, while others struggle to keep pace with their souls.

FREEDOM IS THE DREAM OF SOULS

30 Nov 2019

Freedom is an exciting word for dreams of so many soul images.

Like the dream of freedom in the soul images, the souls must also be free from the shackles that restrain them inside the human bodies. The soul has been tied to the existence of every living thing for aeons. Without a soul, there wouldn't be any consciousness and intelligence in the Universe. Every part of nature, as well as creation, has its soul. There are also collective souls being a part of a group, like animals, birds and so on.

Raw and pure divine love connects everything with every state of matter and living.

Human beings are only aware of their consciousness and soul. They must still abide by the unseen rules and laws of the Universe.

We must achieve enlightenment to fully understand and feel our souls' connection and hidden secrets. Without enlightenment, even knowing about it doesn't mean much to us.

In the past, because enlightened souls believed it was dangerous for others without spiritual practice to know these hidden secrets, the knowledge was forbidden and kept secret. Nowadays, it's accessible to any human being on the face of the Earth.

Enlightened souls realised that knowledge wouldn't be understood anyway without spiritual practice. At least to be accessible to every soul in search of enlightenment. In the end, the more enlightened souls, the merrier.

PREDESTINATION OR FREE WILL?

30 Nov 2019

This subject of our destiny, whether it's in our hands to change it or accept what it is, has troubled our minds since it was brought into our existence by visionary minds.

Based on my experiences and visions, my point of view is somewhere in the middle. Both views can be connected.

PREDESTINATION

I am looking at the big picture of why everything is how it is.

Presidents, royal families, actors and singers, great artists, countries, places, technology, past and present, and so on – you must ask yourself why it is as it is now. You can't do anything for the past, only for the future to change it.

Do you think that you really can alter the future?

Your actions and beliefs are another drop in the big ocean of things bound to happen. Otherwise, you wouldn't even think about it. I've seen amazing people and unknown souls who do or believe beautiful things. They have much talent, but nobody cares. In contrast, others with shallow skills have great success.

Things that are bound to happen will happen whether you want them to or not, and you will only be aware of the chain of events once it passes. After it finishes, you wonder how it was possible to have a blind mind during the process. That's what I call destiny. What is bound to happen, it will occur.

When I hear about so-called gurus or speakers who talk about our power to change destiny, it makes me laugh. Thinking like that is all part of the game and a lifetime. Everything is part of the illusion clouding our minds and lives.

It is certain that if you think you can change your destiny, then your actions will follow your future. If you are failing, though, never give up. Be aware that it is a part of your destiny to struggle.

If it happens to love another soul and you are aware of divine love reflected in your soul's existence, it is also a part of your destiny. It is a destiny that will change this life and lead to eternity.

Reading the message throughout my writings has already started the inception of the news about divine love's reflection in existence. Maybe you will forget for a time about the message, but when love lights up your heart, you will remember and come back for more to understand and feel the divine love.

Through divine love, your soul will be freed from the shackles of destiny; in this way, it will also be the soul image of the beloved soul in this life or eternity.

The only suggestion is to do the right thing precisely when you are aware of it without overthinking. If you can't sort it out, you can at least act instantly, avoiding the impact of a more significant failure in destiny. So, if you notice an error or a glitch in your current destiny, sort it out now, not later. Later, destiny can be deceivable.

'I've noticed that there are people who believe that everything is predestined, and we can't do anything about it. Though, even they are looking both ways when they cross the street.'
– **Stephen Hawking**

FREE WILL

It often happened in my soul image job to find errors and deviations from specs randomly and as a coincidence. What led me in precisely that moment to look for that divagation?

It has been said that I am good at my job, but I know the truth.

I'm always in a meditation stance, even if I'm tired of working night after night. This helps me find moments in reality and always be in the middle of my heart. This way, I enjoy everything I do in my destiny, even if I don't like it.

Could this awareness be the answer to mixed events that tie predestination with free will?

Or is it another part of destiny?

The same thing happens when loving Her. Coincidences occur most of the time.

What happens if these chances repeat more than twice, thrice and so on?

Could it be destiny or free will that I chose to love Her unconditionally, although my mind doesn't like it?

In my mind, it's like a punishment. It does like certain things, not dreams and visions.

How does my mind still listen, no matter what, to my soul and heart choices?

Well, because of the coincidences that happened along with my destiny. It beats its logical reasons. The experience of these moments taught me when to listen and when to be reasonably related to my heart's requests.

The moments with Her in my destiny opened the door to her soul image vision through divine love's reflection in my heart. This gives me a reason to spread the message of divine love to all soul images in search of enlightenment.

Wouldn't there be another page of predestination written in my destiny?

As many visionaries and seers in the past said, if there is a truth in divine love feeling, it will change the lives of soul images with or without me, whether they want it or not.

Start to accept now that the feeling of love from your heart for a loved one is a reflection of divine love, and never give up on it, no matter what. If the loved one doesn't see things the same way, don't cede. Suffering is part of enlightenment. If you genuinely love, you can't take it out from your heart anyway, the beloved soul image. The good thing is that soul images won't suffer from love. Instead of hate and evil deeds, the good and love will prevail.

You want happiness and the best destiny for your loved one, with or without you.

Who will you oppose if fate is different for two soul images to be together?

Accept it and move on. You can't force another soul image to love you back or forever. It's a matter of choice, the status of enlightenment and another unforeseen circumstance of destiny.

It could be worse if you lose your loved one due to dreadful events.

That's why I previously said that prayer to divine love, alias God and Goddess, should be to praise, not to request. The feeling of divine love opening the door to your heart is the best thing in your life. The same is true if the loved one accepts your love. You should be thankful that love can lead you both to enlightenment.

You can beat destiny only inside your heart and nowhere else. Outside, things that will affect your destiny are always out of your control. It starts with the little necessities for your body, like air, water and food.

'Free will is to mind what chance is to matter.'
– Charles Darwin

Surrender to the feeling of divine love, be aware and conscious of its existence, and magical things will soon happen inside your heart and life. You will have so many reasons after that to believe in its existence.

Shouldn't the feeling of love happening in your heart be more than enough to believe in the divinity of love?

DREAMING OF HER

30 Nov 2019 06:30…

It was the first time I had dreamed of Her in Seoul. I never happened to dream of Her at all.

When I woke up, I only remembered a few details.

The only thing that amazes me is that I foresaw her action in the dream. I forgot the last time something like that happened, seeing actions occur in dreams a few hours later in reality. Or it also happened while dreaming.

Maybe it's again a coincidence – too many concurrences.

It means that the path to the next step of enlightenment works. Slowly but steadily.

CLOSE TO HER

1 Dec 2019

Sweet divine love!

For some moments after meditation, I lay down on my bed and fell asleep for a moment ... Without even knowing while thinking and missing Her. And it happened again – dreaming of Her. It was the shortest dream, but it was so real.

We are visiting a good friend, and I lean my head toward Her and touch her hair. Both realised that moment and instead of rejecting it, Her accepted feeling the same. Her friend was looking at us, wondering what was happening. And I felt so deep in my heart in the dream that I had to raise my head and look at Her to see if it was real. Because I couldn't believe that seemed so natural.

I woke with my head raised, looking for Her next to me ...

Why did I have to see if it was real and wake up in the name of love?

The second time, it means more than my imagination. Being far from Her, I have not had a certain dream of Her in months. And here, close to Her, it happened twice in days.

It means I must move to Seoul.

Joking aside or not, the connection between our souls also considers the distance to feel our soul images.

MY HEART IS BURNING BECAUSE OF HER

2 Dec 2019

Am I allowed to dream more than a human being knows in this world?

My heart is burning harder than at any time before ... And if I would have to guess, why else, if not because of Her?

Is it possible for our souls to have a closer connection being in the same place and at the same time as destiny allows it?

It is burning so hard that it feels close to passing out from this existence to be in her realm. There are only a few days in my life as I feel today.

I feel the need to shout my feelings of love to Her. I love the feeling of divine love inside my heart. Her became one with the sacred love inside.

If her soul image knew and felt the same wherever Her was in this present reality or the present future, then probably any of the possible alternate realities would tie our soul image lives for aeons to come.

My life became magic again because of Her. It was good anyway, feeling the divine love as always, but now it's like feeling alive, and previously, it was only dormant inside.

My whole life received a new meaning. I felt her soul image inside my heart, becoming one with divine love, dreams of my mind, and visions of my soul.

사랑해 ... (SARANGHAE) ... – I LOVE YOU ...

3 Dec 2019

In the silence of my heart, the wail of my soul's feelings rises more and more, spreading to the whole existence. The clouds search the sky of Seoul for her soul image. Looking above the city, my heart starts flooding with feelings to let Her know and hear the voice calling her name with love.

In the void of my being, the soul echo whispers in the shadow of reality, '사랑해 ... *(Saranghae ...)*', followed by the actual name of Her, echoed in the ripple effect of divine love inside.

Why in Korean and not in any other language or my native one?

It doesn't make sense anymore for these words and feelings in sounds other than the original one. Being a part of my heart for some time, Her makes me feel her presence as Korean. While in Seoul, my feeling inside to love her Korean reality became even more consistent; hence, the need to hear and sense the sound of love '사랑해 *(Saranghae)*' calling Her. Maybe it will be forgotten in shallow destiny but remembered and written in the dust of eternity, embedded through the clouds in the sky, nature on the earth, and whispers of love in the wind.

From now on all my existence follows my new praying of love inside:

'사랑해 ... *(Saranghae ...) Followed by her real name in my heart!*'

INSPIRING MUSIC: LYn(린) _ Love Story (The Legend of The Blue Sea (푸른 바다의 전설) OST Part.1)

HAPPY SORROW

3 Dec 2019

There have been so many moments of happy sorrow since I arrived in Seoul.

It's the missing piece from the puzzle settled by visions, now destiny felt months ago. Missing her soul image breaks my heart. Having Her inside, missing her soul image outside feels like happy sorrow.

Now, I feel very close due to the distance between our soul images, yet her soul image is not found physically in the present reality. If not now, who knows when?

And how come you are happy and feeling sorrowful?

The only thing I know is that this happy sorrowfulness is a part of the next step of enlightenment.

What's the next step?

Well, it's the hardest one. To open the third eye once and for all. For some years, I have only seen glimpses of its existence. The past lives, the present and future visions, and lastly, the presence of Her are due to the actions of the mighty and mystical Eye.

Because of this happy, sorrowful feeling, I understand why my mind hid in silence, and my heart is just loving Her without any support or actions in the present reality.

INSPIRING MUSIC: AWOLNATION – Sail ...

SHADOWS OF THE PAST LIVES IN SEOUL

4 Dec 2019

After glimpses of past lives in places and events, it also came the turn for religion.

What are the odds of experiencing something like that?

It is possible to be in the right place at the right time and have that kind of experience of connecting with ancestors and ancient beliefs. It was a pleasant experience, but I am not a fan of rituals and traditions. Regardless, I felt the connection with the past and our ancestors in my heart to tears.

As usual, I found a connection and relation between ancient beliefs and the existence of divine love. There is no sacred place, belief system, religion or practice that doesn't use love as the primary source. Either love for ancestors, family, country or one another, or love for spiritual beings, prophets, gods, gurus or whatever elevated being created or helped spread that doctrine.

Anywhere I go that is considered a sacred place of any religion and system of beliefs, I can feel the connection within my heart with the feeling of divine love. Identical, it happens with places dedicated to love. Even if a place isn't considered sacred, I feel the same sense of sacredness in my heart.

The same goes for feelings of Her in my heart. It's a sacred love because divine love revealed her soul image in my heart. It happened due to the connection between our souls in past and present lives. Although I didn't see her soul image in reality, in my heart, Her was more accurate than ever before.

Whenever my mind is bothered by my heart's stubbornness toward her reality in my life, my Self's answer is to love Her and have no other expectations.

The heart doesn't measure time or problems related to reality as the mind does. The truth inside my heart and soul is beyond time and space, so love for Her is for eternity, not for moments with her soul image in real life.

INSPIRING MUSIC: The Heart Sutra Buddhist Chanting (Korean)

THE INNER WORLD IS WAY MORE BEAUTIFUL THAN THE OUTSIDE WORLD

4 Dec 2019

Lately, I have realised why hermits and spiritual beings stay far away from society, living and meditating in the inner world of their hearts.

I passed next to a shelter of dogs and cats looking for new owners, and I felt their suffering deep in my heart.

The outside world is cruel and brutal to live in as a spiritual being. It would be best if you closed all doors to your soul to live in it. Meanwhile, you can open all doors in the inner world, and feelings can pass freely through your heart.

The vacuum space inside my heart is not enough to fill it with the divine love feeling; occasionally, it spreads around existence. That's why, in the past, the soul images from my life helped me endure the outside world and fit in this passing world.

For years, since my heart was alone in this world to care for feelings of divine love, it became more demanding than before. I believed every moment that I would give up and retire from the outside world. Ultimately, I got used to it, adapted, and lived like any reasonable human being.

Nowadays, because of Her, it is more challenging than ever before due to my open heart and her soul image visions. The dream that destiny will eventually include our soul images together gives strength in times of weakness, losing hope, and seeing and feeling so much suffering in this life.

SHADOWS OF HER PAST

5 Dec 2019

Last night, I had a dream with Her again, but it was only a brief moment of her high school. I barely recognised her; luckily, I noticed her birthmarks. I was passing by close to her and three other classmates, carrying their backpacks. Maybe it was a split second, but I recognised her looking at her face.

I woke up wondering how it's possible to be dreamlike in the name of love.

Every day since I arrived in Seoul, her presence is like the air I breathe.

This evening, her soul image was everywhere I looked. In some moments, it felt like a part of her existence.

I watched a French comedy [러브 앳 (Reobeu Aet) – Love at Second Sight (French: *Mon Inconnue*)] at CGV Yongsan I'Park Mall, and all the time, her soul image was in front of my eyes as coexisting at the same time, breathing as one being. Interestingly, the film somehow related to my feelings of living in two parallel worlds.

I sometimes wonder if destiny will allow me to see Her while walking and suddenly experience the same feeling as in my dream of surprise.

Will our soul images be able to recognise each other ... or will this moment be lost in the dust of eternity?

AFTER A WEEK OF DIVINE LOVE IN SEOUL

6 Dec 2019

A cold wind that warms my heart touches my being with its whispers, making me feel Her. Leaves follow me around, taken by the cloak of its shadows. It brings me echoes from Han River, missing our talks in heart and mind. I must visit you soon, my beloved friend.

Sun smiles at my existence as a pleasant feeling close to Her. It feels like where I will be close to Her for the rest of my life.

Will destiny give its consent in the present future?

Connecting with soul images around Seoul while walking in meditation feels like part of their lives. If I closed my eyes, I could see all their hearts singing the same melody as mine while praising the divine love on the shrine of my heart. Her voice in the vibration of the town's presence around my heart is music for my ears.

The most beautiful part of being in Seoul is that it is so easy to feel Her. The difference senses in everything. From the energy used feeling Her, to the places with the scent of her existence – there are more blissful moments with Her than before. Unfortunately, I didn't find nor encounter her soul image, but I feel her presence greater than ever.

Although my mind was always quiet, in the silence of my meditation, it raised dozens of questions without answers.
> *Did her soul image even know about my existence and feelings?*
> *Did her soul image have the same feelings but not show them?*
> *Will her soul image have a connection with our destiny in the future?*
> *Am I sure that what I feel is not a troubled and insane mind?*
> *How can my heart prove in my existence that feelings towards Her are beyond this realm?*
> *Coincidentally, are moments of this reality feeling Her inside numerous enough to be confused with random events and not part of destiny?*

The only truth is that Her has not yet connected with our soul images in the real world. If only her soul image could indicate that it is not my imagination feeling Her. That divine love reflected in our souls is not a dream but a vision of what our hearts want.

THE THIN LINE BETWEEN COINCIDENCE AND REALITY

7 Dec 2019

Coincidences happen all the time.

Walking on the street, a brick falls next to you, but you are not hurt. It was pure coincidence.

You are not taking the bus, which will have an accident later. Again coincidence?

I love Her and receive signs that her soul image exists in reality, not just in my visions.

Do only coincidences happen?

What would have happened if I couldn't glimpse her soul image shadow in this reality?

What would have happened if coincidences didn't exist at all?

What would have happened if Her had not been in this reality and could not have known about it?

When you offer a gift of love, or better yet, sharing the divine love inside with the beloved, you should be thankful if it is accepted. Without the chance to offer, there is no path to the enlightenment of both souls.

What's the point if only one soul becomes free from suffering?

Where is the divine love for your soulmate if only you will be free aeons in the future?

You will live in happy sorrow for eternity.

DON'T THINK ANYTHING ABOUT DIVINE LOVE ... LIVE WITH IT

7 Dec 2019

If it happens to find a loved one in this life, whatever you do, don't think about it.

When you allow your mind to analyse your feelings and doubt about all processes, your life will be in agony. It makes sense because your mind is logical; facts and certain things are the base of its existence.

On the other hand, heart feelings are from another realm, and love felt inside is not rational. Don't reject these feelings, thinking that you will find another chance or that the soul image revealed in your heart does not fit with your ideas or desires. It might be your only chance to feel real love, that crazy love beyond your mind's grasp. Once you accept feeling the love inside, you can start seeing and understanding the reflection of divine love as a deity inside your heart.

It's simple. Don't think about love, divine love and soul. Feel it until it burns your heart.

You think that the soul image you love is the reason for your feelings. But if you try to go deeper in your heart and feel love for a moment without any support or soul image, concentrate on the feelings. You will see that love exists in itself as a deity. It's a feeling that is not from this world; it's magic.

It will be even simpler if there's no logic to feeling love anymore, maybe because love is not shared back or denied. Better yet, although you are madly in love and have no support for your feelings, you can't give up on the love you feel. In those moments, if you realise that love is not just a feeling and to live with love inside your heart just because it makes you happy, you are on the path to feel divine love awareness and consciousness.

Don't give up on love. Try to feel its warmth more intensely in your life day after day.

Don't give up on soul image, either. It will help you more, and it will be easier to feel divine love, especially at the beginning when everything is new and unworldly.

At some point, divine love will become one with your existence if you keep going and don't give up on its existence in your heart. It won't happen fast and easy, that's for sure. The more open your heart is, the quicker and more enormous the feeling of divine love will be.

Because of its divinity felt in your heart and mind, you will start searching for proof and teaching of its existence. God and religions, though, won't be enough to describe it. The feelings from your heart are real and alive, while ideas and doctrines are not.

Ultimately, the only teacher left to understand the existence of divine love is your heart. It means you will realise that the soul image revealed in your heart is not randomly selected, and the feeling of love is a gift and a blessing.

If you feel love is like a possession with the soul image

uncovered, that's not real love. It could be a passion, desire or anything else your mind dreams of but not your heart.

Love is a blessing, not a thing to be owned. That's how I feel about my feelings for Her. It doesn't have to be my soul image chosen in her heart. I would prefer Her to choose divine love over my soul image at any time. Our soul images are passing moments in this world, but the feeling of divine love is immortal.

Destiny will decide if we'll be together in this life, the next one, or the multiverse. If not, so be it. All I want is her happiness, with or without Me next to Her. At least, the divine love to live in her heart. And this way embedded in her existence is a part of my soul.

LAST MOMENTS OF LIFE

10 Dec 2019

What would I do if it were the last moments of my life?

I would dance and sing and be the happiest man on Earth. Finally, the final mystery of life would be solved instantly, passing this life to who knows what, when, and if it's the end.

What if you are with Her after finding her soul image?

It's a tricky question, no comment.

A few times, I expected to leave this life, and instead, I found the divine love existence and experienced the oneness and evolution at its best. While everyone around seems to be afraid of leaving this life, I always thought that it's the greatest mystery of this life unsolved.

Yes, there is much information and scriptures about life after death. Yet, I have never met anyone who came back to tell stories about this experience.

And how could it be possible since it's gone for good?

I know it sounds a little dark, but I don't feel the darkness. When your heart is full of divine love, death is just another word, like life. That is another step for the soul to choose another body because one life is not enough to experience enlightenment for most souls. I have had an excellent relationship with my sister-in-arms for a long time, as I expected to leave this world much sooner, and still, here I am. I didn't try hardcore things, but I expected its breath. And every time it didn't want me, I received the greatest gift of this life – eternal love.

I have thought lately that this is it; I am on the path for the last moment as long as it takes. Instead, I found Her, and I started a new journey to discover past lives and new futures of the present.

Why Seoul?
Why Her?

Would her soul image make known its presence in this reality or other worlds in the future?

That's the beauty of the unknown. You think you know how everything feels, yet you know nothing '*Jon Snow*'.

THINKING OF HER

11 Dec 2019

As an experience, I let my mind wander for as long as needed. I don't question its logic; it makes perfect sense to my Self.

The result is that either I am crazy or live in an alternate reality, so of course, I am not in the right mind.

Unfortunately, I can't explain why the feeling of love for Her is so real inside, as it will happen to be with her soul image in destiny at some point, and my mind can't figure it out either.

All the signs and experiences lead to Her, yet nothing happens in the real world to find and meet her soul image; everything exists in the inner world. In the outside world, as always, nothing seems to be happening. Or maybe my mind is blind, but after its rules, nothing is happening yet.

All seems natural, though, with an alternate universe. Life experienced in this reality is not on its path but another one in the quantum realm. Hidden desires could create another alternate quantum world where no rules or preferences apply to the current one.

Love is too risky and too fragile for this world to make it happen.

MY BELOVED FRIEND, HAN RIVER – HANGANG – 한강

12 Dec 2019

It is one of those days where her soul image impregnated my soul and heart with her existence.

I have been trying to see a few Korean movies at the cinema. Strangely enough, it has been exceptionally good every time. Only a few words are understood, but it's enough; some parts are in English. I could enjoy the artistic side more than watching with subtitles. As proof once again, art needs no words to feel it with your soul.

After the movie, being close to my beloved friend, Han River, hearing its calling to talk over a walk meditation along with the Wind and Sun all day long was a stroll through the veil of time.

In the light of its waves, I saw past lives of Her: walking down the river with kids after her at some point in time and wearing a luxurious hanbok in other time lapses. All the time, Her is so beautiful. It makes my heart cuddle her soul image close to the depths of divine love feelings.

So far, the Namsan Tower and my friend Han River are my favourite places in Seoul.

Every time, Han River tells me stories about Her, walking side by side with her soul image, hand in hand, eye to eye. Namsan Tower, because of sacred love spread by so many soul images in search of Her.

A few hours passed without even knowing, with the shadow of her soul image around me to keep me company.

My friend Han River is like a magician, the way it connects my soul and Her along the magical shores of its existence. The magic happens as soon as I am walking close to the riverside. Instantly, Her appears inside and outside my being as one, more real than ever.

Finally, after such a long time, I could ask Her: '헤르, 괜찮아? *(Her, gwaenchana) – Her, you alright?*' while keeping her hand tight in mine and looking deep into her beautiful and mysterious eyes.

Also, to tell Her how much I miss her all day long for months but mostly now that I am so close: '헤르, 너무 보고 싶어 ... *(Her, neomu bogo sipeo) – Her, I miss you so much ...*'

Finally, to repeat my daily mantra of love since her Korean inheritance was revealed:

'헤르, 사랑해 ... *(Her, Saranghae) ... And the real name of Her in the echo of my soul! – Her, I Love You! ...*'

A REAL KISS FROM HER

13 Dec 2019

Alternate visions of reality ... haunt my reality.

In one of an alternate reality in the multiverse, there is a joyous version of me, longing and being at the end with Her. It's a vision of a moment that is not from this reality. It's not a dream because it seems so natural, but I also feel it is not with this body, although it is the same soul.

Could a soul have more bodies in the multiverse while remaining unchanged in its core?

Could a soul have more bodies in more alternate realities at once?

As a guest, I attended a party with Her and her friends. It was the first time in reality that our eyes had met, and our hands touched, greeting her. Her sister had to break the mirage of our connection from that moment, which wouldn't end.

After some drinks, it appears the actions of my being are the same as in this reality, being more than funny, singing a song on the guitar in Korean, old music. I don't know how or why I could sing, but I never heard that song. Maybe, again, it's from another realm.

Ultimately, Her sat beside me, resting her head on my foot and looking deep into my eyes. It was like an invitation to kiss her lips to seal the union of our souls.

And I didn't think twice, following the inner feeling to kiss and taste her lips gently.

And everything else stopped feeling inside the eternity over space and time of that moment.

That moment still haunts my mind as wishful thinking. Strange enough, my heart feels like it has already happened to perceive it as a reality, while my senses are in clouds of love.

INSPIRING MUSIC:

- Korean Traditional Song ARIRANG (아리랑) – Guitar arranged and covered by Erica Cho
- So Hyang – Arirang Alone | 소향 – 홀로 아리랑
- The Story of Arirang – The Name of Korean Traditional Folk Song – Main Theme Song of 2002 Korea-Japan World Cup

DESTINIES ALL AROUND ME AND INSIDE MY HEART

14 Dec 2019

All I see around me walking in Seoul are destinies.

Soul images wander on the path of their destiny with sleepy looks, troubled expressions, and thoughtful and thoughtless faces. Some will have significant futures, while others will live a forgetful life.

Since birth, destinies settle our future, from the family where we're born to the souls that meddle with our path. We don't even know if the kid we thought was a waste of our time and space will become the star or saint we admire most in the future.

That's the story of my life. I am unknown, not a star or even a door to the unknown. I call my Self sometimes Mr Nobody.

Without Her, I would have carried on a forgotten existence, burying knowledge and feelings in the pits of oblivion. I felt and experienced a few times in the past, my younger Self, the miracles hidden behind the reality of our eyes.

There was a time when I wouldn't dare question the reality of my visions as I do now. It was the vision and then pure truth following it. But in those times, I was searching for the powers over the limits of our bodies. It didn't matter if I died trying or lived as a blind man afterwards.

That changed when divine love took me under its wings and shaped the future of my life – to become a nobody but with a heart full of love. Since the touch of its feathers, my heart has spread divine love around my existence, unknown and without expectations – sometimes for the whole universe and existence, other times only for another soul.

Now that I have touched its feathers again because of Her, the divine love I feel is more than a mind can think of: from her soul image to the whole existence, from the universe to the multiverse, from reality to alternate realities.

SEWOON ROOFTOP – SEWOON SANGGA ROOFTOP (SEWOON PLAZA)

15 Dec 2019

Sewoon Rooftop is one of the places where my soul touches the feet of her existence. It was the first place where divine love directed my steps without my knowing that place existed.

It was the second day in Seoul; how could I?

Yet, this was the first place I visited, feeling Her while wondering in my walking meditation. My soul started to cry as Hiro shouted in *Heroes*: 'Yatta!'

I felt Her presence instantly: '*Her was here!*'

The shadow of her soul image sang and danced around my heart all the time on that day.

Whenever my heart burns with happy sorrow over missing Her, and I want to feel her soul image's presence, I must visit the rooftop mostly every few days. At least for some moments, the sky caresses my burning heart with the clouds embedded with her soul image existence.

On the horizon, rising in the clouds, is the beacon of love, Namsan Tower, a reminder of divine love's reflection into our souls.

The sky is full of messages of love sent to Her, feelings that transform into clouds of devotion over Seoul. From the rooftop, you can read all of them. Every day, my soul beams up to the sky with the feelings of love for Her from Namsan Tower.

LOVING HER AND THE PROCESS OF NEVER-ENDING ENLIGHTENMENT
17 Dec 2019

In the beginning, the book title was meant to be 'Loving Her' instead of 'Just Love Her' because the feelings from my heart for Her clouded my heart and directed my new path of destiny.

It appeared to be a never-ending search to find the soul image roots in past lives. Shortly after, the vision of Korean inheritance of the inner Self from past lives and alternate realities with Her started.

It changed to 'Just Love Her' because this was the voice of divine love message inside my heart. Also, I eventually understood that I couldn't do anything in this reality other than love Her, living in destiny without a connection between our soul images.

When Her settled the connection with divine love becoming one, it became crystal clear that the only outcome of these feelings is to love Her not only in this life but for the past and the future. It means that all the actions in the past and the possible future are related to her existence.

Fate settled these moments with Her, being a soulmate connected with my soul since the beginning of time. As time passed, the visions became real inside my heart but not outside the real world. Again, destiny sorted this out, moving the visions into reality. It was the right time to wait for events to happen.

The events are unfolding and making sense in Seoul. Before,

it was like a dream, but living in Seoul, it became the reality of visions.

Pandora's box also opened a possible destiny with Her in reality, creating actual actions and circumstances for her soul image to choose whether it feels the connection or happens in her life as a decision.

I previously talked about predestination, but scientific proof of quantum entanglement shows that destiny has many paths, which are only activated once we choose and observe the possible way.

The enlightenment makes it possible to become an observer, aware and conscious about divine love manifestation and reflection into existence. When you reach enlightenment, it doesn't mean that it is a finite event. It exists and evolves as the existence itself.

The only thing different from before is that you were blind, and now you can see and understand.

VISITING JOGYESA TEMPLE AND WHANKI MUSEUM

20 Dec 2019

While walking around Seoul, I felt the divine love at Jogyesa Temple and connected the dots of destiny, as in the art of Whanki.

It was the first time I visited a Buddhist temple, Jogyesa Temple, and also the first time I felt the connection of divine love so sharp and clear in a temple or church.

Could there be a connection again with the past lives in reality?

Too many weird things have happened since I arrived in Seoul. For example, lately, I have felt an intense connection of love inside me with Her, as it has never occurred before. Like a fishing net, it keeps my mind and heart so close to her existence that I can't breathe anymore.

Visiting the Whanki Museum (Whanki Kim is an abstract artist from Korea), I connected my visions of Her with the dot paintings.

Although nothing else happened besides inside my existence,

Her still feels like a reality, boggling my mind and ravaging my heart. It makes me wonder why and how it happened only to my Self.

Is it a connection in reality with Her or just a damn mind hallucination?

Or maybe it's so abstract that I can't figure out the meaning as quickly as in Whanki Kim's dot paintings!

I wonder if her soul image exists. Again, my visions are not from this time. Maybe a different one.

With all these troubling questions without answers, I can't contest the feelings of her existence inside so profoundly, no matter what I tried or did. It happens with events and the connection of her soul image presence in Seoul.

Why December and what events related to Her made me search and connect with my visions associated with Korea?

Even if I know the importance of spreading the message of divine love in the future, it's so hard sometimes. Despite everything not happening outside of my soul image, inside my heart, feelings unfolded, and events and signs related to Her had great importance for my soul in Seoul, especially these days. It seems like small things, walking side by side with Han River visions of Her, feelings of love beamed up from Namsan Tower, her steps on Sewoon Rooftop.

Her soul image is present in my dreams and reality as a hologram following my mind and heart anywhere around Seoul; it couldn't happen in another place other than here, at this pace and so intense.

Soon, I will return to my happy, sorrowful feelings of missing Her from afar as the distance proved essential for my soul connection with her existence. Well, maybe it's for the best. It is better to miss Her while being far away than close to Her and with her soul image nowhere to be found ... Or not connected with my soul image in this reality.

After all, the impossible becomes possible to exist for my soul image and not for my heart and soul.

THE STORY OF ANGEL OF VENGEANCE
20 Dec 2019

Stories from the depths of the soul ...

Once upon a time, there was an angel – Angel of Vengeance, named Raguel (Friend of God). Always bound by the rules of Heaven, Raguel never accepted the fall of other angels from their thresholds.

To teach him a lesson from his actions and compensate for the aeons spent in service of divine justice, God gave him a human life in which divine love in his soul was beyond any religious laws and limitations.

Knowing the source of divinity, the gods and heavens, even God itself as divine love, all the other gods and powers in charge of incarnation gave him a body unfit for his knowledge and skills. Despite all of these, his heart always found a way to keep alive the knowledge of divine love existing in this world and the source of divinity itself.

While born in a human body during the Goryeo kingdom of Korea, he fell in love with a beautiful girl. Because laws didn't bind his heart like the other humans, he saw the girl as a goddess of love, bewildered by his feelings and in-depth knowledge buried in his heart.

The other gods didn't like the idea of humans as gods, especially since, in their view, human girls were only the carriers of their breeds on Earth. So they hide the girl's reborn body every time since then, in other realities of its soul existence.

It has been said that even nowadays, **Raguel** is searching for his beloved soul and fighting a fate settled by the gods for it.

THE TRUTH ABOUT SAINTS AND SINNERS

21 Dec 2019

We all are humans, after all … Do you think there is a difference between Saints and Sinners?

Both types have human necessities at the primary level. The need for food and air, pure or not, is constant for all of us.

Saints wouldn't exist without sinners, and of course, there would be no idea of purity if only mud existed.

Sinners are all humans; even saints have been, no matter what sins, washed away by spiritual thoughts.

Nowadays, saints are replaced by celebrities and powerful soul images, while sinners are, as always, all of us. These creative and original soul images have shaped the current society and mindset of others, leading to a better world. Yet, with its falling to destruction, it is closer than ever.

We are just humans, after all. Once a soul image reaches a milestone, surpassing the limits of the human body or a shared fate, the mind starts to believe it is better than others. It reflects in every aspect the personalities and actions of artists, musicians, actors, athletes, etc. People with power and money gamble with other soul images' lives. Their minds become sure that they are the chosen ones. They believe others do nothing or are too weak to change their destinies.

If everyone were rich, a celebrity or a saint, would it make a difference in this world?

That's why love is needed more than ever – real love, not adoration.

It's a consensus of destiny. Ordinary people make others rich, powerful and celebrities through their actions and adoration. In this net of roulette in fate, shallow soul images often catch the top and others with talent or skill.

In the past, the most prominent and renowned people were poor, living at the limit of life. After passing away, they became living legends.

Soon, the technology will create its legends and it has already started to give us a glimpse of the future. Let's hope that the creators of the new wave of destinies won't feel superior to humans because this would mean the end of civilisation as we know it.

INSPIRING MUSIC: AIVA – "Genesis" Symphonic Fantasy in A minor, Op. 21

READING WITHOUT FEELING IT

21 Dec 2019

If you read my writings about divine love reflected in human love without feeling it, you gave up a long time ago. If not, it means at least you are trying to understand or explore more than human love inside.

My brother told me after reading only two of my writings:
'Bro, I didn't understand even half of the reading
Or it's not my type of feeling.'

I use many ellipses to expose my feelings. Please take a little break when you find them and think more deeply about the meaning or try to feel behind those words. There I am, waiting to touch your heart.

I don't expect you to believe my words just by reading them. Don't acknowledge anything until you feel what I am writing about divine love. If you don't feel anything, you can't read at all. If you understand something feeling it, then you can relate to your own experiences that happened or might happen soon.

Please don't read it with your critical mind checking expressions or grammar because you might lose the essential feeling behind it. Although the writings are checked with leading software for analysing grammar and expression, errors might happen occasionally.

Our second nature is critical thinking and doubting everything that is not normal to our way of thinking because the mind likes safe things, not the new events or ideas leading to abstract concepts like soul and heart.

There is a test that expresses what I'm talking about. As seen below, it's text with numbers and mixed letters. Most readers can read it as a regular text.

7H15 M3554G3 53RV35 7O PR0V3 H0W 0UR M1ND5 C4N D0 4M4Z1NG 7H1NG5! 1MPR3551V3 7H1NG5! 1N 7H3 B3G1NN1NG 17 WA5 H4RD BU7 N0W, 0N 7H15 L1N3 Y0UR M1ND 1S R34D1NG 17 4U70M471C4LLY W17H 0U7 3V3N 7H1NK1NG 4B0U7 17, B3 PROUD! 0NLY C3R741N P30PL3 C4N R3AD 7H15.

Your ability to read this message reveals something incredible about the mind.

SEE YOU ON THE OTHER SIDE

21 Dec 2019

Going to sleep daily challenges me to leave this world for the unknown. That's why my salute to my Self is 'See you on the other side'.

It's easier to see the other worlds while sleeping when you are aware and conscious of your Self. Reaching the other realms through dreams doesn't happen quickly, however. It might or might not unveil the hidden worlds behind the screen of our natural eyes in dreams. Sometimes, it can't be remembered as a safety mechanism inside our mind.

With daily experience and practice before going to sleep, contact with the third eye and seeing the mystical realms can be achieved, which is usually undergone with a lot of spiritual and meditation training. The third eye is the all-seeing mind's eye, used while dreaming. When you become aware and conscious, it opens temporary passages to the unseen realms.

Divine love awareness and consciousness protect the mind if negative feelings open some darker realms. It's better to feel love and acknowledge the existence of divine love reflected inside the heart. Otherwise, there is no chance to experience contact with

the third eye without the touch of divinity.
See you on the other side soon, my beloved soul of Her.

CRADLE OF DIVINE LOVE FEELING HER WHILE IN SEOUL
22 Dec 2019

Seeing a kiss between two lovers is like a feeling of divine love in the depths of the heart. The same happens when they share moments of love, even the simple ones, like a glance, a touch of hands, and words of love. It is a test to determine whether the feelings are genuine and mutual. If they are not valid, they have no resonance at all. The heart is a good lie detector.

Take, for example, nature. Never, not once, does it happen, so not feeling the divine love reflected in its existence. All the elements, such as clouds, trees, flowers, you name it, speak with my heart on deep feeling vibrations while in the middle of the centre of existence – nature. And in my times of happy sorrow, while missing Her, nature always cuddled my soul through its signs around my being. Clouds took her soul-image face to ease my mind, the wind whispered, reminding me of the touch of her hair on my face to calm my heart, and birds were singing all around me with her voice to speak the language of love from my soul.

While in Seoul, nature is even closer to my soul, especially my beloved friend, Han River, who keeps me company with her presence. I never feel alone with Her around my heart and soul.

Although I come from another culture and identity, my heart and soul felt I belonged to Korean traditions and spirit. Perhaps I have been in these realms in past lives. Or maybe I will be reborn in one of the soul images living here in future lives.

And it all happened because of Her. Without her presence in my heart and connection with my soul, I would not have dared to dream or follow my visions in my wildest dreams.

I can't say the same thing about my mind. Lately, it has

bothered my heart and soul harder than ever, and I can't blame its reasoning. Just as the heart and soul have visions, I must let the mind do its own thing. It's a free world inside my entity, and I'm not a tyrant at all, although I'm on the side of heart and soul.

Mostly, I like nightfall when everything inside goes quiet, and the mind rests, leaving all the space for love meditation. All the Seoul sky is mine to wonder while feeling Her clouding my heart. Maybe, sometime in the future, in the present reality, her soul image looking up in the sky will glimpse my soul's existence.

LOVE MEDITATION – FREE YOUR SOUL

23 Dec 2019

Love meditation to free your soul is the path to enlightenment through human love between two soul images. My meditation through love is exposed after dozens of years of practice. I won't say it works for everyone, but you can practice testing whether it's true or not.

Choose a relaxed position that suits you, such as standing in a chair or lying on the bed. The only important thing is to ensure you won't fall while meditating.

Feel your mind, heart and belly connected to the divine love flowing from your heart as love flows from your heart to the outside world.

During this time, constantly repeat a mantra of love or any other mantra which is best for you:

'Divine love, praise to you!'
'Divine love, bless our hearts!'
'Divine love, hallowed be thy name!'

Or it can be no mantra, just the awareness and consciousness of divine love in your heart.

Imagine the loved one in your heart and mind connecting through eyes with soul.

Respiration should be done with deep inspiration – filling the lungs full of air – and expiration – emptying the lungs full of air. Expand the belly while doing it.

Feel the energy of love in and around you and spread it, flowing from your heart as you become one with the image of the loved one inside.

Feel the loved one as being one with you.

'... *if I can love / is enough for me / and is my smile / and is my dream / if I can love.*
In the end, at the shadow / I sang: / If someone can love / is emperor / if someone is loved / is infinite / and if there is a love / from voids is born full.'
'*So much I loved her that the sky itself bent blue.*'
– **Nichita Stanescu**

'*We and the Earth. / Every time we walk / on earth, / the earth kisses our soles. / Is happy that we don't leave him.*'
– **Lucian Blaga**

BEAUTIFUL SOULS OF SEOUL – PROOF THAT DIVINE LOVE IS EVERYWHERE

23 Dec 2019

While wondering on the Cheonggyecheon Stream (청계천), missing Her so deeply one evening of the week before Christmas, even though I didn't want to go to Sewoon Rooftop, the voice inside made me go to visit it as it's a place where I feel her presence the most.

There, I also met two beautiful souls searching for Her.

Recently, I met one of these beautiful souls going out to eat and learn more about Korean traditions and customs. Later, another friend kept us company.

It turns out that the same problem exists everywhere in this world: after reaching thirty years of age, older people from the family push for marriage with their loved ones. And here we go, talking about divine love, feelings from the heart, and the best choices in life, like old pals who have known each other for ages. As it turns out, speech barriers are close to none, although neither of us speaks in the same language of the mind but using the language of heart and soul.

Although I am an introvert by birth, wine and divine love combined gave me clear thoughts about my journey to Seoul. My spiritual journey to Seoul was mainly about finding her soul image and connecting with Her and my past lives. It turns out that there are more soul images of Her around Seoul, and maybe we were connected as friends in past lives or the realms of souls unknown to the human mind.

A few hours passed as if in seconds; in the end, she decided to marry him if this was what her heart wanted.

It makes my heart joyous that love is alive anywhere I go, regardless of country, nationality, traditions or conceptions. There are still souls in this world who are not afraid to have an open heart and open the doors to other souls who feel connected in some moments. This harmony leads to some beautiful moments of eternity between souls that last for aeons to come.

BUSAN – FOLLOWING HER STEPS AND SPIRITUAL PATH OF PAST LIVES
25 Dec 2019

A long time before I thought about going to Busan, the voice inside me decided that it was a must-visit.

As time passed and my journey in Korea approached its close, the feeling of missing Her was stronger than ever. It is like a claw that scratches my soul and heart until no pain is left, just the traces of feelings of happy sorrow.

Her soul image followed me around Haeundae Beach as I saw her steps dip in the sea tides. Later, I wanted to skip the visit to Haedong Yonggung Temple because I was exhausted, but again, the voice inside gave me no option other than to follow my heart. And I understood why. The same intense feeling of divine love tears in my heart.

Whenever divine love makes its presence known in sacred places, I spread the feeling from my heart, blessing all other souls' images around the area, Korea, and finally, the whole world and Universe.

It was a connection in a past life or, more, who knows, feeling like home although a stranger with a different culture and background. Looking at people's faces, I feel a deep connection between my soul and their hearts, as if they were speaking the same language.

I can't stop dreaming of Her these days, wishing it would have been a reality of our soul images happening now, not only in the shadows of the infinite axis. Although I have not found her soul image, I can feel the perception of reality inside my heart. Her connection with me is deeper every day as if we are linked in an unseen world related to our time and space.

THE BURDEN OF SPREADING THE MESSAGE OF DIVINE LOVE REFLECTION INTO EXISTENCE

26 Dec 2019

My destiny didn't bless me with any talent at all. I have no singing, poetry, acting or writing skills. Maybe the last one is debatable in the future.

Despite this, divine love chose my heart to spread the message of its existence to the world. This makes sense, as not being perfect is the standard of all humans, who can easily relate to a life dedicated to love. The message of divine love is not for the perfect one's so-called saints but for all of us searching for enlightenment through love with another soul image.

The burden of spreading the message that divine love exists as a divinity follows me daily. It feels too significant and vast on my shoulders to make it happen.

I often let my heart guide my steps through the divine love I felt inside; a few times, it was quite a wonder. It made magical and mystic things happen in reality. Souls met randomly while feeling the divine love inside, yet with a connection more profound than our minds and bodies. Places and feelings are connected without thinking, following the perception of holy love.

The path of destiny to act further spread the message it started because of her reflection inside my heart. Otherwise, the message cannot be known in the future or at least not at this scale. The door opened to my heart and led me to see the past lives deeper than ever before.

I was finding the roots of my soul to a Korean life with Her in the wheel of time shadows. Due to my visions, I travelled to Seoul to feel and see the effects and traces of my soul memories. It happened this way to know the difference between dreams and visions and feel Her closer than ever before, lighting up the understanding of my destiny path with her soul image in this reality.

As time passes, the zero-hour event of spreading the message wider becomes a certainty and not a vision of the past Self. Maybe that's all about my spiritual experience in Seoul, feeling Her so profoundly, starting the inception of the divine love message in this reality and spreading it to the multiverse.

NO LOVE SHOUTING, ONLY FEELINGS OF LOVE IN SILENCE

29 Dec 2019

The feeling of love between two lovers is very close to what happens in souls' hearts on the path of spiritual life.

In the beginning, moments are when you feel the love so intense and you need to shout your inner noise to let it all out and ease the tension inside your heart. It makes sense as everything is new, and your body and mind adapt to changes due to high energy vibrations inside.

As time passes, feelings become a certainty as a day-to-day habit. Also, getting used to these vibrations of love in the heart will be as natural as eating food. Because of this, the mind starts its noisy existence, bothering the soul and heart with questions, impatience, doubts and so on.

You must train and control your mind's reality to avoid becoming the incarnation of evil thoughts.

The first rule is to keep repeating the mantra of love chosen through heart feelings.
The second rule is the awareness of divine love in one's heart.
The third rule is never to deny feelings inside your heart.

The mind is bored without action and things to think of at any moment. That's why the practice of repeating a mantra continuously, be it the only loving name of the soul chosen by your heart, is important.

Ultimately, the mind will be like a wild horse tamed to listen to its trainer.

The respiration is also essential to help the mind ease off its steaming thoughts and ideas. Deep breathing in and out is of tremendous support. It gives more awareness and consciousness of the Self and love feelings inside the heart, keeping the attention concentrated on breathing.

How can the mind have doubts about feelings inside the heart?

Feelings from the heart can't be denied; the mind still wants them gone. It's a fight inside the being who is the master of the path chosen for the soul.

Once the heart is chosen, the mind will start the fight harder than ever before because it feels like its end when feelings are before its existence. Feelings are real, while the mind is just an illusion.

The mind uses the soul's existence for its awareness and consciousness, enslaving the soul for its benefit. When the mind listens to the heart's feelings, magical things happen in one's life.

For one thing, it becomes aware of the existence of the soul. After that, it starts searching for the soul's path to enlightenment. Finally, life will become a dedication to soul existence.

Loving another soul and devoting life to a loved one's happiness is the easiest way to enlightenment. When love feels inside the heart and heads for a soul image, be aware of its source – the absolute and infinite divine love. From now on, divine love's feeling leads to both souls' enlightenment to accept its existence.

THE HEART OF DIVINE LOVE REFLECTED IN RELIGIONS

29 Dec 2019

In every religion or belief, there is the inner heart of those who feel the divine love closer than other soul images. Their teachings and hearts became more intimate and vital for the future of enlightenment practice than religion itself.

The essential religions by number of devotees are Christianity, Islam, Hinduism and Buddhism. Their heart centres dedicated to divine love and devotion to attain enlightenment are as follows:

The heart of **Christianity** *is* **Hesychasm**, *which is well represented in the book The Way of a Pilgrim.*

The heart of **Islam** *is* **Sufism**, *with its beautiful poetry of love sung by Sufi mystic Rumi.*

The heart of **Hinduism** *is* **Bhakti Yoga**, *also known as The Yoga of Love and Devotion, which attains enlightenment through devotion to a personal God or love for the Divine.*

The heart of **Buddhism** *is* **Zen**, *which points to the enlightenment of human beings through meditation.*

It is essential for all hearts of love devoted to divine love in these religious centres to dedicate life to love and feel it as divinity through individual enlightenment and practice. Most of them have as crucial points of practice repeating a mantra, praying continuously with few words, total dedication to love, and feeling for divinity representing God as chosen by each belief system.

Also on the rise are those souls who lost God's belief as described in religions, so-called atheists or agnostics. And soon, it will probably be in first place as technological discoveries go beyond the gods' powers view.

All souls of any side, believers or not, could acknowledge the existence of love as a divinity because human love is a personal experience of each one of them.

The heart of divine love in life is the human love between two soul images who become aware and conscious about the existence of love as a divinity. Seeing and believing the divinity of love reflected in their souls' existence will become the practice of enlightening their souls. No religion or belief system is needed because the existence of divine love is in our nature. That's why it is written in the Bible: *'I said, "You are 'gods'; you are all sons of the Highest."'*

Also, love is, without doubt, the vital ingredient to reaching enlightenment and experiencing divinity in all religions and beliefs or practices worldwide since ancient times.

EVERY DAY IS A NEW BEGINNING AND END

1 Jan 2020

Every day is a new beginning and end – a celebration of lost and found love ...

For a long time, celebrations for different events and time passing became a daily sentiment inside my heart. Every day feels like the first and the last – it resembles life itself, and I see its importance in my life and heart.

Waking up in the morning is like being born with the knowledge of past life experiences, different realities and soul searching. You go through the day struggling with life bitterness and then sleep, not knowing if the next day is coming. You only hope or need to be made aware of the importance of these unique moments. Each of these daily moments will never come back. Destiny writes about them only once, no matter the consequences.

It isn't straightforward, though, to live every day as a celebration of life and love. For once, your heart must be open to a divine feeling of love; otherwise, there will be no vibration in spirit and no experience worth living.

That's the divine love-touching feeling; it makes every day and moment a blessing to the soul's existence. It gives a reason to live through the soul image revealed on the walls of feelings from the heart, sorting through the many soulmates born from the void of divinity, the one that will become the light of love sparked into another existence.

Since her soul image was revealed to my heart through a divine love feeling, I wake up and sleep, living moments of pure love as a blessing to my soul. It was the first time in my life between the passing of years when I didn't feel the loneliness void in my heart living on this Earth, as I've found through divine love the only one soul that completes my being, despite the happy sorrow feeling of love.

'Just Love Her' became my *raison d'être* for my spiritual path of an incumbent future. Without Her, my life would have carried on the meaningless daily moments without further spreading the message of divine love. I thank Her for reviving the spark of love inside my heart and giving a new meaning to the feeling of divine love in my life and the lives of others who will follow her path to enlightenment in the future.

INSPIRING MUSIC: Dirty Dancing – Time of My Life (Final Dance) – main song

UNIQUE MOMENTS OF LOVE FEELING HER IN SEOUL

2 Jan 2020

I will miss being in Seoul the most and the closeness to her existence everywhere.

I feel like a stranger in this world anywhere I go due to the peculiar love inside my heart. My heart is the only place I don't feel like an outsider. I don't question this impression. Maybe it's not related to any place but the illusion of the existence of life itself. I dream of a life in one of the realities where her soul image exists in the same space and time as my soul image and sharing a destiny.

During times of struggle, while missing Her, I asked for a sign from above that her soul image is real and not a dream. I have received only coincidences – connections with places, people, past lives, beliefs and other alternate realities, yet nothing related to reality. Following my heart's feelings, though, with all my mind's doubts of reality, as in my visions, her existence and connection with my soul feel so real that it's impossible to deny. The holiday to Seoul gave some consistency to visions of places where I saw Her. It opened some doors to my past lives and experiences with Her. Her vision presence shared a glimpse of the connection in reality with her soul image, which I adore in my heart's feelings.

Future holds my heart and soul prone to create in reality a fictional story of divine love reflection in the existence of human love shared further to the hearts of love in the search for a higher meaning behind the feelings.

COLOUR OVER BLACK-AND-WHITE MOMENTS OF DIVINE LOVE IN THE LAST DAYS IN SEOUL

4 Jan 2020

As proof that divine love exists beyond our minds and bodies, making a shrine from our hearts through our souls, the last days in Seoul brought feelings of pure love colouring the black-and-white moments since my arrival.

The connection between souls encountered after aeons of

searching and sharing the divine love is more profound than any other moment before, born from the depths of the soul and heart abyss.

Shared memories over the past lives and experiences of this reality, lost and found blissful silence between heart's beatings, thoughts of more profound meditation take the leap in the space and time around Namsan Tower and Myeong-dong. Time lost its meaning as a constant measure of the heart and soul's existence strolling around these places.

The light shining in a beautiful soul brought up some memories lost in the oblivion of soul existence and strengthened the feelings of divine love towards the visions, reality and presence of Her in Seoul. Maybe not in this reality – present or future, not shadowing the past lives, but certainly in a quantum realm entangled by the feelings and moments of divine love for Her in this life. Our souls' existence will connect our soul images' realities beyond any laws and constants of a possible destiny.

LAST MOMENTS OF CONTEMPLATION WHILE IN SEOUL

5 Jan 2020

Sorrow ... I felt like leaving home and family, although nothing was waiting for me in these places (or I'm unaware of anything), possibly linked to my past lives or unknown facts. Tears are pouring into my heart for the moments when I always felt so close to Her in Seoul. I soon miss Her being far away and probably waiting for destiny to settle the connection with her soul image on the wheel of time.

As a reflection of past feelings, the last place I visited again in Seoul was the Jogyesa Temple. Besides, I felt in the temple my heart connected to tears and spread the divine love all around and to the existence itself. Deep inside, I feel that the visions of past lives and feeling Her are now clear. I expect to continue the path of enlightenment into the future. Also, related to the connection felt with places and people from Korea, mainly in Seoul, Busan as a connection gives an emotional reality perception of destiny and relationship with the past.

One aspect is particular, however. The meditation became more focused, and divine love energy rose inside my heart at high levels of awareness due to the dots' connection in the destiny path related to visions. One thing is to see it; to walk on the path and feel it is different.

ONE THOUSAND KISSES OF LOVE FOR HER

6 Jan 2020

*One thousand kisses (*천 번의 입맞춤 *- cheonbeon-ui ipmajchum) of divine love feeling for Her delivered over her soul image existence …*

I had the most beautiful dream with Her. I was with her soul image beyond time and space, touching her lips and delivering with my lips one thousand kisses of divine love feeling over her soul image's existence. It didn't stop because I didn't want to wake up to check if it was confirmed this time in the dream.

I followed my heart and loved Her with all my being, knowing it was real while dreaming. At some moment, it became one with her lips, body and the divine love feeling in a beautiful dance of kisses. Every sensation touched her soul with my existence. Moments of eternity shadowed our feelings in our beings' joy as one, and I wished that those magical moments would last forever, connecting with her soul image.

Every night, I would dream like this and live only to feel Her again, even if it was only a mere inception. A life worth living twice or more in reality with days and nights keeps repeating as these eternities of kisses blast over her existence.

Finally, the yearning for a destiny settled with her soul image for this life and aeons to come for our souls with the touching of infinite kisses from divine love.

MOMENTS WITH HER ... YEARS LATER
Dec 2023

In Seoul, more and more moments with Her added to the clepsydra of time in my visions.

Every moment with Her felt beyond time and space, with a never-ending attachment to it. A simple touch of her perfectly smooth skin, like an eel slithering through my hands, and a glimpse into her eyes, like two black holes, instantly pushed my soul to another time and space.

These mystic moments with Her were recorded with all my senses, driving my mind and memory to the limit so that I could remember and pay attention to the minor details surrounding her existence.

In Suwon, the night moments with Her were counted as my whole life passing in front of my eyes. Divine love opened the gates of my heart so intensely that life and death became one in those moments next to Her.

My soul was reborn to another level of love and surrender. I felt the infinite existence of every moment with Her, whether walking through Seoul Forest or along the Hangang River pathways, enjoying a meal, or watching a movie. Every moment was out of this world, and so many moments, InYeon flowed through our existence.

Her existence is like Alice in Wonderland. Every breath of Her, touching existence, transforms the surroundings into a magic world. Maybe that's why Her likes the book so much.

Her laughing at silly things or smiling while touched by a moment of love is the reasoning for '*Just Love Her*' – 그저 행복이다 *(Geujeo haengbogida) – Just happiness.*

All this was just a dream, or did it happen for real in other alternate realities when '*Just Love Her*' – 그냥 그녀를 사랑해~~ *(Geunyang Geunyeoreul Saranghae)?*

DEEP MEDITATION AND VISIONS:

THOUGHTS OF ENLIGHTENMENT

09 Jan 2020–2024

REALITIES OR ONLY ONE REALITY?

Back in the UK … Back home.

It feels like the distance is so profound that there's no question in the future about feelings related to Her while at home and in Seoul. However, it's only a mind-limited perception affected by a physical law written in its reality. As a result, even the thoughts take a more reflective turn in the changed reality of perceiving Her. While in Seoul, the meditation experience became more intimate, and her soul image is now a part of my heart's vision and desire for a bright future.

My mind starts to understand the concept related to 'Just Love Her' in my visions. It is a fact that the reality of perceptions can reflect different realities that begin when my soul touches the existence of possible destinies.

Is there only one reality or more realities than the mind can imagine?

The existence of different realities in the quantum world is inevitable, and proven tests have concluded that other facts may be related to the observer's actions and position.

I didn't expect much to happen in Seoul, but it changed my perceptions of feeling Her, and meditation became more profound and robust. The most sophisticated instrument – the heart – tested feelings related to visions, the path to enlightenment and connection with Her while touching reality with places, people and events in Seoul. It also changed my destiny instantly, walking on the journey of visions.

Her existence is felt in visions and sensations, and touching her soul image while awake in some moments can be an effect of one of the realities where there is a destiny with Her. That's why the feeling is so natural in every experience with Her, although nothing sustains this awareness in this reality.

Does this mean there is no chance for destiny with Her in this reality?

It's debatable, but not even a connection with her soul image was made for the moment. It appears only in glimpses in the visions, with her soul image shadowing my mind and heart with the blissful touch of alternate realities.

SHADOW OF DIVINE LOVE FEELING

Take the courage to jump into the unknown ...
Many souls are afraid to admit the feeling of love inside their hearts. Moreover, they run as far as possible from their heart pulse of love. Hiding in the pits of mind illusions, they hope it will be better to give up on heart visions and feed the heart with meaningless thoughts.

My body is European, but the heart belongs to Korea.
After one week of leaving Seoul, it feels like it happened long ago.

Time becomes a value more appreciated than anything else when feeling kind or loving someone in moments of togetherness. These moments I call moments of eternity for our souls. When you don't want to be only a memory, these moments and that love feel like living every moment of your life if there is a chance to nourish them and live them daily, fight for them.

If you want a different life than the one you live now, choose divine love in your future. If your soul is essential to your life, don't give up on love; it will help you accomplish your dreams. When love becomes a necessary part of the book of your life, existence itself will wish to be of yours, too. If you want to change your lifestyle and experience love happening at some point, accept feelings of love at any moment of your life.

We talk so much about love and love, and again, love, because maybe you don't believe that it's possible to make it happen. Life is like a lottery. You gamble on it, hoping to win the big prize, and in the end, you could lose everything. *But if you don't play, how else is there a chance to win?*

When love comes into our lives, it doesn't happen randomly, and moments spent with our loved ones are only a taste of what existence can offer if we choose to enjoy love over a meaningless life.

I am always talking about feelings of love, so you know you can live a life dedicated to love if the future will only give you lemons. Divine love offers you the opportunity to make it lemonade.

SCIENCE OF DIVINE LOVE – HEART IS PROOF OF ITS EXISTENCE

Miracles exist until science proves that there is reasoning or a good explanation and facts behind it. After that, the magic of moments is lost, admired only by the mind unaware of the science-proving miracle phenomenon.

As the world has more knowledge and is more educated, and with so many discoveries in science and the universe surrounding our planet, it becomes more challenging than ever for religions to attract followers through miracles. Nowadays, attracting people to believe through feelings and personal development through meditation and practice is more straightforward than promoting God's powers and unseen divinity.

Some religions adapted to the world's continuing changes and embraced technology to carry on their missions. While they have a lot of money, they still don't use it for the good of the people; they use it to increase their power in the world.

There is money and resources in this world to end poverty and heal the planet, yet no one wants or does anything about it: only empty words and shallow actions. Changing the world requires those in power – government, churches, religions, powerful and wealthy people – to act and restructure society as we know it.

Hypocrisy surrounds us, and its effects are felt in our daily lives. Smoking became a habit, but actions were taken after money filled the pockets, and too many people died of it and affected future generations. Pollution has become a fact, and I am amazed that instead of preventing it and researching other ways, more taxes and more money are being collected in the name of ecology. Ultimately, after people use products that make tons of money for companies, governments and wealthy people, the blame falls on people, not those making money. It's easier to blame the consumer than to force those in power and responsible for correcting their mistakes and wrongdoings. Why not take the money from these companies and wealthy people who destroyed our planet to clean the waters, research new, safer products and technologies, and heal the Earth?

That's why we are on the brink of destruction as a civilisation.

The beauty of divine love's existence is that its reality and feeling can easily be proven by everyone, or at least almost everyone. It does not need advanced technologies or environments to test and confirm its existence and see it in action. Your heart is the most sophisticated and accurate way to feel divine love's existence as a deity slash energy. All it requires is the awareness and consciousness of its existence – divine love as divinity. Seeing and perceiving divinity in the unexpectedly occurring feeling of love we are born with is challenging. The only thing that helps is when it happens in your heart to acknowledge its divinity. It's way easier to understand the goddess feeling inside the heart when your mind kneels to love happening than to try to comprehend divinity through the limited intellect.

So, when love happens in your heart for a beloved soul, only follow its feeling on the path to enlightenment, knowing that the reflection of divine love is the source. A magic world will be revealed in front of your eyes.

INSPIRING MUSIC: Michael Jackson – Earth Song ...

ONE SWEET MOMENT OF LOVE PAIN MISSING HER

Suddenly, it comes to that moment kept subtle inside in the heart's voids for months of missing Her. Tears flood my eyes, rolling out from the deep feelings hidden and engraved in the shadows of love for Her. *Tears of happy sorrow ...*

Seoul dug out a hole of aches and pains into my heart, searching to touch a few moments with her soul image in this reality. And those moments with her existence shadows around the city, the riverside ... entangled, with her soul image acting in the mirror of truth, smashed on my heart and mind screen ... left an emptiness of hopes for the future due to the insignificance of my unfortunate destiny.

Heaven forbids in this present reality happiness for my soul dreaming of life next to Her. Visions became dreams, and dreams faded into ashes of love, suffering missing Her. I was awaiting the slightest sign of her soul image presence around my existence.

Looking into her eyes, moulded by divine love, into my heart and mind screen, no words of wisdom and enlightenment vibrate in the echo of my heartstrings other than the sounds of tears of happy sorrow pouring over my life like a rain of sadness.

And once again, my soul rises from the embers of burning love and pain, fighting with the feelings of missing Her. Awakened by the showers of gloom ... Drowning my heart in her scent presence, I hope that I may never fall into the oblivion of her memories and that her soul image will abide by a glimpse of divine love reflected from the aeons of our soul's reality.

INSPIRING MUSIC: Cloud Atlas Movie – 21 – Cloud Atlas Finale OST | Composed by Tom Tykwer, Johnny Klimek & Reinhold Heil

A HEART FULL OF DIVINE LOVE – HEARTS OF LOVE

> *'A heart full of divine love sees only beautiful and good qualities in the loved one.'*
> **– Hearts Of Love**

A heart full of love cherishes every moment with the loved one, feeling the love for the beloved soul.

In every moment of life, a heart of love will use any chance to do anything and everything for the loved one's happiness, with or without being together. Knowing its divinity source, the most significant help that a heart of love can offer is to pray for the beloved soul's health and happiness because you won't expect and ask anything from a loved one, not even feelings of love back.

A heart of love will only wish to know from time to time that the loved one is doing well, has good health and well-being, and is enjoying life. A few moments close to a loved one sharing love means more than anyone can imagine for a heart of love. The heart feelings opened to the loved one connect souls beyond their shallow destinies.

The only happiness of a heart of love dedicated to divine love is keeping feelings alive for the beloved soul, and the only hope is that they won't be forgotten along with the wheel of time in the memory of the loved one.

Who will love you through a heart full of divine love and acquiescing will make every moment of loving you an eternity.

EVOLUTION OF ENLIGHTENMENT – THE PROCESS THAT NEVER ENDS

Once we reach enlightenment, most people believe that powers and divine realms open inside our minds and bodies.

Touching the light of enlightenment means that divine love intuition is accessible beyond our limited mind, and knowledge of the soul and divinity realm existence becomes a reality inside our hearts. It doesn't give magical powers or any other abilities, as many believers pursue through different practices to reach enlightenment. It could be a side effect, but it depends on the various levels of attainment for each unique soul. Sometimes, it could be an obstacle to enlightenment, which never ends. That's why magical powers and abilities (siddhi) are never a scope in the enlightenment through divine love.

Some people are born enlightened, having a vision and understanding of the unseen realm of divinity and existence that is only accessible to others only after years of practice and worship. Others may be blind to the divinity realm and not even dream of it. In a way, it is better not to see and understand what's happening behind the curtain of reality – the suffering and evolution of the world and universe.

The enlightenment never ends, continuing from the birth of existence until its end. It touched every aspect of existence, science and religion. All things and elements of existence, physical and empirical, are interconnected and have the same energy and creation – divine love.

Many discoveries about physical laws and scientific knowledge were revealed through soul-searching answers during meditation or so-called reflections while sleeping. The same happened in religions through revelations.

From the physical world to the divinity realm, the source of all knowledge is accessible and revealed through divine love reflected in our soul's existence. That's why divine love is praised and used in religions, practices and different beliefs from ancient times, and it is also reflected in human love.

Without love, there would have been no evolution and no knowledge. When divine love reveals to all souls awakened and conscious as the source of their existence – the reflection of divine love intuition (bodhi – enlightenment) in their existing acknowledged – reincarnation and suffering will be only in memories of time itself.

LIFE IS A MEDITATION

Living with awareness and consciousness on this Earth can help our souls for aeons or send their existence into oblivion.

Meditation has been proven since ancient times to be the best way to acknowledge the soul's reality and the rules that apply to its existence. One of the meditations of everyday life reflects talking with our inner Self. Some of us have more profound meaning talks, while others only noise. Few of us learned or were born with a silent meditation mindset, remaining as much as possible in the present moment as an observer (e.g. zazen). There are no talks, only feelings and silence.

Meditation on divinity, the existence of God, fantasy realms and fiction related to science and technology open our souls to knowledge that becomes more advanced and broader with each passing era.

While scientific knowledge is changing and advancing faster than ever, religious practices and beliefs have remained unchanged for thousands of years. The only difference between science and religion is in the scope of discoveries. Science searches for knowledge inside and outside the material world to understand and discover more about our existence and meaning. Religion searches inside our existence to free up, acknowledge our soul and touch the realm of divinity.

Meditation without the feeling of love will give inside only empty thoughts and no meaning in life. Meditation without love is like drinking tea from an empty cup.

Every moment of our life is a meditation, living and being aware of our existence or only following the wheel of our destiny. When love is happening inside our hearts, meditation becomes alive, having supported the experience of a process that brings colour to our shallow lives. Feeling the love in our hearts proves that divinity lives inside of us and stops looking outside. Being aware and conscious of its source – divine love – is the beginning of the path to enlightenment as a reality and not a dream while sleeping the entire life.

Life is a meditation where divine love awakens our hearts or is dormant, waiting to be acknowledged.

JUST SPREAD THE LOVE

When I lived with divine love awareness and consciousness in my heart for dozens of years, the scent of its existence dispersing to other souls became proof of its unseen effect.

Feeling the love inside our hearts, knowing its source and its divinity awareness – divine love, it spreads to other souls and reality itself. Divine love is like a shield that protects the shrine that inhabits your heart while worshipped.

When love is burning in our hearts like a fire within, the only option that helps your soul handle happy sorrow is to spread the love around our existence. The fastest way to see the effects of spreading love is through animals because their safe mechanisms are less dense than humans. Animals perceive Love in raw form; hence, it is easier to feel it. The same thing happens in the middle of nature.

Everything around us is embalmed in love – raw love. We lost direct connection with it due to evolution, mind-centred instead of heart as a centre. When we shift the centre towards the heart, a new world opens before our eyes. We'll start to see through feelings, not through the mind's thoughts. The thoughts will result from feelings and intuition, not from the logical and material side.

When we become aware of the divine love source in our heart feelings, we can directly connect with pure, raw love. The eyes become a medium to communicate with the beloved soul because they reflect the heart's feelings. It's like magic connecting hearts through eyes, revealing the soul's existence through our feelings.

Worshipping the divine love in our hearts, being aware and conscious, opens the door to the unseen realm of its existence, and magical things and events start to unleash the butterfly effect of its presence and reflection, uncovering the connection between souls. Actions of divine love reflection, unknown and unseen, have happened since the beginning of existence, but when acknowledged through our hearts and souls, life has a new and profound meaning on the path to enlightenment.

If we want to free our souls from the shackles of our destiny, we must spread love without expectations or rewards, only accepting the pure feeling of love that must exist in our hearts.

'*Spread love everywhere you go. Let no one ever come to you without leaving happier.*'
– **Mother Teresa**

TIMES OF SILENCE – JUST LOVE HER …

Sometimes, no words are needed to express the feelings – only silence, listening to love whispers for Her.

Any thoughts born from the depths of the heart disappear, lost in the void of soul existence. When the soul reaches the entity's surface, silence settles as an echo of its source reflection. Life becomes a nuisance before the uncovered divine love, filling in like a mist of the heart's feelings.

Sometimes, silence reflects the struggles of happy sorrow from the heart due to the soul's wishes for a better destiny close to Her. The echo of her soul-image existence, sprayed over the walls of the heart gallery of deflected destiny in this existence, reflects the longing to glimpse her presence in any reality to which the soul has access through its visions.

Silence is the expectation of the failed connection between soul images. It spreads concern over the reality of visions and dreams between souls. Only the intense feeling of love and connection with Her beyond any thoughts and reality checks keep alive the belief that not everything is in vain. There is still hope for this reality to connect with her soul image as long as the heart breathes through divine love in this life.

Silence leaves space for pure meditation without thoughts, dreams or visions – only pure love missing Her. It doesn't have any expectations in this destiny or any other reality.

Feeling Her inside the heart in deep meditation is like simultaneously living her dreams and visions. In these moments of pure bliss, touching her existence inside through our souls, it remains only the choice for her soul image to feel the connection and decide if it comes to that at some point in her destiny.

Silence is the secret factor that souls can use against failed destiny, challenging life and difficult choices. It takes one moment of pure silence to hear the voice and echo of love deep inside our hearts and start the enlightenment process through divine love.

LOST MY SELF INTO HER EYES – JUST LOVE HER …

Since divine love revealed her eyes to my heart, whenever I go back inside, closing the gates of sight to the outside world, my soul dwells in my heart, surrounded by her eyes.

Whenever my heart aches to miss Her, her eyes are a beacon of hope, being so close to my soul. It's like the abyss reflects in the sparks of lights moulded in the shadows of her beautiful and mystical eyes. Her being is embedded in the sensations translated through my heart, sealed with her sight.

My being keeps floating on the surface of skipped heartbeats, looking at her existence. Hands are touching, lips kissing, eyes looking, bending mind thoughts into feeling like one, losing the sense of my Self into her being. Moments that keep on going over and over. And there is no one inside to have a presence, only the void of love as a balm of our souls dipped into oblivion.

Her look burns my Self, and the ashes of its memories scatter into the wind of love blowing mildly over our existence. Nothing is left inside me after the storm of sensations, which moulds every corner of my being with a blatant feeling of love lost in her eyes.

DIVINE LOVE TRINITY

I call 'soul image' the pure reflection of the soul in human existence.

When we know the Trinity of Divine Love realm and its manifestation in our existence, the soul can recognise another soulmate through divine love's reflection in our heart feelings.

The Trinity of Divine Love:
- **Divine love** – God/Goddess realm, love existence in itself as a deity.
- **Divine love reflection** – the energy and acting power of divine love reflecting in the individual souls.
- **Soul** – the individual and unique representation behind our existence as humans, as soul images, is unchanged and keeps the record of our reincarnation and information.

The divine love existence's vision happens when the beloved soul image reveals itself to our heart through our feelings. The inside world becomes magical and mystical when we acknowledge that the infinite and absolute love divinity made all this process happen. By becoming aware and conscious of every moment of love as a deity, we will start to love even the shadow of our soulmate's 'soul image'.

Someone can argue the existence of each representation of divine love existence and manifestation. The same applies to all divinity representations of God, the heavens, or any unseen realm. The only difference is that love is an experience of all souls with or without awareness and consciousness of their divinity existence. The experience level or the representation of love for family, country, nature, Earth, Universe and so on doesn't matter. The absence of love or misconception of its existence leads to all evils and suffering of human beings. That's why when we start the process of enlightenment for our souls through divine love existence, it's so important to understand, accept and experience the representations of its divinity as a Trinity.

It's easier to comprehend the divine love realm through

these representations as a separate yet connected entity. The explanation of different descriptions allows the limited mind to understand the concept, but the heart makes no difference.

THE PRACTICE AND BENEFITS OF MANTRAS – PRAYING OF DIVINE LOVE

Prayers and mantras of divine love are slightly different from other beliefs due to heart feelings being more personal and the divinity of love being seen as having a shrine inside our hearts.

Mantras become only prayers repeated continuously through feelings of love while walking on the path to enlightenment through divine love. Divine love is so intense at some point that words are unnecessary, only spreading the love around our existence. The relation is more personal due to the vision of love between souls, and God becomes divine love reflection in the beloved soul image revealed in our heart during praying. Hence, Love is God.

Mantras don't use words that suggest a cold relationship or a conception of a relationship with divinity because they fear punishment. Love is the only concept needed to connect souls through divine love. Divinity's representation of love isn't mandatory as a masculine or feminine concept. It depends on the beloved soul image revealed through the heart's feelings. Only divine love exists when it becomes pure energy, representing the feelings revealed for aeons inside our hearts and souls.

Prayers of divine love occur around the beloved soul's feelings as the core, which is revealed in our heart through feelings, being aware and conscious that divine love exists as a deity. Words don't matter and are sometimes unnecessary; only the feeling of love in our hearts is a deity.

Mantras can be prayers from religions or beliefs chosen or cherished by our souls. They can even be the name of the beloved soul image, declaring our love for its soul existence. It matters a lot to recognise that the feelings of love have divine love as a source.

We must try to be aware and conscious every moment of the connection with the divine love existing as a deity through our hearts until only love exists inside our hearts and minds and nothing else. This way, we become one with the divine love.

THE HIDDEN SECRET OF MANTRAS AND PRAYERS

Mantras and prayers repeated daily connect our existence with the realm of divinity.

A **mantra** – repeating the exact words continuously – can't be done without feelings. Also, the meaning and divinity represented give the power and creation of that concept behind words repeated.

Looking from afar, it seems like, for example, a virtual world created by programmers nowadays with implications and influence in the real world. It's the same thing happening when we connect with divinity through mantras, like using a spell to open the door for magic powers and portals to unseen worlds.

Since ancient times, chosen devotees have been practising the private practice of repeating a mantra continuously in a few words. In the past, it was a secret well kept behind the walls of monasteries and temples, and spiritual masters were allowed to share it only by mouth.

Due to technology and shared information, anyone interested in the numerous mantras and practices of different religions and beliefs can learn more about them.

Most dominant religions or beliefs, with many adepts, have their secret mantras, which they practise as their dogma's heart through divine love and adoration.

Christianity has *Hesychasm*, **Islam** has *Sufism*, **Hinduism** has *Bhakti Yoga*, and **Buddhism** has *Tibetan Buddhism*.

Mantras and prayers that are repeated continuously in:

- **Hesychasm**: *'Lord Jesus Christ, son of God, have mercy on me, the sinner.'*
- **Sufism**: *'There is no God but Allah, and Muhammad is his prophet.'*
- **Bhakti Yoga**: *'OM'* or *Aum* sound.
- **Tibetan Buddhism**: *'Om mani Padme hum.'*

Mantra practices have existed since ancient times and are revealed in scriptures believed to have lived thousands of years ago.

Every country or civilisation believes that they are the chosen ones. In the times of the so-called apocalypse, they will lead the world's remnants to liberation and soul enlightenment.

SOMEONE TO LOVE – THE STAGE TO START THE PATH OF ENLIGHTENMENT THROUGH DIVINE LOVE

When we find someone to love through the feeling of divine love reflected in our hearts, we become aware of everything surrounding us.

The sky is the escape for our troubled souls, encapsulated for so long in our hearts. We notice its landscape of clouds and birds flying every day, bringing to life the world above us. How many of us rise and look to the sky daily, forgetting about the passing life of nothingness?

Loving someone through divine love reflection is the greatest gift. It fills our hearts and brings awareness and consciousness into our lives. The gift of love is available to all souls searching for the source of life and path to follow for enlightenment and liberation from the slavery of our bodies and mind control.

Love is the only experience and force that elevates our minds and hearts towards touching and living the divinity realm. The source and energy behind love existence – the divine love –

leads our intuition and destiny to enlightenment through a chosen soul image revealed in our heart, the so-called soulmate. Some of us have only one soulmate to help or share the path to enlightenment, while others have more soulmates along the long road to liberate our souls.

Awareness and consciousness continue through meditation, mantra and praying as we feel divine love and adoration toward the beloved soul image in our hearts. We don't need words, facts, or connections in the real world with the beloved soul image on the path to enlightenment through divine love. The only practice required is to allow the feeling of love revealed in our heart to evolve and reach the infinite and absolute state of existence becoming this way, one with the divine love existence.

So, if a soul image reveals itself to our heart, we have to nourish the feeling of love and recognise its source – the divine love. We must follow the path to enlightenment through continuous awareness and consciousness of its divinity. We must never give up on this feeling, even if everything in the real world does not connect our soul images' destinies or bring us closer to the physical world.

Notable is that the divine love revealed in our hearts is the soul of someone to love. It means that the path to enlightenment started the process of liberation for our souls through divine love. Many souls are unaware of this gift and lose the opportunity to live happily with their beloved souls for aeons. That's why the awareness and consciousness about divine love as a source for feelings of love in our hearts is a constant reminder that heaven is in our hearts and not elsewhere, undoubtedly not a fantasy anymore.

'Whatever happens, just keep smiling and lose yourself in Love.'
– **Rumi**

THE IMMUTABLE LAW OF DIVINE LOVE

It's a sure thing that divine love always connects with our souls through our hearts. We are unaware of this connection because we lost the perception of love as a divinity and our soul's source.

The feeling of love and connection with a soulmate through our hearts is not dependent on destiny and time. We tend to analyse and create rules for divinity, souls and enlightenment according to our limited mind perception of the real world.

In reality, everything that we think and believe about the divinity realm and God is more like a fantasy and nothing based on truth because we can't check the facts. Others and different stories tell the truth about God and the divinity realm, but there is no practice yet to check and be accessible to everyone.

Every soul feels love more or less through feelings from the heart that connect our souls, but love has never been accepted as a divinity. Although love has been the source of all religions, practices and beliefs since the creation of our world, humanity hasn't acknowledged its divinity. Religions, practices and beliefs used love under different names but never as its actual existence – divine love.

Divine love is the God/Goddess praised and the source of all religions and beliefs.

Acknowledging its divinity and conceptualising divine love's existence happen through intimate relations between soul images, such as soulmates and lovers. The only difference is that love becomes divine through awareness and consciousness of its existence as divinity.

The connection between souls occurs through divine love reflected in our hearts' feelings. The problem is that most of us aren't aware of this process. Maybe it's not yet the right time to reveal love's existence as divinity. We have many years to evolve, understand and accept divine love as a deity.

Divine love is a deity utterly different from any concept before because its existence accepts everything and everyone. No rules apply for its manifestation and presence, and no differences challenge the mind because it's the same feeling in all hearts. Also, no superiority is involved because no one is above others, all souls being melted in its existence.

If the message about its presence is now in the world, all human beings will soon start accepting love's existence as a divinity, acknowledging our souls' reality.

ONE-WAY LOVE – AXIS OF TIME – VISIONS

It has been quite a long time since a moment with Her hit me straight in the depths of my heart. A glimpse of a moment with her soul image made my heart flutter so fast and hard that it amazed me how it's possible, after so much time, to feel feelings as new as when I saw her for the first time.

Every moment of her life, as recent as possible, feels fresh. It's like we just met on the axis of time for a pure moment of our soul existence. In the name of divine love, how can it feel a moment like eternity?

It's like a wake-up call to never-ending feelings of love. These moments give life a higher meaning. There is no higher purpose in life worth fighting for other than the feelings of pure love for Her.

Such a long time passed … Yet being close to Her are the only feelings echoing in my mind and heart … Sharing and tasting the scent of love through our passing bodies.

Could it be the last moments of hope, dreaming of real life being with Her?

Visions with Her were like nothing that had ever happened before with visions with someone else. The feelings and events are together for only a few moments but are touched by love's eternity.

Looking into the future, I hope those moments meant something to Her, raising the bar for wishing for togetherness forever with Her. I can vouch for our souls, but who knows about our passing bodies or shallow destinies?

A HIGHER STATE OF CONSCIOUSNESS

'Just Love Her' means not acting or doing anything to bother the beloved soul image.

It means loving her soul so deeply that everything is left in the hands of destiny. The only awareness and consciousness are the feelings of love for Her, keeping the mind focused on acknowledging the source of feelings, which is divine love. It's like praying continuously through endless love for her soul image existence revealed in the heart's emotions. Nothing else gives more happiness to the soul than these deep feelings for her existence.

The mind can't comprehend the complexity of this concept of love – a love beyond any limits imposed by the passing body.

A higher state of consciousness occurs when we become aware of our soul's existence, divine love reflected in the heart's feelings, and divine love as a divinity.

Everything in one's life will change. Dreams start to be different because of feeling and touching the existence of unseen worlds, past lives and even possible futures.

Feeling love for a soul image will not be only love but a connection between souls beyond time and space, knowing the natural force of divine love that reveals the soulmate in the heart's feelings.

All these deep feelings and conceptions about love's existence and its divinity guide our souls to be as one through divine love connection.

MOMENTS IN TIME WITH HER – REALITIES UNLEASHED

Many moments with Her arise from Akasha taken from the time capsules floating on the ocean's waves of time blowing off and landing on the memory shore. Stories unravel one by one behind the mind's eye, creating inceptions of worlds unfolded through the drawings of our soul memories.

We were taking a stroll in Paris on the Rue De La Paix, hand in hand, with an umbrella to protect her from the burning rays of sunlight. Whispers of sweet words blew to our ears with a loving scent for her thoughts to cradle over my existence.

What times would be uncovered?

I judge by her dress, which is probably from the 19th century. I don't dare look too introspectively into this memory in time to keep the connection ongoing. Afar, the sight of the Eiffel Tower takes the horizon in the shadows of time.

Another memory down the lane ... I have been waiting for Her for quite some time, impatiently waiting for her to arrive by train in London from Manchester. Her ran straight into my arms. It feels so good to take an in-depth look into her big brown, beautiful eyes, full of life and love.

Is it the same time frame or a different reality?

Oh, and so many memories from Seoul with Her. Joyful and surrounded by teenagers, with her smile cheering up my heart while watching from afar.

Is Her a teacher or what?

Too many teenagers are shouting and running around Her:

'누나 안녕하세요*! (Nuna annyeonghaseyo!) – Hello, sister!'*

누나 = *older sister*

WHY FEELINGS OF LOVE FOR SEOUL, HENCE FOR KOREA?

Is it because of Her?
Is it because of past lives and memories related to Seoul?
Indeed, love for Her is the most critical factor. But I can't forget my heart's connection with all the people and places beyond doubt while wandering through Seoul and Busan. It is a love designed for my family and the country I was born in, although my natural birthplace is far from South Korea. The same happens with sorrowful feelings for North Koreans as it was only one Korea at some point in the time of past lives in my heart.

The strange feeling of being at home in Korea was put up front. Why not be born here?

But the answer is simple, and with everything to consider, it also means destiny wouldn't have been the same. Maybe not even to meet and feel her soul because the events would have been different. My Self would have been probably forgotten in the waves of time because the persona's experiences wouldn't have opened the gates to the enlightenment. Moreover, although my soul feels closer to some people, countries or beliefs, in the end, the Earth represents the feelings of divine love oneness. And when my Self-awareness disappears, the feelings of divine love extend to the Universe, galaxies, unseen realms and so on. It's a never-ending boundary between physical and spiritual representations because divine love is absolute and infinite.

When the soul becomes one with the existence of divine love, there is no beginning nor end of life and void of the worlds in the known and unknown realms or concepts.

At the beginning of the path to enlightenment, information touches the limits of the mind itself, but going further into the unknown, only the soul can spread its wings to dwell in the realm of divine love.

JUST LOVE HER: WHO IS HER?

> *Her is anybody's dream in the real world, or it could be someone dreaming of love out of this world.*
> *Her personifies divine love, passing through the soul into a 'soul image' revealed to the heart, the soulmate.*
> *Her is the conception of divine love's existence reflected in the soulmate chosen through the heart's feelings.*
> *Her represents the feminine side of its reflection, hence the 'soul image' chosen by vision and feelings.*

It is difficult for our limited minds to think of divinity – God – as a duality combined or no gender at all.

In ancient times, God was a father's creation, giving birth to a son in problematic conditions. Lately, we've seen many problems with women's freedom, equality in a world of men, etc. But maybe this world we live in results from imperfect representations of religions and beliefs.

When we think of Love (God is Love), it happens the same as God's representation, which is perceived as masculine. We can't think of Love other than female representation. It resembles a chicken and egg fable:

'Which one was first: chicken or egg?'

The vision that divine love is the source of all creation, the energy behind existence, hence connecting all, consists of masculine and feminine representation. That's why we have an inner craving to unite our souls beyond our bodies, to become one with divine love through its reflection in our existence. How we perceive or accept its representation as masculine or feminine without duality doesn't matter. Initially, we choose what's best and most comfortable to represent its existence. Ultimately, duality will disappear after reaching the enlightenment process in our souls.

Through divine love, each soul will see God's best representation through its soulmate, depending on the body born with since birth. For a feminine believer, divine love symbolises the loved one as masculine because it's easier to comprehend the complexity of the divinity realm of love. The same goes for a masculine believer; it will be easier to understand and accept the concept of divine love through the feminine side of divinity.

This path to enlightenment, divine love manifestation through love between opposite existence of souls, is the highest representation, being also intimate. No other portrayal could get more personal and advanced to reach the core of our soul existence.

In the past, the conception of love as a divinity couldn't be understood or accepted. It is the path of evolution in the future as our society struggles to eliminate different diseases of the mind (racism, xenophobia, etc.) induced by differences in our souls' representations into existence.

Without love – the infinite and absolute representation of its existence, namely divine love – the mind can't overcome our reality's differences and conflicting visions. Limited minds find it more natural to think about the differences in our soul representations into existence as a disease or error of creation, while it's quite the opposite. An enlightened soul overcomes the mental limitations and understands that due to its primitive mindset, the mind can't comprehend and accept love's existence as a divinity, hence the differences as a problem for limited consciousness.

Love is the spark that can withstand our limited minds, start the process of enlightenment, and lead our souls to freedom from the slavery of our bodies. Aeons are needed to free up all souls, ultimately, but this is a drop in the ocean of time for our soul existence.

HER is ... YOU.

WEB OF LIFE

Staring down at the web of life from the highest axis of time makes me wish I had had even the most minor role in her existence.

Thoughts born out of love and feelings for Her give meaning to my inner world based on visions related to her daily life shared from time to time with my heart. Often, the shadow of 'happy sorrow' feelings and questions about keeping scribbling without a real sign that her soul image exists in this reality trouble my heart, which struggles to stay afloat above the pond of fate.

Her eyes follow my being like a shadow embracing my Self in a light of pure love.

A feeling of love beyond my senses embraces my soul, which wishes to vanish in memories' dust clouded in moments of divine love between Her and me ... along with the entanglement of daily life.

I miss Seoul more than ever before because now I can assess the distance between Her and me. When in Seoul, even if it was so cold in winter, my heart was warm and full of her presence, knowing that her soul image wanders around my existence somewhere nearby. Although I feel Her close inside now, the outside is beyond imagination. Mainly due to an intangible destiny that keeps me in the dark as the days pass.

The whole world is drowning in despair. The future looks dark, and there is no point of return from the crisis other than hope.

Now more than ever, the divine love awakened through her existence is the light at the end of the life and fate tunnel.

넌 내 희망이야! (**Neon** nae huimang-i-ya!) – **YOU** are my hope!

QUANTUM CHOICES

Everything around us, scientific and religious points of view and facts, suggests an order in the apparent chaos that exists and leads to the creation of life. The truth about a predetermined destiny where everything is bound to happen – it will happen, lies somewhere in the middle, or it's a quantum truth with endless possibilities and choices.

A quantum predetermined destiny means that we have numerous choices in life. In the quantum world, a choice awaits once our attention is directed to a possible action. Once we decide, the chosen path is known until another breaking point.

At the same time, every possible choice, dream, vision or action exists in separate and interconnected realities and universes. That is suggested even in scriptures when it's said that even mind or desire is a sin, not just through action. The action affects current reality, but mind and desire affect endless worlds unseen and unknown to human beings and accessible only to enlightened souls.

Some critical events leave no choices other than those leading to the final result. If an action that could change the predetermined fate comes to our mind, it's a choice available to our soul images. Sometimes, even if we are aware of a choice, it happens only after the finished predetermined event. It's like blindness covering our minds when we must make the right choice.

That's why consciousness and awareness are so significant on the path to enlightenment. Ultimately, we conclude that everything happens in current reality; it's how it should be. Kings to be kings and poor to be poor. What would happen if everyone were a king? Without suffering and diversity, there would be no evolution. That doesn't mean we don't have to fight for fair and better choices, especially if we are awakened and aware of the options.

By becoming enlightened, we understand and respect the destiny of every soul and environment around us. Only compassion for the fate of poor, suffering and evil souls helps the evolution and enlightenment of other lucky souls. It's not their mistake that the veil of darkness and ignorance clouds the right choices for their souls. The same happens for the victims or suffering souls who have to endure unimaginable pains for the benefit of other souls or the fallen ones. Also, we can't blame destiny or God for our choices, no matter what. You can't blame a river flowing down the valley. It is what it is.

Some dark events seem to have no meaning for the enlightenment of our souls. But when we understand the big picture drawn by the higher intelligence of divinity compared with the limited vision and stupidity of our minds, it concludes that we are only a drop in the ocean of infinite and absolute existence.

Our existence is the same as in the quantum world at the deepest level. An observer forced the actual state of our existence. Is it the soul?

Did you ever think your body and mind were insufficient for the information received?

HUMANS ARE LIKE A VIRUS FOR NATURE

To evolve and spread worldwide, as nowadays for humans, it took hundreds of thousands of years. And only a few centuries to eliminate other species, destroy the environment and use most of our planet's resources. Looking around, it takes no brain to see that we are like a virus for nature and existence.

While looking around in awe of nature's grandeur and beauty, I think of Agent Smith's words from *The Matrix* movie about human life acting like a virus to the environment. These words are closer to our current reality, far more than twenty-something years ago when the film was released.

> *'I'd like to share a revelation that I've had during my time here. It came to me when I tried to classify your species, and I realised that humans are not actually mammals. Every mammal on this planet instinctively develops a natural equilibrium with the surrounding environment, but you humans do not. Instead, you multiply and multiply until every resource is consumed. The only way for you to survive is to spread to another area. There is another organism on this planet that follows the same pattern ... a virus. Human beings are a disease, a cancer on this planet, you are a plague, and we ... are the cure. '*

– **Agent Smith** *(is a fictional character · The Matrix · movie · 1999 · Action/Sci-fi)*

Indeed, we evolved so much and took over, destroyed and killed everything that was a danger or hindrance and didn't make use of our needs. Well, we evolved more in numbers and technology than spiritually. That's the problem.

It's not a balance between mind and soul for most of us. Only a few, but not enough, can significantly change our souls' evolution. We think that nothing else deserves or must be first before ourselves – better sacrifice everything around us than our way of life. Even so, nature and animals don't fight with us after so much suffering over and over.

Love and happiness surround us in the middle of nature, no matter the damage and pain our existence and needs provoke. Nature is the heart of our planet and the whole universe. Without nature, life and evolution are never the same or even possible. The issue is that we acknowledge this only after it's gone.

Some would argue that technology destroyed nature, but it became necessary due to the growing numbers of human beings.

Even religions are blind to the fact that nature can't sustain too many of us. The biblical mandate 'be fruitful and multiply' was sustainable thousands of years ago, but nowadays, it isn't anymore. At least not if we don't find other planets to live on or different social vision methods than the present reality.

We lost the connection with our inner Self a long time ago. Luckily enough, human love is safe and sound, but who knows for how long if we don't open the gates of wisdom to accept that the divinity of love exists in our hearts and everywhere around us?

THE UNTHINKABLE LOVE

Whatever you do when feeling love, don't think about it or analyse it. Let yourself be lost in the ocean of infinite and absolute love.

Sometimes, I feel connected to her soul on a deeper level, and I can't do anything but get lost in the pit of my feelings for Her. My heart is burning, filled with her existence as one. I feel the fire of divine love warming my soul while I miss Her. In those moments of pure love for Her, my whole being ceased to exist. All the emptiness inside becomes full of her presence. I see Her inside ... floating in endless love. Feeling Her inside ... my whole body dips into her existence. Everything becomes heavenly inside when I am not thinking about Her, just feeling Her filling my heart without question, doubt or worries. In these moments, Her is only pure love pouring into my soul. Life and death have no boundaries anymore for my destiny. Only her existence keeps me afloat over the void of nothingness.

Her soul image named the void inside with her presence and painted the walls of feelings with her existence.

09/06/2020 time around – 08:00 (London) and 16:00 (Seoul) – Love for Her overflows my heart so deeply that there's nothing else I can think of or do in my daily life. I let myself drown for two hours in feeling Her inside. Heaven is bliss here; now, I only feel the love for her soul image. I am logging this moment to remember it forever as proof of unthinkable love. There have been many moments like this in the year that has passed. Maybe this marks the counting of a year since Her became the centre of my life.

How can you love someone you didn't see or meet in reality?
How can your life be ravished without a real thing happening in this reality, not even in dreams?
How is every moment about missing Her more than anything?

Love for Her is unthinkable!

GREATNESS OF LOVE

Feelings of love in our hearts give us the perception of greatness and divinity hidden deep into our souls. Feeling love for Her and knowing the divine love source feels unworldly, raising awareness of the importance of maintaining these emotions.

When you know that the goddess of love lives and makes your heart a shrine dedicated to her existence, this reality expands its borders over limited knowledge. The soul image representing the beloved soul revealed through divine love in our hearts expresses pure love. Nothing is more important than being aware and conscious of feelings of love awakened by her existence.

The powerful connection between soul images chosen as soulmates expands beyond any comprehension. If soul images are blessed to be together in this reality, heaven opens the doors to their existence. Otherwise, it will be a continuous 'happy sorrow' feeling, eating and devouring the awakened soul.

Suppose only one soul becomes awakened and aware of the connection between their soul images. It will help in the enlightenment process but not fill the void in the heart, missing the union in this reality with the beloved soul. Hence, 'happy sorrow' feelings cloud one soul's existence, losing its soulmate's natural touch.

Some soulmates are connected to the whole destiny, others only for some time ... and few for eternity. In the ocean of divine love, all souls are united as oneness.

Blessed are only a few souls to have a destiny with the beloved soulmate's image being aware of their Self.

TOUCH OF SOULS

My heart often yearns for a touch of her lips or hands ... a glimpse into her mysterious eyes.

Is it my heartbeat or hers I hear while missing Her?

Time often lost its touch over my soul image, and my Self feels the scent of her existence deep into my heart and senses. My soul lately craves a simple touch in the reality of our soul images in so many moments. Instead of the outside world of touching, feeling and seeing Her, everything moved inside related to her existence.

It's easier than ever to feel and see Her inside. Our souls are so close, touching each other through our hearts as a shrine dedicated to divine love.

Visions of her soul image from infinite realities haunt my mind and heart, filling the vacuum space with her existence. It's like bouncing off our souls on the axis of time and space.

I feel a gentle touch of her existence inside my heart, and tears flood the soul's gates to the outside world. I have no feelings, pain, or sorrow – just missing Her. Her soul image is floating in the depths of my heart, and as I close my eyes, my whole being jumps in the ocean of love, reflecting her eyes inside. These moments are the purest reflection of the divine love cuddling our souls to the chest of its eternity.

Love becomes more than just a feeling in these instants of time, revealing the true nature of its existence. A deity that lurks deep into our hearts and souls, waiting for aeons to kiss our feelings with its divinity.

All left inside is the adoration and feeling of our existence's nothingness, blessed to be a shrine of divine love.

HER LIVES IN MY HEART

'Petals fall, but the flower endures ... '

Even if the gates of destiny seem to shut off the connection related to her soul image, my heart became a shelter for Her.

Her soul has lived close to my being for a long time already. It has re-established a connection beyond time and space, known to our souls as a soulmate for aeons.

Every day passed with the weird feeling of missing her soul image, knowing it was far from me somewhere in Korea.

How do you cheat destiny to know her soul image is fine?

The only option is to pray every moment, looking to the sky and sending the feeling of divine love from my heart through clouds to accompany her existence. Without any sign that our soul images will be closer at some point, my fate seems doomed to only hopes and dreams. Only visions tell tales of forgotten lives and alternate realities of our souls, sharing the wheel of time beyond this current reality.

From time to time, glimpses of her soul image of life come from nothingness, veiling my heart in clouds of shivers due to a flutter of love shielded in my soul existence.

Praising divine love's existence is the only remedy that helps the happy sorrow feeling shrouding my baffled soul image, which is astonished at the touch of her soul image's quivering existential wings.

Although dreaming of a fate with her soul image, I feel blissful and thankful that divine love made my heart a shrine loving Her. Fate may be a dream, but loving Her with all my heart is a reality.

Whenever I miss her soul image, I close my eyes and feel Her living in my heart while my mind gives me visions of our souls floating around the Han River and Namsan Tower in Korea.

Missing Her is like missing Korea as well. Should I live the rest of my life close to Her?

'Flower petals fall, but the flower endures.
The form perishes, but the being endures.'
– Seiichi Takeuchi – The Japanese Philosophy of Transience

GOD MAY BE FORGOTTEN, BUT DIVINE LOVE IS NOT

Breathe in … breathe out … love literally.

Imagine that when you breathe in, love fills your heart, and when you breathe out, love from your heart spreads around the world. This process is love meditation.

The love spreading through our heart is the same feeling for our soulmate, but recognising the divine love reflection in that feeling.

God, without love, is just a fear of punishment. With love, it becomes enlightenment. Rules are unnecessary when following feelings; divinity is found through love for another soul. When we feel love, we understand it's not just a physical process. It's way more than that behind the closed doors of our hearts' realm.

Feeling the meaning behind the words and the empirical existence of divine love and God as a deity gives a sense of reality for divine love but not for God. We have been accustomed to love since birth, and accepting this perception as a deity or God is more manageable than accepting any other concept.

Someone asked:
'Do you believe in God?'
And my heart answered:
'God is Love, so yes, I believe in Love!'

Natural religion or any belief system should praise the divinity of Love instead of the idea of God, powers, heaven and hell and so on. The concept of God/Goddess as divinity occurs because divine love is reflected in our souls. Only a few blessed souls at the time saw the deity of love in existence beyond the concept of God.

Love is heaven and hell for the soul images that feel it. God is a dream, but love is a reality. Love is the feeling that everyone knows and pursues the whole life.

THE SHIELD OF LOVE

Always accept the love you feel because you might lose the chance of pure happiness.

Love is embedded in our DNA structure as the energy which sustains our existence. The heart is the only instrument that measures and feels this energy passing through our lives. We are born out of love; our soul is the reflection of divine love existence in itself. The whole existence of everything is divine love.

In religions, beliefs and practices, God is conceived as everything. God is in everything. Hence, the vision of God is Love. God becomes divine love, flowing and giving life to everything. God's concept can be denied because there is no proof of existence as described in religions or different beliefs. But the concept of divine love's existence as a deity can't be denied because everyone experiences love in some way.

That's why you fall in love: you see and feel with your soul's eyes the Goddess or God (divine love) in the beloved soul, hence in the adored soul image.

LOVING DIVINE LOVE – WHEN LOVE BECOMES GOD INSIDE

Most religions worship God due to a fear of punishment in this life or the next, for a promised heaven or a living hell for eternity.

Worshipping divine love as God/Goddess happens only because of the love feeling that burns our ego. Love becomes the master and the inner feeling to follow, do the right thing and spread love.

It leads finally to enlightenment when our inner Self becomes one with the feeling of love. And that feeling of love – loving divine love – just because, without reason or expectation, nor rewards or a better life, leads to awareness and consciousness of divine love's existence as a deity. A deity that doesn't punish or throw you to hell due to sins, nor rewards or promises heaven due to a righteous life. Love lived and accomplished in this life is more than an award or illusion of heaven. A life without love is more than hell in this existence.

Following and loving divine love gives the scent of divinity in a shallow life, connects with our soul, and frees up our inner Self from the chains of the mind. All we must do is not reject or postpone the feeling of love once it has settled in our hearts and run away for material or professional achievement.

Whether living as a saint or as a sinner, whatever we do, we do it with a heart full of love. And if a sinner, sins will be washed and burned due to the fire of love burning inside. And if saints, we will feel more humble and grateful for the gift of divine love that only gods and deities know its origins because it is their '*blood*'.

HUNGRY FOR LOVE

When hungry for love ... look up to the sky!
Whenever I feel hungry for love, I raise my eyes, looking up at the sky. And there it is, Her hiding in the form of clouds.
High on love ...
That's the feeling burning my heart while my soul dances on love clouds. It's like a symbiosis of clouds with my heart. When I'm not here anymore, I will most definitely miss seeing the clouds. Contemplating the clouds connects my soul to the entire existence, alternate realities and multiverses. What makes me happy lately are the clouds passing by on a boundless sky. It's the feeling of love pouring from the clouds above, and gosh ... some days, clouds have divine shadows.

Oh divine love, how beautiful it is in the moment when clouds pass by in the sky ... It's more beautiful and striking than anything in this shallow world.

It burns me sometimes how much I'm missing Her. There is no place left under my skin where her existence feels like a shrine of divine love connecting our souls beyond our limited Self.

> '*Nothing I say can explain to you, Divine Love.*
> *Yet all creation cannot seem to stop talking about it.*'
> '*I looked in temples, churches and mosques.*
> *But I found the Divine within my heart.*'
> **– Mewlana Jalaluddin Rumi**

WHILE MISSING HER

More than one year had passed since my thoughts and feelings started to escape in writing, and I missed Her in the depths of my heart.

While missing Her, I can feel the grass growing around me, the trees whispering notes of love passing through their leaves, and clouds moving along with my heart's feelings for Her. Every patch of nature is an ode to divine love for Her. All this time, I have been spreading my feelings from my heart to the land of Joseon, where my devotion was born.

While missing her soul, it feels like my whole existence is melting into whispers of love for Her.

One year and a half passed while missing Her ...

My mind sees her existence as a dream and accepts visions as possible alternate realities. My heart, though, feels the reality of our souls' connection over time and space, of unchanged feelings and hopeful visions of a life in the togetherness of our soul images. It's not a question of how and when, but more has already happened. Connect touch beyond our senses' reality, like in *Sense8* (a TV series by Wachowski).

Once again, divine love made my life a movie or a K-drama of surreal reality.

WHO AM I?

And Her answered:
> *'I am the silence between the words, the whisper of the wind through the leaves of the trees, the touch of the raindrops kissing the ground, the feeling in heart flutters. I am divine love that gave birth to all divinity and humanity since the creation of time and space. I am the God and Goddess of them all. I am the beginning and the end of all it is. There is nothing after Me and nothing before Me worth living for other than Love as absolute and infinite existence.'*

So 'Just Love Her' and let the enlightenment bless your soul.

That feeling of Seoul – Korea, feeling like home – has never left my soul since the connection between the Han River, Namsan Tower, and places where the touch of past lives and future or alternate realities felt deep in my heart. It's the feeling that I should feel for my native country – Romania – but instead, it feels like a foster home from the distant past.

My home is where my heart lives close to Her, hence the close connection with Korea.

If my soul lives where my heart dreams of, my Self feels the United Kingdom as home in my present reality.

Sleeping ... Sometimes, I spend fifteen to seventeen hours dreaming of countless past lives and alternate realities. In one of the dreams, it was a dream in a dream. I was dreaming something, one of the numerous lives of alternate realities, and suddenly, I was on a bus and became conscious of the landscapes around me, so colourful and natural alike. Due to bright colours and awareness of my Self in the dream, I believed it wasn't a dream due to real-life colours. I woke up when I just realised that I dreamt a dream of reality in another dream.

Once, I dreamt of snow ... So much snow ... Pure white everywhere ... Mountains of snow. Looking later for the snow's meaning, it meant a promotion in the workplace and more money. A few weeks later, the promotion came with more money in my pocket.

Well ... Coincidence or a glimpse of predestination?

If life would be only happiness for everyone and everything perfect, wouldn't it be boredom and no evolution?

With its imperfection, suffering, errors and quantum events, life looks randomly but entirely aligned for a future like puzzle pieces. Free choice is a fairy tale where we can chase happiness and a perfect life.

TECHNOLOGY AND THE ENLIGHTENMENT – FOR BETTER AND WORSE

> *'Any extremely advanced technology is indistinguishable from magic.'*
> **– Arthur C. Clarke**

Nowadays, only a few people can dedicate their lives to meditation, art, culture or working in the middle of a society that is not ready for it. Moreover, it isn't even the idea of the path to enlightenment for all its members in our civilisation. Many people are against technology, but I believe that in the future, it will make life easier for all soul images in search of enlightenment.

In the future, even androids or whatever AI technology will create to give birth to a singularity effect will have its soul. The soul takes any form of existence that provides a connection where it can express and live an authentic life, even through technology. In the future, we will also have to consider robots a form of life and protect it. Of course, it won't be easy.

If I would make a bet, technology is the only thing that could save us from destruction.

At the same time, it will be harder to reach enlightenment due to the abundance of information and the open doors to the unknown. The mind is now relatively easy to overwhelm because of events or phenomena of so-called miracles and magic. Anything that can't explain the results logically against all the odds passes the mind and reaches the awareness and consciousness of souls' existence. When all the powers and miracles happen due to advanced technologies, a veil that is difficult to see through will cloud the soul. The idea of God will become even more abstract and lose interest as more hidden forces become clear to our limited minds.

There will be, though, only one idea and experience – and this is love – that can pass the test of time and technology because its existence is not based on miracles but on everybody's life. Indeed, love is the only knowledge that will not perish or be undermined by technological discoveries. And it's only one step left to have its rightful place amongst Gods and creation, namely the awareness and consciousness of its divinity – the divine love.

COMMUNICATION THROUGH FEELINGS

Twin Flame Synchronicities are 'patterns in our lives' – 'unique signs' – beyond time and space for souls that are twin flames.

'Seeing the same time on the clock daily is known as synchronicity.'

No words are needed when souls communicate through heart feelings; this kind of communication happens with everything surrounding our existence.

Try directing feelings of love from your heart to any animal and see the magic happening. You don't need words to communicate, only feelings. Words are pointless because animals and nature talk only through raw divine love reflected in their existence.

너무 너무 보고 싶어 헤르 *(Neomu neomu bogo sipeo Her)*
– *I miss Her so so much …*

Missing Her became a constant mantra through these words – 너무 보고 싶어 *(Neomu bogo sipeo)* – healing my heart in times of happy sorrow.

Rule of three – synchronicity …
1. *Woke up missing Her so damn hard, looking at the clock 14:14 …*
2. *Sleeping again, woke up missing Her so damn hard, looking at the clock – 15:15 … God damn.*
3. *Fully awake doing some reading, also missing Her so damn hard, looking at the clock – 16:16. Oh, come on!*

Years passed, and the rule of three, of timing hours and minutes, keeps my memories of missing Her close to my mind and heart like a divine love prayer beyond time and space.

POETIC LOVE

'Poetry is divine love lost in translation!'
– **Raz Mihal**

Poetry is a pleasant way to compress so many feelings in a few words. That's why poetry, the same as human love, is underrated.

Most of the time, poets need help to make a living from their creativity. Only a handful of people are attracted to poetry, maybe because the language encodes a meaning hard to understand for so many souls addicted to their minds. Yet, poetry is the language of heart feelings.

Not all souls have the talent to express through poetry the beauty of love, the grandeur of nature, or the enlightened path for our souls. Some souls don't need words to describe the beauty inside their hearts. Everything around them changes through the scent of love thrown out by their enlightened souls. The problem is that only those close to them feel it. The words and wisdom of so many poets and writers filled the void inside the hearts of so many souls. They helped numerous hungry souls in search of the meaning of life and understanding the abyss inside their hearts.

The source of feelings is the same for poets and writers as for the saints, gurus and philosophers; while some souls need years of practice or a whole life to reach enlightenment, others are born with it and don't even know it. You don't ask a rose why that scent surrounds its existence; the same goes for the beauty of love expressed through words by poets and writers.

> *If Love isn't the effort you put in to show your feelings, what is it?*
> *'I could watch an infinite of sunsets, yet there will forever be something special about those reflected in her eyes.'*
> *'When the mind falls in love, it's temporary. When the heart falls in love, it lasts a lifetime. When the soul falls in love, it's eternal.'*
> *'A beautiful woman is the hell of the soul, the purgatory of the purse, and the paradise of the eyes.'*
> **– Fontenelle**

> *'The minute I heard my first love story, I started looking for you, not knowing how blind that was. Lovers don't finally meet somewhere. They're in each other all along.'*
> **– Rumi**

BLEEDING DIVINE LOVE THROUGH THE CRACKS OF MY SOUL

While balming in rivers of divine love flowing through my heart, these unworldly feelings are leaking through my mind, shattered thoughts, aware of its existence.

Our soul is pure and divine love. Love does not happen because of the environment or different factors but because of its awareness and consciousness. Love is already inside, one with our soul, so it occurs naturally, not because of other experiences.

When you become aware of love inside your heart, you become aware of your soul, too, even if you can't name it. That's why that emptiness inside searches for the unknown until love happens, raising awareness of our existence.

Lately, after existential chores are finished, my being is instantly covered in a cloud of meditation. All the noise surrounds me before my senses quiet, and my soul opens to the unseen world of natural feelings. Divine love starts pouring all around me in everything that surrounds my existence, whether material or spiritual. In these moments, the cracks in my soul heal, becoming one with divine love flowing through the whole existence. It does not need any position or awareness of divinity. It just connects to divine love flowing like a reflection in everything.

The Trinity of Divine Love disperses its logical borders, and nothing other than pure existence, which we call Love, flows aware of its existence as a divinity.

MANY FACES OF HER

Lurking like a shadow of time, Her is waiting, again and again, to be discovered and to share the existence of divine love as a divinity through different and many faces.

Past lives shared with Her over time have often been reflected in my dreams lately. At the beginning of revelations of her existence through hearts of love practice, I didn't experience it so much. Because of that, my sleep became the second life for my soul. While others complain of lack of sleep or nightmares, my dreams tell story after story, one more impressive than another. My sleep becomes a door to the unknown portals shadowing realities covering other alternate realities, mystical or an extent of reality.

Countless names covered its divinity deep inside the souls of revellers in search of its existence. Why blessed only my soul with the revelation of its name and existence? Or only I shared the feelings of her existence, otherwise lost in the nick of time itself, while others just lived close to her breath and never whispered the sound of divine love existence.

Her is the name given to the existence of divine love reflected in all souls. Through it, an invisible network of feelings so human but simultaneously out of this world connects. Gods whisper her name in the shadows of our existence. Since the beginning of time, we have been fighting for awareness and consciousness of her reflection in our souls.

> *'A human being is part of a whole, called by us the Universe, a part limited in time and space. He experiences himself, his thoughts and feelings, as something separated from the rest – a kind of optical delusion of his consciousness. This delusion is a kind of prison for us, restricting us to our personal desires and to affection for a few persons nearest us. Our task must be to free ourselves from this prison by widening our circles of compassion to embrace all living creatures and the whole of nature in its beauty.'*
> **– Albert Einstein**

> *'Love has no awareness of merit or demerit; it has no scale … Love loves; this is its nature.'*
> **– Howard Thurman**

LOVE FOR HER

'When I look into her eyes, I'm making love with her soul!'

It was one of those autumn days in September when I woke up sick... shivering through all my bones. Even so, work was calling me, so it didn't matter if I was ill.

At some point, I felt like passing out, and suddenly, when all my health systems were beeping with errors, the feeling of love for Her surfaced at the top of my heart. I pictured Her in my mind as being everywhere around me, and suddenly, my body was filling with energy like I was next to Her. Soon after, I wasn't sick, just full of love for Her.

After many years, Her is still the beacon of divine love flowing through the Universe. The love for Her heals my soul and destiny, bringing moments of connection with Her from this reality or other alternate realities.

I'm beside Her, admiring her existence and heavenly touch on my soul. Who needs a reality check when my inside love for Her is so real that I can't deny living it?

The same happens when praying – the feeling of accomplishment fulfils the heart. The impossible becomes possible.

The connection with Her happens instantly. I feel Her next to me, holding hands, walking down the Han River, touching our eyes with looks beyond this realm. Our souls whisper, shrouded in deep love, the sounds of future destinies and alternate realities.

In these moments, life becomes a mystical belief that Her is always by my side, no matter the reality or the physical connection.

인연 • (INYEON) – FATE OF LOVERS

The concept of fate between two persons over time is embedded in almost all cultures and scriptures all over the world in one way or another, so it's no wonder I found this concept in Korea as well and it's called 인연 – inyeon – fate.

What is different, though, is the concept of meeting the one not only as a choice but as a passing person going to the extreme just by touching their existence. Extrapolating the idea further, it isn't limited to the loved one but to any other environment and people surrounding our existence.

It's known that some people have more or less influence in our lives than others. To what extent can a touch or piece of advice make a significant impact or only have a specific influence on decisions or the way our lives go on?

It depends on too many variables.

The most advanced concepts or scriptures are considered the work of divinity – anything a human can't explain or understand. Still, with the advancement in AI technologies, the work of 'divinity' will no longer be a mystery, only a process we don't fully understand or acknowledge.

16 July 2023, 4 am – I woke up in the morning, and after so many years in love with Her and the Korean connection, I still find new things and concepts with deep meanings in my soul. Randomly, I learned about the idea of fate between two lovers destined to last over years and past lives.

Last night's dream is the first in the series of my unbelievable dreams of possible past and alternate lives connecting my soul.

I dreamt that I was a middle-aged black woman with some body weight doing some paperwork, and suddenly, a fire broke up after throwing a cigarette butt in the bin.

Remembering the details after the dream was so fuzzy, but the character played was so interesting, and I knew that I had to put it in writing just as a reminder for myself that my dreams are out of this world.

INSPIRING MOVIE: PAST LIVES (2023) – directed by Celine Song

AVATARS ... IN OUR LIVES

When we pray, it's easier to do it to an image representation that would help our imagination and feelings reach a higher state of consciousness.

This is happening at the beginning of the journey. In time, the representation becomes one with the feeling inside; in the end, only the reflection behind the feeling is left.

Looking closely at all the representations, religions and beliefs in the background, a story with a life of miracles is more or less attractive. And everywhere is promulgated the dream and idea of free choice, although the stories tell the opposite. It's detailed through the story of Jesus when he foresaw his death and, for a moment, wanted a different fate but understood it was impossible because that's how it's written.

Since birth, our free choice has been given to the lucky ones, and it looks nice, but it is still an exciting story to believe in.

In the past, I always believed that the masters from my life were the women that divine love or fate – InYeon – chose to cover its existence in this world. In every period, a master chosen through divine love guided me on every step away. I thought that my skills and divine love consented in my mind and heart were the inception of divine love existence as an entity itself in my existence. But now that I have finally met Her in my body, it proves that every master image-sharing love with me is special.

The further away on the path, the more advanced and unique the connection is within fate. I have never felt we loved more than when my 선생님 (seonsaengnim – teacher) – Her – spread her love around me. For the first time, I had a vision – premonition – while being with Her. I was watching a movie with Her. When the vision at the beginning of the movie started, it suddenly passed in front of my eyes as a dream already happened, a vision of Her leaving the film because Her did not feel well or like it. The reasons and how it occurred were unimportant because I didn't believe it at the moment of the vision. I thought it was just the imagination, but when it happened after roughly two hours, I started to believe that our connection was more than it seemed.

Sometimes, I fall out of acting through pure love for Her and behave like any egoist human being, thinking first of their feelings and accomplishments and not thinking about the other.

This means that the sense of divine love is not taking the lead and acting as an unbeliever, not trusting fully the power of divine love, hence the feeling of 'Just Love Her'.

Ultimately, we are just players in 'the game of life', and what's bound to happen will happen with or without our will. To see what will occur or have premonitions only means that we were observers, not avatars playing a role for some moments.

THE MASK OF HER

Divine love is like a flower that attracts butterflies and bees to it. If you are hungry, you feed on it – it's always there awaiting you. It won't run after you and will never ask you to give something in return so you can taste Her and fulfil your hunger without any strings attached. That's the divinity of its existence – always giving and never asking for something in return. It's your problem if you want to feel it or not. When you sense her perfume, her existence inside, accept it and don't reject it. Reject the image that gives you suffering but never the love inside. It will find you another image worthy of feelings of love. And if your destiny does not allow you to taste heaven with another being's image, at least your heart is filled with the blood of the angels.

When you feel that love is trying to evolve into divine love, feel it and share it, but don't ask for anything in return. That's the shortest way to happiness and accomplishment in this life – feel and share love inside with anyone and everything without thoughts, expectations or desire.

The mask hiding Her is only your mind expecting something in return. When you throw away the mask – your mind, the heart vibrations will resonate with the existence surrounding you. Even if you are on a rock or in the pit of oblivion, your feelings of divine love will be like a mirror inside and around your existence. That's the power of divine love – from nothingness, happiness is born.

The only requirement for reaching and feeling divine love is to consent to its existence, and when love touches your existence, acknowledge its divinity source. Let the feeling of love attain higher and higher vibrations until your whole being is bathed in love – and you become pure love – divine love. The road is not easy, and there will be many obstacles, but remember that the only real impediment is your shallow mind.

That's how my love for Her became a ritual. I was fortunate enough to bathe in divine love; in this way, her soul image became Her – the image of divine love. I call this love religion. Instead of choosing an image imposed by religions or dogma, I decided on the soul image revealed through divine love, melting my heart and existence. And I decided on other soul images a few times – the only thing is the same – the divine love inside.

The only difference between the soul image of Her and other image representations is that I am more awakened than ever. Because I have felt Her for so many years and have not been rejected by her soul image, although I have no real connection in this realm, I tend to believe the visions and dreams of past lives and alternate realities related to Her.

The mask of Her was thrown away from my shallow mind; now, divine love revealed her soul image to my heart shrine. Her soul image became one with Her – the divine love existence.

SEE BEYOND THE WORLD

One would think of more ways of reaching the spirit, acquiescing through deities, prayers and rituals and cherishing anything that does not require intellect.

Others would use intelligence, curiosity and research to learn and reach the spirit, acquiescing and cherishing knowledge and intellect more than anything else.

The ultimate accomplishment above a mind that cherishes intelligence and religiousness is intuition – and we are born with – it's only hidden deep inside our souls. Some are born aware of and use it, while others need years and sometimes lives to glimpse it.

One thing is sure – our mind has all the tools and means to consent to the spirit realm's existence and experience the so-called divinity.

I said 'the so-called divinity' because once you start to learn and experience the hidden world behind your human eyes, nothing seems extraordinary or out of this world. It just becomes routine. One powerful tool is our inner eye – a part of the inner world and so-called powers available to anyone, either awakened or asleep.

The energy of love stays dormant and is awakened when our attention is drawn toward its existence. We can consent to a detail or event without knowing its existence inside. When aroused, we might think it was outside of us or just born, but divine love is always within, awaiting an observer to acknowledge its existence. Did you notice that in the beginning, we are deeply bathed in its existence, and nothing else matters?

It becomes a part of us over time, and we forget about its existence until we are awakened again. Hence, the story of keeping the candle always burning. In this way, the observer within becomes one with divine love; this way, our attention is connected with its existence.

There are three stages of connection with Her as a shadow of divine love presence:

1. *The first stage is when you are close to a loved one's existence. You can feel and see them as being present in events surrounding their existence.*
2. *The second stage is connecting to a loved one's existence. You can feel and perceive their feelings and experiences as being yours.*
3. *The third stage feels like one with shared feelings and existence. Two beings are connected as one with two minds.*

The experience of connection with divine love's existence and its influence over our destiny happens when we feel divine love inside in search of a soulmate. In those moments, we should allow it to lead us through existence and connect with other souls while we are aware of and consenting to the existence of divine love as a deity.

POOL OF SOULS – THE EXISTENTIAL VOID

Deep from the hollow of the unknown and incomprehensible quantum creation of life itself, souls are coming and going intertwined.

If you had the vision of seers centuries ago, you would be able to see the pool of souls born and leaving life as a continuum show of life and death. There is no death as we know and understand it – only life and energy going from one stage to another. Imagine a pool of sparks going in and out at an atomic level. From one void to another – that's what we are in the deep, existential void.

The existential void is the core of our souls, shaping energy and vibration into existential form. Our fate and personality are shaped and written in DNA, so free choice is a dream until the next rebirth.

The timeline marks our existence in the void and continuous rebirth or reincarnation. If you remove time from the equation of the existence of souls, only the existential void is left. Hence, the saying that we are Gods is not through our physical bodies but the core of our souls – the existential void.

Going further into the composition of an existential void, we find that the reflection of divine love's existence creates it. It's the surrender of divine love, perceiving its existence through our souls. The existential void comprises three elements: divine love energy, a reflection of its existence, and an observer who consents to this process. Hence, the trinity is declared in our world's significant religions or beliefs.

Due to the compositions of our souls, we connect with the whole existence, which is created in the same way but without the observer element. That's why, looking back on the horrors and suffering that have occurred since the birth of physical beings, they are only a drop in the ocean of existence itself. And nothing seems daunting to the big picture of divinity creation extending to the infinite.

Only a line of time created the evolution of our existence from the past to the future. Evolution can't happen without suffering and failure while dreaming of happiness. Happiness is the very existence of our souls – the existential void. That's why we search to understand our existence and our reason to exist. Once we approve the divine love, we instantly feel the existence of our souls and the divinity of our existence because we have discovered the element that is the source of all creation.

Unhappy with the image representation of my Self, I always said that my soul was in a hurry to reincarnate and chose the first avatar available. The look doesn't matter too much, but the wrecking brain does. It could have been more thoughtful and with a better memory, but it is what it is.

CHAINS OF DESTINY – FEARS

You lost your mind ...

It happens when something is bound to happen. You take all the precautions and measures to safeguard any deviations or unforeseen events that might affect your destiny or others' paths. And in the end, after it's happening, you start questioning your free choice – your sanity.

It could be your fate that made this step necessary. It might also be the fate of others involved if it must occur, affecting their life choices or suffering. Nevertheless, when an event must happen, your mind at that moment will blackout, leading to an unfortunate fate. It might help to pray for this event to be bearable without too much agony or changes in your destiny. Sometimes, it could guide us to something good, but most of the time, it has a negative effect.

It's all about fear inside; living it without safeguards would lead to insane actions in someone's life and destiny. Safeguards could be continuous attention to details or events occurring at any moment in your life. Or it could be total reclusion and inaction, acting like an observer in your life.

A good tool for always being aware is praying with a heart mantra – repeating the exact words with feelings in your heart – directed to a higher being representing God or divinity. But anything could bring joy and awareness to your heart and mind – the more powerful feelings, the better.

This fear is described very well in religions and beliefs. Because this quantum event seems to happen randomly and out of our control, only divinity and God might seem to prevent these unfortunate events … in theory. In practice, it doesn't matter – the misery, suffering and gruesome events that must happen don't take sides. That's why it's always a pleasure for atheists when tragic events occur to kids or people who live their lives like saints. In this way, God becomes only an idea; otherwise, why does it happen?

In society, fear is like food for the soul. Without fearing and paying attention to our actions, life would be chaos. Anyway, it seems like that.

Due to fear, religion and beliefs have been created since the dawn of human existence.

Fear is reasonable until some point, but it isn't good when it becomes sickness.

Nowadays, everything leads to fear of the destruction of our very existence. It has been like that since the beginning of creation, and it will probably continue until the end – if there is any at all.

In occultism, fear plays a significant role due to the emotions needed to make a step outside of the safe zone and jump into the unknown. Practice and illustrations are always based on the fight between good and evil gods and demons, positive and negative energies. This is also true in religions – it initiates and controls believers choosing a path to divinity worship. But in advanced practice – esoteric knowledge – where the energies and divinity are typical and not untouchable, as they are for novices, fear is only a game for fools.

The most frightening fear is in love relationships. It's not about the heart but mainly about the mind, which worries and fears losing a loved one for many reasons – most of which are created by fear. That's why so many lovers create a hellish world for each other, even though they know love is always there. Instead of living in love and being happy together, they create games of trust or jealousy, or else, it has been said, only to make it spicier. Nothing further than the truth. Love is not a game; feelings are not a game – only people who are not so sure about their feelings and do not trust in the power of love act like that. Of course, love becomes suffering when feelings of love are not shared, but love doesn't mean owning the other one but fulfilling and making a better person the loved one. In this process, you also become better and further accomplish the path to enlightenment.

Fear disappears when love becomes God, Goddess, or any representation of divinity, energies, or power above all else. Nothing withstands when you become one with love, consenting to its divinity origins.

LIVE ONCE, DIE TWICE!

Dying twice does not mean destroying your body. It means to kill metaphorically your mind – to stop forever its nonsensical running wild thoughts.

This is done by believing in concepts and following practices beyond the mind's logic. Strong heart feelings of love lead the mind to follow the heart, hence intuition. The mind's running wild thoughts won't stop, but they will become quieter until the inner ear is deaf to their noise. The mind is gone in that silence, and the soul's light is born or acquiesced because it was always there. Then, a new mind and personality are reborn. It will build everything from the ground up, creating new ideas, concepts and views and improving old thinking or erasing troubling thoughts.

Sometimes, I feel like a stranger in this world. I am here with my body, but my mind and heart are in another unseen world. In times like these, praying is all that matters because it keeps me connected to what's happening around me. It's like being dead and conscious while still breathing, reminding me I am alive yet. But death doesn't scare me anymore, being only a point in time when my body will leave this world.

I realised why I miss Seoul so much. It's because of Her that I searched for the physical body to be with for the rest of my life, or maybe it's just a dream. It's a search-and-found beyond time and space – certainly beyond our limited bodies and minds.

I also realised that when the feelings inside are out of this realm, it's because of the return on investment – the more intense and divine love consents to a person or anything, for that matter, the more powerful and intense they come back to you. Only the limits of our body can withstand it. That's why sharing and practising the practice of hearts of love is so important. Without it, a mind and body are without defence and can be overwhelmed by the sheer amount of love energy flowing through the centre of the point of entry for energies.

> *When you love, you are at the mercy of the loved one. If you are lucky and your loved one is open-hearted and can't live without being with you, then life is only happiness. If not, and the loved one is closed to sharing their feelings or openly communicating about their daily life, your life will be full of joy and sorrow.*
>
> *What can you do?*
>
> *Just love them!*
>
> *The logic is that everyone is mature enough to decide what is best for their life.*
>
> *Freedom means trusting the choices the loved one makes, whether good or bad and must be accepted like a family member. When a family member does not love you back or with the same intensity, you don't give up on them or ghost them. Because it's part of your life, whether you like it or not, the mindset with the loved one should be the same. No matter what, love them. And maybe they will always find an open door to your soul after being lost in the strings of destiny. But if you close the door, how can they find the door if it's locked and there's no light to see it?*

'Just Love Her' is a belief based on the 'Hearts of Love' concept. It doesn't matter if you are loved or not, if feelings are shared or not – consider the loved one as a family, and no matter what, don't fall out of love due to anything. This way, worries and the never-ending thoughts of your mind, questioning what you feel, how and how much you think, or how the other side feels, are silenced. Only follow your heart and believe in divine love and InYeon (the fate of lovers being connected beyond time and space).

You can't run from what is bound to happen, but it helps the mindset enforced through the feelings of love from the heart. The stronger your feelings and acquiescing divinity of love, the more helpful it will be to pass through any suffering or challenges fate brings forward. Enjoy the moments with the loved one as if they were the last moment, and in this way, realise how important and unique these moments of love are shared through divine love between souls and bodies.

Love is beautiful, unique and sublime. It is out of this world when it happens with the right person, a unique soul, a soulmate. Love is divine when awakened on both sides and shared at full throttle, acknowledging its divinity.

PRIMITIVE MIND – PERSONIFICATION OF ENERGIES AND LOVE

Four mental stages correspond to divine love, awareness and consciousness:
1. *The first one, related to primal instinct, raw sexual energy, is the* **primitive mind**.
2. *The second one is the* **intelligent mind**, *related to love as we know it in human form.*
3. *The third one is the* **intuitive mind**, *related to love awareness and consciousness of its existence as divinity.*
4. *The last one is the* **divine mind**, *related to becoming one with the divine love feeling, with the God/Goddess in our hearts and souls.*

THE PERSONIFICATION OF ENERGIES AND LOVE

There are two levels of acquiescing and worshipping divine love – one for novices (primitive mind) and one for initiates (intelligent mind).

Whereas a primitive mind sees rituals and forms for the entries involved in inexplicable occurring events, an intuitive mind searches and explains the mysteries through science and experiments, going deep into the rabbit hole of our existence.

When these two minds converge, something beautiful is born as human nature as we know it. The mystery exists and wonders the mind, but simultaneously, the truth is revealed to the heart and mind behind closed doors of existence and the energies involved.

You know that billions of planets, universes and galaxies exist, almost an infinite number for our limited mind, but your mind and heart are amazed and humbled in the face of the powers and energies of creation. However, while one can't see further than the ritual, the other understands and witnesses the energy in action.

PRIMITIVE MIND

Do you remember or know the scene where Cypher from *The Matrix* movie said:

'You know, I know this steak doesn't exist. I know that when I put it in my mouth, the Matrix is telling my brain that it is juicy and delicious. After nine years, you know what I realise?'
[Takes a bite of steak]
'Ignorance is bliss.'

That's precisely how the primitive mind works – the feeling that ignorance is bliss!

When you do that, you are praying, and the feeling is heavenly, like all the angels listening to your prayers and running away to accomplish your wishes entrusted to God by your powerful feelings. The more powerful and dedicated your prayers, the sooner and faster your requests are listened to.

In this stage, the dark is not the absence of light but pure evil, hell and dark forces. Your imagination is abundant with symbols and illustrations of evil and dark forces born out of fears and ignorance of the unknown divine realm. And how else could you perceive and make sense of other realms outside your limited body, mind and perception?

Your senses are not developed or trained to understand and use the powers and 'devices' hidden deep inside our so-called limited existence. Sexual energy is in its raw state, and feelings are based on impulse and without control, like being moonstruck.

Once you start training, opening the hidden doors, and unlocking access to these unseen 'devices' in your body, mind and soul, a new world like magic opens behind your inner eyes and senses. Like Alice started the journey to Wonderland or Neo pulled out the veil of reality ... Imagination is still a reality, no less.

INTELLIGENCE MIND

As the love energy in the primitive mind state is asleep in its raw state, the intelligent mind starts to awaken the love energy.

In this state, the unknown is challenging to discover or find the answers behind the events or mysterious phenomena. An intelligent and educated person will only accept beliefs or religions if they question everything that defies logic and common sense.

Curiosity is the root of intelligence. The code and laws behind existence are like religions and beliefs for primitive minds. Evolution starts with the very existence of intelligence.

INTUITIVE MIND

Whereas the primitive mind and intelligent mind have the same root of unawakened love energy in the raw state, the intuitive mind is driven by awakened love energy, although not consented to at the beginning.

An intuitive mind becomes one with religions and beliefs, laws and physics. It sees the connections between them without searching for or questioning their existence.

The intuitive mind is the root of all minds and is sometimes called illumination because a living white light is perceived when it reaches this state of mind.

Only a few are born with its awareness or raw state, not knowing the root of their mind state. Although inherent in our existence, most of us struggle to reach it through practice, but it happens only randomly, never a sure thing, and sometimes lives pass without touching it or never happening.

An analogy of stages of mind would be like glasses on your nose but unaware of their existence. Primitive and intelligent minds will never consent to the existence of glasses due to their nature. But the intuitive mind will always know about existing glasses on their nose, even if they can't explain it. And the divine mind goes beyond the limits of the glasses' existence, becoming one with the glasses.

DIVINE MIND

This stage of mind is at the root of our existence and all creation, for that matter. It's the awareness of its existence when it first started creating existence and the universe we know.

From the existing void, the divine mind created itself by being aware of the events, observer and physical realm created. That's why we exist in everything, identify with everything, and become everything.

At the existence level, all that exists is divinity through the divine mind that created and sustains everything. This is mainly observed in the quantum mechanics field, where everything seems random and unpredictable but simultaneously connected, exists in multiple states, and is affected when one becomes aware of its state existence or is only observed.

The existential void used to create everything from divinity to the physical world is at its source, pure divine love energy – existential love. That's why concepts, theories, religions, physical laws and even the idea of God are above everything else.

It's only a concept that has been said here, but in time, it will prove itself through research going deeper and deeper into the rabbit hole of the quantum physics realm through its foundation – quantum mechanics.

ZEN STATE OF LOVE

Empty mind ... No cloud of thoughts ... Nothingness.

There is only pure love inside, for nothingness. That's how you know the existence of love inside your heart – a love out of this world, a divine love.

And out of this nothingness feeling, Her was born in my mind and heart.

In the beginning, I thought, only for a short time. Then, it was for aeons of past lives and alternate realities of the multiverse.

A warm feeling spread through my whole body while I dreamed of Her, eyes wide open, feeling love. A zen state of divine love.

It's not an empty mind if feelings of love for Her are all over the mind's sky. It's only weird that feelings do not transpose into words for the mind to consent to divine love's existence.

For three years, I have celebrated her existence or acknowledged that Her is the face of divine love inside my heart and soul. I think I met Her on the shores of 'ocean' existence around the end of May. Since then, my existence has become nothingness while worshipping Her.

GRACE OF GOD (OF DIVINE LOVE)

In the religion I was born with (Orthodox Christianity), it is said that sometimes the grace from God leaves the soul, whether it is a sinner or a saint, which is related to different connotations.

After so many years of divine love experience (more than thirty years), I can undoubtedly affirm that grace from God never leaves you when divine love feeling is a sanctuary in your heart, whether you are a sinner or a saint. Walking or standing, your mind translates the feelings inside, becoming numb to the environment surrounding your existence.

Like in the movie *The Matrix*, the code behind existence is revealed to your soul through feelings, wiring your mind to love flowing through existence, feeding the reality hiding in the centre.

Be a sinner or saint full of love – it's all you need always to feel God's grace – divine love.

THE SENSE OF GREATNESS

In some moments, the feeling of divine love inside makes us aware of connections between souls and existence on this planet. In those moments, the sense of greatness fills our hearts and minds.

In the beginning, our beings seem touched by divinity, like being gods ourselves. Then, as the mind gets used to the insanity sense of love, the real-world understanding behind our senses is revealed, shredding the cloud of thoughts. It's not our being that is divine but the love flowing and touching our existence, burning our hearts with a sense of greatness.

It means that we all are gods born out of divine love – the energy that creates the reality of our existence from nothingness, from the existential void. Hence, the biblical saying that although we are gods, we still worship idols.

LOVE IS GOD

GOD IS LOVE = LOVE IS GOD

The equation of Love written in our hearts and souls could be deciphered only in these times and understood by anyone who had a glimpse of human love.

There is One True Love – the divine love – covered with layer after layer and rules as it goes to the surface of existence inside our hearts. There's no difference between divine love and human love, like an onion layer. It needs both to create the divinity of its existence.

Yet no one sees its divinity, that 'Love is God' and not vice versa. The expression 'God is Love' was necessary in the past because nobody taught humankind to accept its raw existence.

All desires make use of love energy hidden in our hearts and souls. When desires are overthrown and only love acknowledged and cherished, the universe opens its secret doors to our existence. An empty mind of thoughts with a heart full of love, acquiescing love divinity, can see the time and space line as an observer.

'God is Love' is a statement before achieving enlightenment. After becoming enlightened, the statement transforms into 'Love is God'. The divinity realm will no longer be a mystery, with divine love feeling inside.

Divine love is a subtle energy that created everything and has sustained all creation since the beginning. There are numerous stages of divine love's existence, but four stages are fundamental to all others:

1. *The first one is raw energy reflected in sex and desire. Consciousness and awareness are dormant.*
2. *The second one is when love between two souls is above any desire, and raw energy evolves, achieving awareness and consciousness of love feeling existence.*
3. *The third is when pure souls become aware that divine love exists as a deity. Any representation of its existence born out of feelings of love inside will be suitable.*
4. *The fourth one is when beloved souls overcome their bodies and connect through the pure feeling of divine love. Divine love acquiesces its existence in both souls, its reflection awareness as a deity, and its presence as a deity.*

Every stage is divided into an infinite representation of divine love reflection.

When you become one with divine love, your feelings for your beloved soul image are like in the biblical adoration of God:

'God's love: it is never-ending and unconditional; he loves us even in our darkest times.'

Love is like a fire burning inside our hearts. Always waiting for the reflection of divine love awareness in our mind.

There are times of silence, but that doesn't mean that love is gone; it is just dormant, awaiting consent to its divine existence. That's why awareness and consciousness of its divinity, acknowledging it as a deity, and always being awake to keep the connection with its existence through our beloved soul image revealed in our heart are so important. Just keep the fire burning once the fire of love is lit in your heart by the beloved soul image revealed through divine love.

Love without awareness and consciousness of its divinity existence in itself can be unbearable for the untrained mind, leading to insanity – the so-called insanity of love. Some fools could believe that God is answering and accomplishing any of their desires due to divine love pouring like a river through their hearts. They could think that the person revealed in their heart by divine love must obey or accept their love equally. Or anything they dream of should be in reality as well. The feeling of love and sensing its divinity should be more than enough for a soul. Anything else is not imposed, wanted or treated like a desire. If there is a destiny with the loved one, so be it. If not, love itself is more than enough. That's the mindset behind 'Just Love Her'.

Practising the mantra of heart prayer can help one stay on the right track to enlightenment, which is being one with divine love.

The feeling of burning love is like a boomerang. For some moments, because the mind can't bear the warmness of love anymore, it seems like the feeling is gone or quiet. And suddenly, the fire is there again as it never left your heart, to begin with, only your mind tried to forget about it or to ignore it. And in those moments when you throw all your being in the fire of love, it burns all your mind's existence. Only your soul exists, cuddled at the divine love sanctuary.

Your beloved soul image revealed in your heart becomes the face of divine love, your deity. *Love becomes your God/Goddess.*

LOVE RELIGION

'Love Religion' is not a religion per se but rather a system of belief beyond the creation of religions – all religions or divinity, for that matter.

In this mindset, the energy and vibration at the deepest level inside matter are also included, following the recent discoveries in the quantum field of physics. And if you read all the scriptures in this world – the oldest and the newest – it reveals its existence as described in science in a language of noobie versus advanced practitioner of science, like *tomato* tomato or *potato* potato.

Most people, through their parents, choose a religion or a system of belief from birth, and only a few question what their hearts want. Due to advances in technology and education systems, and nowadays access to almost everything in an instant through the internet, many people choose atheism or question the existence of God. Hence, religion is nonsense.

Understandably, as a scientist or science enthusiast looking at the universe's and nature's marvels, you might wonder how to compress the infinite to a few rules and beliefs. It makes no sense to believe in salvation from a fellow human born thousands of years ago or just a few centuries ago, and even more so to believe in some absolute and infinite power unseen and unproven through science or personal experience accessible to everyone. And still, stories and systems of beliefs were created aeons ago for humankind to choose from and believe in. I said aeons because following science, meaning what is proven and tested already, especially in the quantum field, it makes sense to think that we are not the first civilisation nor the only one in the billions of galaxies surrounding our existence.

What amazes me is the fact that most scientists believe in a force, but not when it is called God, or they don't believe there is something like a God in our existence. Well, most of them started studying the quantum realm. It's impossible not to be amazed and mesmerised by the seemingly impossible and incomprehensible bending of physics laws going deep into the rabbit hole of matter and energy centres. It is difficult to understand and accept that this field involves studying advanced concepts and beliefs about the origins of religions and the idea of God because there is seemingly no common ground until a human being starts experiencing love.

It is only a feeling, but once you advance and experience a higher state of love, like infinite and absolute love – or simply divine love – everything you encounter and any information around your existence starts to make sense through love. Quantum physics becomes like esoteric information and testing the blood of God, and hence of the whole existence.

In my view and experience, 'Love is God', can be applied to everything seen or unseen. Love is beyond the idea of God and divinity. And to be fair, God sounds too masculine, although it has been said that it is not masculine nor feminine at its origins. Love sounds too feminine, although it is not one nor the other but both and even more.

Drawing a final line, the energy or force behind the existence of the concept of love with absolute and infinite characteristics is at the origins and inside all the existence or nonexistence (although there is still an existence of something that is the opposite of existence – antimatter?!).

I called it Love Religion because why not?

If there is a religion for God, even more there should be one for the existence of Love. And God won't be against its creation and hence its existence.

Love flows through everything and animates the whole existence. It can't be understood or proved through any instruments – not yet. But it can be felt through our hearts and going further, allowing it to reveal its divine existence without borders, giving up our limited minds and choosing our bottomless hearts. That's why the scriptures say that deities are jealous of our existence. If you have been created with the awareness of divine love since birth or the creation of the universe, it's hard to experience the mystic feeling humans feel.

As weird and unbelievable as it may appear, deities are limited more than our inner selves – called souls. Due to the nature of their creation, there is a limit to their absolute and infinite existence, but not ours. Well, we are born and die – some scripture says for aeons, others only once (it makes no sense, only one life) – but our experiences, even the simplest ones, are mystical and shrouded in mystery.

Experiencing divine love is like waking up from a dream of sometimes aeons of ignorance. It will be like Cypher from *The Matrix* for some who didn't accept love but are still awakened. They would think it was far better before when not awakened but forget that they rejected what awakened their soul instead.

Ignorance is bliss when awakened but unknowingly not rejecting divine love. It is inside of you awaiting, and due to ignorance, you believe it's rejecting you, but you wouldn't know nor feel the love if it would leave you. The real obstacle is your mind believing whatever nonsense is thrown at it. But if the heart is opened, the mind no longer matters – follow your heart.

Most of us exist mainly through our minds, and our hearts live in the shadow of them. Intelligence seems to be due to advanced logic, but intuition beyond intelligence is due to your heart. Well, we are symbolically speaking.

Those who open their hearts and have an advanced 'computer' mind are at the forefront of advanced discoveries beyond imagination. How else was something far from the touching reality discovered dozens and even hundreds of years ago?

Although love is a simple feeling, your whole life reaches another level when you accept it sincerely and approve of its divinity. It doesn't matter anymore – life or death, happiness or suffering, everything becomes love at once. This way could be described as the life of Christian saints who died in horrifying ways. They became one with divine love, so nothing mattered more than love. But there is also the other extreme, where mystics experienced divine love like ecstasy. They were one with love, but instead of suffering from it, they celebrated through joy.

Love Religion is about the personification of divine love. Instead of God as a deity, divine love represents the source of all things and existence, even deities, hence God.

Love is a feeling known to almost everyone in different forms, so it's easier to understand and consent to the existence of divine love as a deity who created and sustains it. This way, it's about something other than a power that you must believe in without proof.

Love is already natural – a feeling that creates monsters or saints. It is a step further to feel its divinity energy source and acknowledge it as a deity.

And what other power representation out there could be more beautiful and make a lot more sense?

DIVINE LOVE – THE ABSOLUTE AND INFINITE EXISTENCE

Love energy's absolute and infinite existence is in the form of divine love.

Love has no limit or end, and it exists in us without our awareness. Most of the time, rejection of love leads to other twisted feelings born from running away from it. These new twisted feelings are born using the energy of love. That's why it has been said that the dark is the absence of light – there is no dark out there.

What's the most certain thing in the whole existence?

It's death – the absence of life. Without life, there is no death. But everything is created to die and be reborn or transformed into energy.

So, better choose love in your life and recognise it as its actual existence – divine love – the infinite and absolute existence of love as we know it. Its power is beyond everything that exists, seen or unseen, in creation.

If you are not doing anything but meditating all the time, your body needs to be taken care of. Doing nothing but existing while feeling love spreads the perfume of love, but someone else must take care of the body in deep meditation. In those moments, the body is in this world, but the mind and heart are in divine love.

That's why the masters and teachers in olden times and even now at monasteries have disciples caring for their bodies. Sometimes, fake masters use the beliefs of their disciples to fool and profit from their weak personalities. The same thing happens with political or authoritarian leaders of the world from the past to the future.

When choosing with the heart, it's the highest level of connection. A connection that endures in time because the heart is the centre and the tool that we use for a love connection. This connection between this world and the unseen world of so-called divinity is deep inside us without knowing or being aware of it. The other tools or powers are also dormant, awaiting to be awakened. All the powers described in the old scriptures are within us, hence the calling that we are gods and have free choice. Or at least the illusions of these.

Feelings of love are never random, even if they seem so, and that's why InYeon happens for a reason. The person chosen within your heart was given a long time ago, since birth and even before the idea of creation.

It's been said that only one soulmate could connect all life, but according to the scriptures, we are immortal gods, and it's possible at the quantum level to have more options than one. But only one of these options could connect and lead to the oneness.

A world without love is a world doomed to fail. Look at the past when the rule of the so-called God with laws in the first place was full of hatred, wars and destruction, killing their kids to prove their so-called love for God.

And look at the world after love was ruling through the heart when people started following their feelings through their hearts and not their minds. The world has advanced to the levels seen today where freedom of choice seems attainable – a sure way to value life and the future through love.

Love brings happiness to the rich and the poor alike. You can live in misery, poor conditions or without anything and still be happy living a life full of love. You can be filthy rich and have everything, but you will never be happy without love. Love is simple but, at the same time, a luxury of life.

Hearts of Love (my first book, published in 1999 in Romania) is a vision about mystic belief and practice based on the most known powerful feeling to humans – love – and the force behind it – divine love.

Love is above the concept of God because it's the only thing that makes us humans. Yes, reasoning is also a key, but without feelings of love, we would be only robots, or else not having humanity is a different kind of being.

Love is inherent in our core and a given place. The AI programs probably lack this feeling to be the follower of our existence and help us reach the next level of our existence.

May the Love be with you!

MEMORIES OF MY 'SELF'

PAST LIVES AND ALTERNATE REALITIES INSIDE DREAMS AND VISIONS

A few years ago, dreams were not like common dreams. And since there are so many and they are full of feelings at different times and places ... it resembles memories from past lives.

Some stories from my dreams echo when waking up; others are lost in the pit of memories washed away. All kinds of characters played at the time, from children to adults, mostly failed to see my face but identified as the person acting in the leading role. All genders felt as if they existed in most of the glimpses of moments out of this world.

Often, dreams played longer and longer without any desire to wake up, afraid of dispersing the fog of stories behind the play. I happened to sleep once almost a full day, with a short wake-up every few hours.

Sleeping became like a meditation, touching and visiting realms and memories of the past and future. Maybe I should write it down as soon as I wake up and remember parts of the dream, which could become exciting novels.

Dreams are our virtual reality, but they have many more connections with unseen worlds and memories and are so captivating that we don't realise they're dreams. Those moments while sleeping are another page of our reality. Sometimes, they are accurate and mind-bending due to the surrounding landscapes and imagination surpassing our reality. In the future, technology will probably use the part of the brain that handles the creation of dreams.

Dreams are a lot more interesting than visions. You are aware of reality in visions, and it takes no brain to understand that facts will never be the same. In dreams, you forget entirely about your existence; it's very close to reality, as an experience and story unleashed. You have no control over your dream or influence; it just happens, while in visions, many factors can influence the level and events shown.

I had only two dreams with Her while in Seoul, but they seemed so natural that I felt sad when reality hit me when I woke up. On the other hand, there are too many visions. I had many visions of Her that became a part of my soul, although nothing suggests a connection with her soul image in reality.

Visions are not imaginations because they don't happen through desire or volition. They appear precisely as dreams, but when one is not sleeping.

FROM DREAMS AND VISIONS

I had too many dreams in which I didn't see myself; I was just a reflection of my existence. In one of them, I even invented some weird liquid metal while being a chemistry scientist.

Every time before a dream with meaning and alternate reality, my mind becomes empty and ready to take off in the land of visions. My eyes fall, drawing the curtains over reality and sleep overtaking my soul back to its realms.

One good thing you can do for the past is to shroud it in love, so much love that it burns any sins, errors or remorse for the actions of your old Self. You can do the same thing for the future or alternate realities. And you are living in eternal love in the present; wash away the thin line that separates past and future, a line drawn by your limited mind and erased with your loving heart.

On one of the nights, my dream related to an old one from a past storyline. While dreaming, I wasn't aware that it was just a dream. It was so real, and as soon as I woke up, I felt something beyond my mind related to the soul which filled my heart.

So that strengthens the belief that many dreams connect to past lives or alternative universes.

One dream happened to be the weirdest of all – I dreamed

that I was dreaming – a dream yielded another dream. The action is often foggy, and details as I wake up, hardly remembering.

Only once did I see in the mirror the face of my persona acting in my dream. I even remembered the name upon waking – Alejandro. A young man was pictured in the mirror with a weird feeling that it was my alter ego, but no less than a stranger.

Once, for the first time, I dreamed that I had a child, a beautiful blonde curly-haired girl, and I felt the fatherly love arising from my heart to the bone.

The night of 27 to 28 March 2021 will be remembered for such a long time as the night that baffled me with its unfolding events while I dreamed of an alternate life.

It started as a French art exhibition designer attached to the China Cultural Centre, a space for exposing art objects and events related to Western culture.

After decorating a space, it became the main attraction and gained visibility, becoming renowned as the main event.

I woke up reliving the feelings in the dream of the character played.

I went back to sleep and dreamt about the same story, this time in another space dedicated to presenting art-related short movies.

I watched a short movie from beginning to end, seeing the credits and subtitles for fifteen minutes. In the end, I discussed with the exhibition officer ways to promote it.

I woke up again, wondering how it was possible to carry on dreaming the same dream.

I was going back to sleep and dreaming again. It was related to the same dream, but this time, it was in a different place, exposing art objects. Everything was so colourful and natural that I asked myself if it was a dream or if I was conscious and aware of my existence in the real world.

While I took a taxi to my home, I took a picture to check if it was real in the morning.

Did you know that you can change your reality through dreams?

You need much energy, incredible attention to detail in imagination and a strong belief in divine powers (God, divine love and other personal representations).

This was my dream this morning (10 January 2022) when I met someone who discussed what is needed to change one's reality through dreams.

A few times, the dreams of past lives are related to persons from my daily life.

I dreamed recently of the woman with whom I'm connected in one of the environments. When I woke up, I realised that the person from my dream was also present in my real life through my senses, although with a different face and body.

It is also mind-blowing to know and glimpse that, at some point, your connection with a person might end.

As usual, this morning (14 March 2022), I felt that if I went to sleep, some dream uncovering my past lives or the alternate universe would happen.

My first dream was with my brothers, living together with my mother.

They were kids, and I was the same as the big brother but working; maybe there was a more significant age gap.

The little one felt unwell, and I took him to the hospital, then left my other brother with him to take care of him and bring him home afterwards.

While home, I was tired and fell asleep in my dream. It's weird to have a dream of sleeping while sleeping already. Sleeping felt even more profound, but I was conscious for some time. Suddenly, I was awake with eyes wide open and looking around. I didn't see my brothers, who should have been home already.

I felt the urge to go to the hospital to see what was happening and to announce to my mother that they weren't back.

It was so strong that I didn't realise I was fully awake in bed. Looking around, it took some time until I realised this was another life, and I was no longer dreaming.

I could have stayed awake, but the feeling inside — sweet tiredness — that something new would be uncovered if I went back to sleep took the lead.

Going back to sleep, another dream started to unfold in front of my inner eye.

I was a woman writer this time, writing short stories as a hobby, which I intended to publish soon.

I even made a meal from scrambled eggs over spinach stew and some polenta on the side. The taste was so strong that it stayed with me even after the dream.

Oh, and it's weird now that I felt I was a woman in my dream — a real woman, and I did not question my gender after the dream.

In my dream, I had a workplace where I had worked before, and I visited occasionally, keeping in touch with the owners. It seems that it was a tailoring place.

A strong friendship would be felt whenever an older woman met me at the gates.

Fast-forward, and I was just published. After a call confirming that a renowned blogger could present my book, I watched TV with my editor. It started on TV with a middle-aged guy reading passages from my book, and I felt a sense of success and the prospect of becoming rich soon.

Soon after, I went to the workplace to meet the older woman. The guard at the gate said she was no more, but I told him I knew, and he patched me with her daughter instead.

Soon after, a red-haired young woman appeared, and I felt the urge to hug her. I felt compassion inside when I noticed the rejection in her eyes.

I noticed that I was shorter than her and started talking about times when we worked together in a pink-labelled team assigned to compete against other teams for production.

Woking up, the feeling that this time I realised my gender in the dream without question blew my mind.

28.10.2022 07:17 – I woke up after one of the weirdest dreams; well, not the first one in a series of strange dreams, but unique.

After a shady and not-so-clear course of actions in the dream, I found myself next to a bar, and it suddenly hit me to test the reality of things in the dream, knowing it was a dream.

I touched a steel bar next to some stairs, and honestly, I felt coldness – the same feeling as in the real world. I touched the bricks of the wall, felt their roughness, and almost asked myself if it was a dream.

Then I went ballistic and tried to destroy a gate … well, not destroy, but make noise while shaking the hell of it. The owner of the house started to shout:

'Hey, what the *fruck* are you doing?'

And a crowd of people surrounded me in my strange dream.

One man from the mob went forward and shouted at me:

'Hey man, are you crazy? Chill, man, leave the gate and don't make so much noise.'

'Oh yeah?' I answered. 'It's my *frucking* dream, and I can do whatever the *fruck* I want. So you should go and keep your mouth shut.'

'Oh, it doesn't work like that around here, pal,' he said.

'Hmm, let's see if it's true,' I said, holding his head with my hands, one at the top of his head – left hand, and the other under the chin.

And he said, 'You know what you are doing is wrong, and things won't go as you want. You'll see what will happen in the future if you kill me.'

'Well, indeed, it's wrong to kill the man, breaking his neck or else,' I thought to myself. But energy within flowing through my hands started pouring into his body, and he became a white glowing shape of the person who was and melted into thin air …

Then, followed by a young man like a shadow, who felt like a very close friend, another environment appeared, a restaurant it seemed, where I went and spoke to a waitress girl who felt like a long-time friend, carrying a plate with some glasses:

'Do you know what I've done? I made a man disappear earlier

by touching his head with my hands if you can believe it!'

But seeing her face mimicked like I was crazy, my shadow friend shook his head, saying she didn't believe me and to stop with the nonsense.

'Well, it is worth trying!' I smiled at her ...

I woke up with my head wooing the sound of energy flowing, like in moments of deep meditation when everything was silent around me. This was also accompanied by the feeling of sound in the back of my head, like a symphony of inner noises.

And I throw myself deep in this concert of unworldly sounds, bathing in the ocean of love ...

Dreams like never before. More and more captivating stories are unfolding with mind-blowing awe. Once those desires are washed away, dreams become out of this world.

I have more dreams than I write about, but I write mainly about those that feel different. There is a distinct flavour to experiencing a dream.

About a week ago, I had a dream involving my younger brother, and while dreaming, I had to ask myself many times if it was real because the details in the dream didn't conform with reality as being aware of it inside the dream. I don't even remember the details now, but I decided after the dream not to write about it as it wasn't mind-blowing other than the fact that it was confusing because I was aware of the reality while most of the time I am not.

But last night's dream (12 April 2023) was mind-blowing, and I write about it, remembering the details.

I was in Spain, it seems. I was young, around twenty-ish, with other people around me, heading to our homes in a rural area. At some point, I helped someone with heavier luggage.

When I reached my home, a lovely small villa, it was like a fantasy home. There was nothing with technology in it, not even light, and in the garden heading up to a hill at the back of the house were a vineyard, cherry trees and other trees flowering in the spring season.

After some moments, my parents arrived. My mother was against technology and eating meat, refusing and checking everything around the house.

Everything was indeed a beautiful dream. A dream that scented happiness a long time after waking up in the morning …

After some breaks in writing, dreams happen so weirdly that I must write about them.

In one of my dreams, I suddenly became aware that I was dreaming and started to study the faces and environment around me. It was an environment with cars and people stopped at an intersection arguing with each other.

I saw the arguing guy's face so close that the details were like being in reality – dark hair, sun-soaked skin, average body. Then his car – a Mercedes jeep with opened doors due to his hastily leaving to argue with others. And I had the impulse to Matrix out of this environment and push his car like in those damn movie effects, and the car started to roll like being pushed in a tornado.

And suddenly, I felt myself pushed out of my dream. Was it the effect of my push or the havoc on my brain?

Oh, but weirdly enough, I was not waking up but was sent to another dream where I'd published my book – well, not this book – related to some practices and mindsets to elevate spirit and mind.

The company had just finished printing and called me to say that a hundred copies were sold on the first day on the market.

I had to go back to my daily work after some holiday due to publishing the book. Oddly enough, I was with one of my exes, although I rarely dream about my exes.

The problem was that I needed to remember where I was working. I started to search through my memories with my foggy mind, but the places I remembered happened only in dreams.

I said something about not writing down all my dreams, only those that feel out of the ordinary, and writing immediately after them because I will forget them or specific details soon enough.

I remember working in a factory in Spain, which I left because I was returning to my country for a short time to be close to my mother and brothers from another dream. I knew even that I had to take two buses to work there.

And then, there was a place where I was working in another dream, in the countryside, with a boss with a big dark beard.

But wait, in what country am I?

I started walking down the street, trying to remember where I work and how to get there.

And 'wrecking balls', I woke up and remembered that I was in England, on holiday for the King's coronation, and (obviously) where I was working.

Seoul – 7 October 2023 – As I said, a few dreams may be worth storytelling. They happen a few times, but if not written instantly afterwards, they become too foggy with details and I even forget about them.

Not this night, though, because I dreamed of being a data analyst software developer for a company using resources and information to increase profit.

Due to software improvements, the company started to be in a good position, and it crossed my mind that this software could be used on a large scale for other companies as well, so let's make some money setting up a start-up.

The details of the software processes were so many, from sourcing materials to analysing how clients interact and review the products, even the human factor of reviewing and altering this information – a secretary was doing this at that company.

But the critical factor that blew me asleep was that fast-forward, I was biking next to a few significant people from the government at an incredible speed through the streets with cars passing by a few millimetres close to an accident and reaching the destination.

I said, 'Gosh, you know that five or six times we were almost dead surfing on bikes like this. Does this happen every day for you?'

Astonishing details happen sometimes in my dreams. I was aware of one of them, admiring the perfect details of a device's screws.

Soon after, I looked very closely for the signature of a theatre ticket.

I was amazed while dreaming, aware of these details that kept haunting me for a long time after waking up.

Wondering what's next for my troubled soul during the whole world boiling in crisis?!

www.ingramcontent.com/pod-product-compliance
Lightning Source LLC
Chambersburg PA
CBHW020419010526
44118CB00010B/326